THE
BAD NEWS
BIBLE

Also by Anna Blundy

Every Time We Say Goodbye
Only My Dreams

ANNA BLUNDY

THE BAD NEWS BIBLE

headline

First published in 2004
by HEADLINE BOOK PUBLISHING

10 9 8 7 6 5 4 3 2 1

British Library Cataloguing in Publication Data

ISBN 0 7553 0296 6 (hardback)
ISBN 07553 0949 9 (trade paperback)

Typeset in Electra by Palimpsest Book Production Limited,
Polmont, Stirlingshire

Printed and bound in Great Britain
by Clays Ltd St Ives plc

Papers and cover board used by Headline are natural,
recyclable products made from wood grown in
sustainable forests. The manufacturing processes
conform to the environmental regulations of the
country of origin.

HEADLINE BOOK PUBLISHING
A division of Hodder Headline
338 Euston Road
London NW1 3BH

www.headline.co.uk
www.hodderheadline.com

For Gemma, without whom etc.

Acknowledgements

A huge thank you to Deborah Rogers for introducing me to the lovely Rosie de Courcy, through whom Faith Zanetti was born.

CHAPTER ONE

The man next to me was scared. White-knuckle all the way. I told him my joke, but he didn't laugh: the plane is going down, cabin fills with smoke, people running around screaming, trampling over each other, when someone says to a stewardess: 'Where are the exits? Where are the life jackets?' The stewardess looks at him condescendingly and says, 'Oh, so *now* you're interested.' Nothing. Not even a smile. So I put my headphones on and leaned back to watch the clouds. Miles and miles of them. A candyfloss blanket around the world. When I was little I used to want to leap into them, softer than cotton wool.

I ordered another vodka and the steward raised a conspiratorial eyebrow and slipped me two. Trevor, his name was.

'Thanks, Trevor,' I said and winked at him.

We were being shown a film about how beautiful Jerusalem is. The sun setting over the Mount of Olives. Look how you can go to these nice restaurants and swim in this idyllic pool, the soothing voice-over was saying. If a car bomb doesn't blow your arm off, I thought. That's

1

the thing about flying El Al. They have this insane security which means you have to get to Heathrow about a year before you fly, and they open your toothpaste and smell your socks. A little girl in front of me was in tears because they were body-searching her teddy bear. Then, when you're on board, they do this patriotic 'Israel the wonderful' thing as though the plane weren't about to be blasted to smithereens.

'Hey. My favourite grace,' said Don McCaughrean, slapping me on the shoulder.

I winced in pain. Oh, he was OK really. The judge had given him the absolute minimum visiting rights and his heart had just broken. Perhaps as some sort of substitute McCaughrean was famous for never letting his cameras out of his sight. He booked them their own seat on the plane. He had them with him now in their battered canvas bag on the floor at his feet, blocking the aisle. He knocked someone unconscious with them once.

I was surprised to see him. I hadn't noticed him get on. He looked as though he had been tipping it back since take-off three hours ago.

'Hey, Don. How are you?' I said, taking my headphones off. 'I'm a virtue, actually.'

'Whatever,' he laughed, perching his bulk on the arm of my seat. It looked painful. 'So, Faithy, what's a nice girl like you going to a shit hole like this for? Hot as a fucking A-rab's armpit out there at the moment, let me tell you.'

'I'll stay in the shade,' I told him, offering him one of my miniatures.

'Ta,' he said, slavering at the sight of it, twisting off the little red lid with fat sausage fingers and sucking the vodka down in one through wet lips.

'Thought Edmonds was still out there for you boys,' he said. He wiped a last lank lock of hair back off a damp forehead.

'He's gone to Rome. Not a short straw,' I said, smiling at the thought of Edmonds sitting at a pavement café with his espresso, watching the pigeons. I liked Edmonds.

'Noooooooooo!?' McCaughrean sputtered. 'Buggered off to Roma without so much as an *arrivederci* and left a pretty young thing like you to get shot at on the West fucking Bank?!'

'There was sort of an emergency reshuffle,' I tried to explain, but Trevor was hustling McCaughrean back to his seat for landing and had picked up the obstructing camera bag. I was glad. He slightly repulses me, heart of gold or not.

'Don't you fucking touch that, you woofter,' McCaughrean shouted, rolling back up the aisle in a dribbling rage.

Actually, it had been more of an emergency frenzy of sackings. Edmonds, not exactly known for his sanity, had finally gone off the rails in a bar in Bethlehem and had been put out to pasture as a matter of urgency. Mary Polanski (no relation to Roman, though she pretended sorority to get into restaurants) had been doing Italy for years, claiming she couldn't leave because her girlfriend was Italian and their adopted daughter was at school there. She had finally been fired for refusing to come back from holiday in Sardinia when that porn star got murdered. So I got Jerusalem. I'm not complaining, that's for sure. I'm half mad with elation. And relief.

After Salvador, I thought they might put me on a features beat. They have this spiel where they pretend that writing for the new tabloid-sized drivel section is actually prestigious because you can do long in-depth stuff and everyone reads it. 'Everyone' being the kind of loony members of the public who write you letters in green ink and get their upper- and lower-case letters mixed up. So, that is, no one. Your actual peer group and anyone you give the slightest toss about only reads the main section and, let's face it, not much of that. 'In-depth' is rubbish too. That just means padded to ridiculous length so they can fill the endless space. They mean 'in-depth' stuff about soap stars who've decided to give up cocaine (why bother? Some people need to come to terms with the fact that they really are just too boring without it), or the agony of mothers trying to juggle a career with childcare. Oh, I don't mean these things aren't hard and all that, but you don't want to read about it every single day. Or maybe you do. God knows.

The whole thing in Salvador was my fault as well. I was hot and tired and we'd been hanging around waiting for these people for days. I think my judgement was skewed by insomnia and I just trusted the wrong person. He said he was taking me to the heads of the Miami-based Mara. We walked about two hundred yards before they started firing. He was killed. I got shot in the shoulder. I still dream about it.

It's strange because, when it happened, I felt acutely practical. By the time I was back in England, it was already well in the past. When people asked me what it was like, I didn't know what to say. They wanted a horror story, but really it wasn't that bad. Not for me, at least. It was bad for the boy who died. It took ages and I was talking to him, trying to comfort him. I held his hand. He must have wanted his mum, not some Westerner he hardly knew.

But in the dream, I can feel the searing heat of the bullet going through me and I can taste the sand on my lips as I hit the floor. The boy bleeding and moaning, people shouting in Spanish all around me, me slipping in and out of consciousness in the back of this Toyota pick-up, a metallic taste in my mouth, wondering if I would die. And the sky so blue.

I wrote the story in my head as we drove: 'British reporter Faith Zanetti was killed in El Salvador today, shot by warring gang members in the hills outside the capital San Salvador.' But she wasn't, of course.

I did win an award, though. Norman Tebbit gave it to me at the Foreign Press Association, God knows why. I still had my arm in a sling, which the photographers loved, so I was in lots of magazines. I was supposed to be brave and intrepid because I'd been shot, but actually I was just stupid. Still, I shouldn't be whingeing about it. I got Jerusalem. I can't believe I got Jerusalem.

*   *   *

4

'Well, Zanetti,' Martin Glover said to me. I use the word 'said' in the loosest possible sense, since really he was just dribbling claret down his chin when some words came out. He is my friend Shiv's boyfriend. No, honestly, he is. They've been together for years. Not that they see each other much. She's always abroad, sleeping with younger, better looking men (and who can blame her). He can hardly be capable of much action when they are occasionally together. She's half his age. Then again, she's always been like that. She was sleeping with the teachers at school by the time she was fifteen.

We decided together that we were going to be journalists after we saw that film with Katharine Hepburn in it – the one where she smokes decadently and slams the door to the editor's office a lot. Great suits.

Shiv actually did it properly. English degree (basically a lot of punting and vomiting), journalism school, and clambering up through the ranks showing off her shorthand. I ended up filing stuff from Russia in the early 1990s after I'd met a correspondent in a bar who spoke only English and Finnish and was looking for an assistant. I never meant to do this really. I'd rather have been a pop star.

So Martin and I were in El Vino's on Fleet Street and this was the second bottle. It's all banks on Fleet Street now, of course, but they miss it, the old ones. They get taxis all the way from Wapping and Canary Wharf just to be there, pretending Goldman Sachs is still the *Express*.

It was midday. He ordered a round of tongue sandwiches (I don't think these are served anywhere except El Vino's) but he didn't touch them. It was more as a sort of gesture to convention, it being lunchtime and all. They say he has a vitamin pill with his whisky at supper.

'Well, Zanetti,' he burbled. He has been promoted. He used to be the foreign editor but now his position is nameless. Lofty but nameless. Senior roving drunk. 'What about Jerusalem, then? Fancy Arabs much?'

This was a job offer. You have to be alert to them, because they can be very cryptic and you might not notice that you've just been made editor-in-chief. At my first job, on a more left-wing paper, my boss came up to me and said this: 'Fucking Portillo, eh? What a cunt.' Then he wandered off. It was only later I realized that he wanted me to write a three-thousand-word profile of Michael Portillo for the tabloid section front by four o'clock. You have to be alert.

I put my glass down and nodded energetically.

'Love them,' I said, my head spinning from the wine. I was trying to give up smoking, but I had some in my jacket just in case. I lit one now, leaning forward to take the book of matches out of the glass ashtray.

'What about those Yids?' he wondered. It was a test. Would I be offended? Was I prim and prissy, or was I one of the lads?

'Oh, them too. Them too.' I beamed. 'You know me and dark men.' That was me accepting the job.

There was a little scrap of me that would like to have kissed him, to have told him how grateful I was. But it wasn't the form. Instead, I held my glass up to chink with his, the thick wine slopping against the sides.

'Shivvy's out there. You can keep a bit of an eye on her for me,' he said sadly. I suppose he knew.

Trevor shook me awake. I was sweating and my face was wet with tears. 'Ready to disembark?' he asked me. Ready to drink myself into a stupor. I was shaking with fear. I had my dream again. I am lying in bed – not quite asleep, but unable to move. I can hear someone coming towards me and can smell the alcohol on her breath, but I daren't scream. When she puts the pillow over my face, I writhe and twitch, I try to shout and to push her off, but my mouth is stuffed full of cotton and I am passing out. The woman is my mother and I know it isn't a dream.

'Thanks. Yeah. Just give me a sec,' I said, smiling.

*   *   *

And here I am. I went through immigration at Ben Gurion airport in Tel Aviv, got my bag from a decrepit carousel, and went outside to find a cab. It was hot and chaotic. The air was thick with dust and exhaust fumes. A tired soldier with his M16 cocked against his chest rested in the unreliable shade of a palm tree, his head slumped forward over his gun. Cars honked and screeched, music blared out of an old Mercedes window as it passed me, sending up a wave of heat from its tired metal and choking exhaust. The strap of my bag dug into my skin and I was already soaked with sweat.

'Get in, Zanetti,' Don shouted, his face livid red, a fag hanging from his lips. I threw my stuff into the boot and did as I was told. There were prayer beads swinging from the rear-view mirror. McCaughrean gasped in the heat like an asthmatic, handing me an open pack of Marlboro.

'Thanks,' I said, and fell back into the sticky black plastic behind me. The driver turned his radio up.

'Colony, right?' McCaughrean breathed.

'Mmmm,' I confirmed, blowing my smoke out in a stream that seemed to cut through the dense heat. 'Got to get a flat.'

'What about Edmonds's place?' McCaughrean wanted to know.

'Dunno. Too weird,' I said, looking out of the window at the mountains of watermelons being sold in the dirt at the side of the road. Anyway, I love the Colony. I fell in love with it the second I saw it. Years ago. I was doing some feature about cross-cultural marriages. I think it's the lizards.

There was one scuttering across the stone floor of the lobby when we crashed in, bags and voices in the echoing gloom. The entrance seems like a hole in the wall from the outside. The sandy streets were deserted apart from a few small boys with donkeys, and the air was singing with crickets and scented with lemons. An avenue of trees leading up to the lion mosaics near the doors, the fruit big and bright and unrealistic on the branches. There was a boy I'd never seen before on the desk, crouching under a ceiling that hung with brass lamps.

7

'Ahlan. Salaam. Good evening, sir, madam,' he said, inclining his head towards me as though I were wearing a taffeta ball gown, and not old jeans and battered cowboy boots. He had black, flashing eyes and skin the colour of toffee.

'Hey, Zahir. How's the sex life?' McCaughrean asked, slapping his passport down on the old brass counter.

The boy laughed. 'Nice to see you again, sir,' he said, and tapped a key on his computer. 'Number nine.'

McCaughrean slung his bag over his shoulder and shuffled off down the narrow stone corridor, slits of windows to either side, the ceiling arched Islamically high.

I leant my elbows on the desk and smiled at Zahir. 'Oh, courtyard, courtyard, pleeeeease,' I begged. He dealt with this request every day of his life. Anxiety flickered briefly across Zahir's face as he peered into his screen. Who wouldn't want this room? I couldn't believe Don was so blasé about it, taking any old thing he was given. When you had the courtyard room, you felt as though you were the pasha himself, striding manfully across the cobbles, past the fountain, the light filtering through the citrus trees, to the cool, spacious gloom of your boudoir. Or whatever.

Tap. Tap. Then Zahir lit up, a smile spreading from ear to ear. He dangled the key tantalizingly before my fingers. I grabbed at it.

'Courtyard, Miss Zanetti. Number six,' he told me, almost as delighted as I was.

I shooed two lizards out of the bath and ran it burning hot. BBC World was showing a piece from Iraq by that idiot Pip Deakin. He's short and he dyes the grey out with an awful Paul McCartney orangey-brown. He's had his teeth bleached too, and he does pieces to camera with his shirt open halfway to his waist as though he's just in too much danger to be bothered with doing it up. This is on the rare occasions that he actually takes his flak jacket off. He always does stories about himself and the hardship he's enduring on the mountainside or in the trench or whatever. He was wearing full combat gear outside the Intercontinental Hotel in Baghdad once. A crowd of locals going about their business, shopping, hustling, stopped to laugh. They had to be carefully edited out later. Pip Deakin hates me. It's not my bloody fault he faked being sniped at in Kosovo. Basically, he said his bit and then ducked and ran as though someone was firing at him. The trouble was that he messed it up the first time so the tape that was sent round to the pool had his frankly pretty pathetic piece of acting on it – twice. It was no secret. In fact, it is a story as famous as the one about the cameraman (I know who it is as well) who set his equipment up on a tripod to pirate himself a video of the hotel's porn channel. He didn't bank on the reflection in the television screen. Then he accidentally sent the wrong tape back to New York.

Anyway, the thing with Pip was that I was at some drunken dinner in London one night (at his ex-wife's house, to be honest) and I told this story about the fake Kosovo sniping. Unfortunately, I was sitting next to a newspaper diarist who was a bit short on material. It took Pip about thirty-two seconds to find out whose fault it was. Relations have been a bit chilly between us since then. I was sorry really. Embarrassed anyway. But I think I aggravated things last time I saw him. We were in the Mille Colines in Rwanda and by the time he arrived in the bar I was already a bit pissed and tired. I asked him how come he wasn't wearing his flak-jacket because you never knew when the barman might turn on us. Everyone laughed. It was meant to be flirtatious. Me trying to make up.

'Fuck yourself, Zanetti,' was what he said though.

I considered saying something awful back, like: 'Rather that than fuck you, Deakin', but it didn't seem worthwhile. Plus which he can't complain: he's easily the highest-paid British television correspondent on the planet. Supports two families.

I switched over to CNN, but it was *Style* with Elsa Klench, so I got in the bath. I shut my eyes and let the water burn the journey out of me. A muezzin was calling evening prayer.

* * *

9

I shouldn't even have been here yet. I'd like to have just gone straight up to see if Shiv was around, but there is a kind of protocol about getting straight off the plane and straight to work. We have a conspiracy of silence about the fact that we're all on holiday. During the Yugoslav conflict, people were fighting each other for the assignment because everyone spent the whole time on the beach in Split. Came back with all-over tans, rested and happy. Genocide notwithstanding.

The foreign desk, having spent weeks hassling me about living at Edmonds's place because they were paying rent on it for decades to come (no way), had booked me in here for a month's time. Then Glover said he'd got some tip-off from a bloke who'd been his fives partner at school (now foreign office) about an Israeli army mole who was masterminding Palestinian suicide-bomb attacks. This is the kind of story nobody ever manages to prove, but also the kind of story it would be so fantastic to break that everyone gets their best people on it. Usually it's not even true, of course. I was once forced to work on a story about Mark Thatcher for a lurid Sunday that makes the headlines up on a Tuesday and has the journalists write the stories to match them by Saturday night, truth or no truth. They'd decided Mark was probably tax dodging and they wanted to run a piece saying: 'IRS Investigates Thatcher'. So we called the IRS in America and told them we thought he might be dodging his taxes and they said they'd investigate. The story ran on the front page.

Anyway, Glover insisted I come out now and had prodded me in the ribs about arranging an immediate meeting with General Meier. A mole meeting. Not, of course, that the General was likely to tell me anything. Not without seeing my tits, at any rate. Glover actually set it up himself in the end. Ooooh. What a treat.

The General said he'd pick me up at the hotel an hour and a half after my plane got in. I was surprised he was willing to drive into this area in his big black assassinate-me car, but when I said as much, not quite in those words, he told me he'd survived two car bombs – God wanted him to live. In that case, God was pretty much alone in this desire. This guy was 'rumoured' (i.e. it was true, but nobody dared do anything about it) to have presided over so many massacres of Palestinians that even right-wing Israelis found him to be a bit on the extreme side.

I rubbed my hair dry with a big white towel and shook it loose. I gave up on my spirals years ago. A blonde Afro. The General seemed to warrant a skirt, I thought. I do own one skirt – it is tight, black and short for exactly these occasions. Someone once told me I had good legs. 'Fuck off,' I said, but I bought a short skirt anyway, just in case. I also travel with a pair of black stilettos for the same reason. I find it hard to believe that anyone would actually choose to wear these things for anything other than strict professionalism. Maybe they don't. And never mind make-up.

The first time I met Colonel Gadaffi in Tripoli I was so nervous I went as far as borrowing someone's lipstick, but I felt like a clown and I haven't tried it since. Not least because Gadaffi sent his aides outside, locked the door and tried to get me to wear an apricot silk negligée that he seems to keep under his desk. I want them to feel relaxed, superior, complicit. I'm not trying to get raped.

I assumed the knock on my door was a beautiful boy with a chocolate for my pillow and a carafe of iced water for my bedside table. I opened it wide on to the courtyard, a towel in my hand. In fact, it was the General – early, and holding a bottle of champagne. He was followed by Zahir, the brass buttons on his green uniform glinting in the evening light. Zahir carried a pewter ice bucket, two glasses and a vase of roses on a tray.

'The delectable Miss Zanetti,' said the General, his eye smiling lewdly.

I say 'eye' advisedly. He's only got the one. What may or may not remain of the other is hidden under a patch. He took my hand in his and turned it over to kiss my palm. I tried not to flinch. The combination of his dry lips and his blown-off fingers was enough to bring bile up in my throat.

'General,' I said, looking admiringly from his face to the champagne. 'You read my mind.'

Zahir arranged the flowers on a blue mosaic table. I half expected him to spin round and cut the General's throat. Instead, he poured the drinks and took his tip from the mutilated hand with a perfectly deferential bow. There was something about the way the General licked his lips as he lowered his immense weight on to the edge of the bed that made me want to get him out of my room. He wore shiny black loafers with a gold tag. I threw my champagne back in one gulp, eyes watering from the sharp bubbles.

'I'm starving,' I said, standing up and slouching my leather jacket on. My Dad's leather jacket, in fact. He was wearing it when he was killed in Belfast. They sent it back to our house in a plastic bag. I remember Evie whimpering over it.

The General stood aside to let me out of the door, holding my elbow as we walked across the cobbled courtyard. Chivalry so often tips over into sliminess when overdone. The lemon trees rustled above our heads and the sky was turning orange. A waiter crossed our path, starched linen cloths piled high in his arms. He looked at my dinner date and bristled with visible venom. The General was no doubt responsible for the murder of half his relatives. This, after all, was the man who, when I interviewed him about a Palestinian prisoner who had been tortured with sleep deprivation, said: 'It must have been his conscience keeping him awake.' It was basically my friendship, if that's the word for it, with Meier that got me sent over to do all these big Saturday foreign stories, even when I was based in London. Pissed the then correspondent off no end. This was before Edmonds, and I won't name him, but he once sent me an email calling me a bitch. Not my fucking fault they were sending me to big foot. If he could have made the contacts he'd have got the story.

An armoured car was parked outside the hotel gate, its engine running. I could see the driver's silhouette behind the blackened glass and a uniformed soldier stood by the passenger door, his M16 cocked at his shoulder. A group of ragged children had gathered to stare, their bare feet kicking up the dust. I waved at them and they giggled and pointed at my hair so I patted it for them and got a squeal of delight in return. The long knife of a watermelon man caught the light a few yards down the road and the soldier flinched.

Inside, the car was extravagantly air-conditioned and I immediately got goose pimples all over. No danger of my legs sticking to the beige leather seats.

The General sat too close to me and I watched the city glide by outside. A strange mirage of first and third worlds like a newsflash watched from the safety of our silent capsule. Palm trees are so familiar to everyone now – Marbella, Florida, the neat manicured boulevard palm trees of Los Angeles. But these ones are not peaceful or controlled. These ones are random – taller, and planted in red dust. Even the affluent shopping streets with tourist shops selling silly T-shirts and Beanie toys of comical, head-dressed Arabs and Hasidic Jews are illusory – not really peaceful at all. The young mother's perfect smile is strained – she is used to glancing over her shoulder.

'You have become even more beautiful than the last time I saw you,' the General told me. What did he honestly expect me to do? Giggle coquettishly and bat my eyelashes? I tried it. Apparently it was exactly what he had expected me to do, since he leant back, satisfied, one hand draped across the seat behind my shoulders, his fingers just brushing the collar of my shirt. What was left of them.

We went to a depressingly flashy restaurant in downtown West Jerusalem with spectacular security, Russian prostitutes in high heels, and a casino on the second floor. The menu was foie gras, caviare and pheasant. The staff oppressively obsequious. The ladies' loo, mausoleum-like in black and white marble, was stocked with hairspray, major brands of perfume and spare pairs of tights and stockings. I took a few packets of tights and the woman who handed out the towels scowled at me. She was in a kind of French maid's uniform with a frilly white apron and a preposterous bonnet.

'*Na vsyakii sluchai*,' I said to her in Russian, and she grinned and passed me a couple more.

My first husband was Russian. OK, my only husband. I was eighteen, and it seemed a good way of getting out of London. We lived with his mum and granny on the twenty-seventh floor of a suburban apartment block in Ryazan where the lift broke down a lot. Before the wedding, he told me he lived in Moscow where I'd met him. I got followed around by the KGB all the time. In fact, the local KGBeshnik was a boy my husband had been at school with so it was all a bit of a joke. Not a very funny one, though.

'Everyone's Russian,' I said to the General when I sat back down on my gilt chair.

He leant forward to light my cigarette with a delicate gold slip of a lighter.

'Ten per cent of our population now,' he told me, with a disappointed nod of his huge head. Not only had he lost an eye but his face was sprayed black with shrapnel. A violinist approached our table playing 'Don't Cry for Me, Argentina' and the General waved him away with a gesture which made the candle flicker and die. He served his purpose though. General Meier *is* the scoop. And he's mine. On the other hand, I would have to file something tonight for tomorrow. It's all very well having long-term investigations and God knows what to be working on, but I was also going to have to be doing daily news. I wasn't at all sure I'd get enough out of him for that. Time to plunge in.

So, basically, I thought I'd probably better touch his hand when I asked him about the mole. One of his soldiers butchering his comrades and all that. Brothers-in-arms.

Before he started wildly denying any possibility of army infiltration, he looked surprised. I couldn't tell if it was because I'd been so physically forward or if it was because I seemed to know about a huge military secret. Could have gone either way.

Once he had calmed down about what he had apparently taken as an accusation of personal ineptitude (which I suppose, if true, it was), he started droning on with the predictable tediousness of a politician about how he had nothing against the Palestinians as a people. 'They wish to annihilate Jews, but as an Israeli I can assure you that we have no intention . . .' Blah blah blah. Also a lie. He'd done plenty of annihilation in his time. Was famous for it, for God's sake. Might be tried for it one day. As part of his spiel, he promised to introduce me to an English Jesuit Priest who took in Palestinian orphans – a project very close to his heart. When he said 'heart' he touched his wallet.

He claimed to be very interested in child welfare. Personally, I couldn't imagine children being anything but terrified of him. Was he naïve enough to seriously believe I had been diverted by this?

'You are obviously a very kind man,' I said, lowering my eyes and smiling at my food. OK, so I brushed my foot against his. I can't deny it. I did.

'But, the mole?'

He sighed deeply and leant towards me.

'If I have not made myself clear enough on this issue, forgive me,' he hissed into my ear. 'There is no traitor in my army.' I felt the spray of his saliva and my throat constricted in that pre-vomit way. I nodded what I hoped might come across as appreciation of his devastating sexuality.

'If you are looking for a demonstration, my best men are out near Ramallah at the moment. Getting ready for a raid. I'll talk to the captain. Arrange a press visit.' He pulled back, smug, as though he'd just actually given me a story. A nice feature, sure. But not exactly Watergate. It would do, though. I could probably manage to drag a few hundred words out of it for tomorrow – talking about a planned raid. You see, then you can pad it out with a history of the Israeli special forces and how hard they are and stuff.

When we got back to the American Colony he leant over and kissed my neck, his hand wedged between my thighs. I pushed him away as non-violently as possible and said: 'Oooh, General! You move too fast for me!'

He said something like: 'You little minx, you!'

Then I leapt out of the car and ran into the hotel to the extent that I could in my stupid shoes. I wish he wasn't so useful. I would like to punch him in his good eye.

By the time I'd changed back into something normal and made it down to the bar, McCaughrean had already pretty much had it. He was cheek-down on the zinc, his fingers still wrapped round a shot of tequila, his eyes half open.

'Faith! Faith! You're here!' Lovely Siobhan Boucherat shouted from over in the corner. My Shiv. I beamed and went to join her. We stood and hugged for ages and she even started crying. More the drink than the emotion, I should think. I haven't seen her since Salvador. I love Shiv. She has a phobia of unattached buttons (seriously) and a thing about men under twenty-five, though Martin's got to be fifty-five. It was a bafflement to everyone, but presumably they both got some kind of comfort out of their theoretical union. It would take a good shrink to find out what kind, though, if you asked me. Which she didn't.

'This is Misha,' she told me, winking. 'He's over from St Petersburg to do a piece about the Russian underworld.' She said 'underworld' as though it was something unspeakably exciting and delicious. She was being ironic. I shook hands with Misha and he blinked nervously from behind his glasses. He was one of those pale types who had devoted himself to post-Soviet journalism; thin, married to the truth, though unable to uncover it. He had dust-coloured hair and grey eyes, nervous fingers.

'Everyone is Russian in this country. I just had dinner with old sleazoid Cyclops in Hippodromica and the whole staff was Russian,' I said.

'Ugh. I hate that place,' Shiv groaned, lighting a cigarette. 'Anyway, how come that creep's still alive?'

'Dunno. Nearly killed him myself,' I said.

Misha shuffled in his seat. He was not comfortable here, and I felt a bit sorry for him. Shiv was always pouncing on innocents.

'Pleased to meet you,' he eventually managed. 'Siobhan has told me all about you.'

I laughed and went to get myself a vodka. There was a group of tabloid hacks at the bar talking about going to Ramallah the next day.

'Fancy a bit of action, Zanetti?' one of them asked me. I certainly did. Couldn't have been more convenient, though probably someone or other went out there from the Colony every morning, it being where things were happening, militarily speaking. I suppose I could file an edgy sort of battleground piece while I was there, as well as having a look at the mole thing.

I said I'd see in the morning. I needed to call the desk first. Didn't want to give anything away by seeming too keen. I think though that I was the only one on the mole story, but you never can tell. We shared most stories, but I wanted this one to myself, thanks.

'Planning to take time off from your busy poolside schedule, then?' I wondered.

They usually just listen to the BBC World Service and file their copy by sat-phone from the sun loungers.

'Yeah, yeah, yeah. Your paper's bigger than ours!' Grant Bradford sneered, offering me a cigarette. Grant Bradford is everywhere. He's the kind of tabloid hack who used to be described as a brothel creeper. He liked to pretend he'd never done exposés of soap stars' love lives. His hair is short, spiky and bright orange.

'A2,' I boasted taking it, and went back to Shiv.

I had barely sat down when McCaughrean roused himself and started picking a fight with the gutter press.

'Don't know your tits from your arses, you lot,' he began, cutting straight to the chase. Bradford stared at him, waiting to see what tack he would take.

'I'd have thought that was the one thing they do know, Don,' somebody else chipped in and everyone roared with laughter.

McCaughrean ignored the comment.

'I have won awards, fucking awards, for my work,' he shouted. 'I show the fucking world what's going on, and what do you lot do? Crop my picture down to a fucking two-inch, fucking photo-booth—' He paused, losing his train of thought. The point he was trying to make was, however, clear. Bradford slapped him on the back.

'You're a genius, man,' he told him. 'You're a fucking genius.'

At this, McCaughrean burst into tears.

'Thanks, man,' he said, his head in his hands.

Misha was telling me about Jerusalem's Russian crime wave when he stopped dead and looked up, eyes large. Terrifyingly, McCaughrean had begun to stagger towards us, recovered now from his crying. He knocked a table over on the way and glasses smashed to the floor, the little plastic stirrers bouncing on the terracotta. His approach silenced us and we watched in bewildered awe as he attempted to aim for the seat next to me. He missed and crashed to his knees, clinging to the table edge for support.

'Bollocks,' he murmured, his face swollen and sweating.

Misha helped him up, losing his glasses in the process. McCaughrean trod on them with a crunch that made the rest of us wince.

'I've got to fucking screw you, Zanetti,' he dribbled. Shiv and I looked at each other.

'Hello?' I said, peering into his face.

'Gonna fucking split you in half,' he told me, making a lunge for my arm. 'Fuck you. I'm gonna fuck you,' he said, clinging to me now.

Peeling his fat fingers from my skin I pushed him off his chair. He slid easily to the floor, his blubber quivering. I felt guilty as soon as I'd done it.

'I love you,' he burbled, eyes closed. 'Zanetti.'

It occurred to me that perhaps he did.

By now a pair of waiters was dragging the lifeless McCaughrean out of the bar and up the stairs and conversation had resumed.

'Oh, gross,' Shiv concluded, laughing and reaching out to take Misha's hand. Misha was practically shaking with fear at what would now be expected of him. Sexual intercourse with Siobhan Boucherat, or, as she liked to put it, 'full penetrative sex'.

'You gonna take Don up on the offer?' she asked.

'Tempting,' I said and stood up to go to bed. It must have been 2 a.m. already. 'See you tomorrow.' I kissed Shiv and left.

I skipped upstairs and left the noise and the boozy fumes behind me, emerging suddenly into the thick dark and heavy silence of the deserted courtyard. I heard something rustle as I crossed and my throat closed up slightly in response. What if McCaughrean had sobered up a bit? I didn't much like the thought of him lurching at me from behind a tree. A lizard darted out in front of me. Far away in the gardens the crickets were screaming.

The heavy clunk of my key in the door echoed off the white walls and when I flicked the light on I found myself quickly scouring the room for danger. Stupid, I thought, giving myself a disapproving tut like a school teacher spotting some graffiti on a desk. It must be something to do with being drooled over all evening. Always makes me feel like someone's out to get me, trying to paw me when I'm not expecting it. I've had it since I was a teenager. The hour or so after the end of the date that hasn't ended in sex makes me nervous. Like someone's going to come after me in the night.

What I did see, though not spectacularly dangerous in itself, was a cream envelope on my pillow, 'Miss Faith Zanetti' written with an expensive fountain pen, the colour seeping slightly into the coarse grain of the paper. It was a note from the General.

'I will not give up so easily,' it said, and a signature. Why couldn't he have left it at reception? Who let him in here? I drank the dregs of the champagne we had abandoned. For the briefest sliver of a second, but long enough for butterflies to creep into my stomach, I considered ringing Eden Jones. Eden Jones, with whom I am absolutely not in love. Not and never will be.

I set my lap-top up on the desk, moving the stationery wallet out of the way and flicking on the big green globe of a lamp. Write the mole story with absolutely no evidence whatsoever but break it myself, or wait a while and let everyone else get started on it as well? I decided that Glover's foreign office friend would have to do as the main source. It was enough for the paper to splash on. Then I could go straight into Meier's denial. I lit a cigarette and started tapping. My Internet connection didn't work so I had to talk it over to copy: new sentence, If Israel – capital 'I' for Israel – is going to find the traitor in its midst – m-i-d-s-t – comma . . .

I was just finishing when Shiv barged in. I hadn't locked the door. She was carrying a bottle of beer.

'Asleep. He just went to sleep. One blow-job and out like a light,' she whined, stealing a cigarette off me and lying down on the bed. 'What is the point of that?'

I shut my computer and smiled at her, wandering over to get a swig of beer.

What is the point? I wondered. None, as far as I could see. But I could have told her that before she went to bed with him. She humphed dramatically.

'Where did you find him?' I asked her.

'He found me. You know that piece I did about the children's mental hospital in Haifa?'

'No.'

'Well, I did. Fuck. Don't you read the papers?'

'No.'

'Anyway, he wanted some of the numbers from it. He read it on the Internet while he was researching his story, apparently. Sounds really grim,' she said, wincing at the thought of it.

'You said he was doing Russian underworld crap?' I said, leaning my elbows on my knees and peering at her. It was starting to get light outside. Or, at least, less dark.

'He is. Sort of. Russian underworld and child trafficking,' she sighed.

'Oh God.'

'Yeah.'

We sat in silence for a bit, being tired and trying not to think about Misha's story. Eventually Shiv hauled herself up.

'Might try and rouse him now,' she said. ''Night, sweetie.'

When she got to the door she looked back at me, her face somehow different. Pinched. Or perhaps she'd just stumbled into some bad light and the fact that we weren't sixteen any more had shocked me more than it should have done.

'Listen,' she said, and bit her lip.

'Listening.' I nodded, bouncing my curls.

'I know one oughtn't to be too pathetic about this sort of thing, but Misha's story is getting a bit sort of . . .' she paused. 'Someone phoned my room and threatened to kill me. Arab.'

She sat back down on the bed and I put my cigarette out.

'Why?'

'I don't know. It's definitely Misha's thing, though. He asked me not to tell anyone, but if you . . . if anything happens to me . . . to Misha or me . . . will you?'

'Don't be so fucking ridiculous,' I laughed. 'People are always phoning up threatening you.' In her case usually someone she's slept with and not called. I reminded her of this but she didn't even smile.

'No. It's not that,' she said and then she laughed – all fake and irritating.

She kissed me on the cheek and slapped me on the back. It was a sort of acknowledgement that we'd made it. Abroad. In danger. Well-paid. We couldn't say it out loud, but here we both were. Goal achieved.

I cleaned my teeth and spat my evening's disgust at the General and McCaughrean down the sink. I hate it when someone like Shiv gets scared. It's a breach of protocol. Other people are scared. Not us. Taking comfort in my old grey T-shirt, I climbed into the enormous white sea of a bed. But I couldn't sleep. I heard footsteps in the courtyard. There was scuttering in the bathroom. The phone startled me with a deafeningly sudden ring, but it was a wrong number in Hebrew. When finally I put my head under the duvet and curled myself into a protective ball, I swear I heard someone tiptoeing across the tiles.

'Who the fuck is that?' I shouted, sitting up. But then I felt silly. I hated myself in this edgy mood. First-night nerves. I went into the bathroom and took a diazepam with a glass of water. I suppose I must have fallen asleep some time after the call to dawn prayer because when I came round everyone was already having breakfast outside my window, McCaughrean included. Seeing him there I was surprised at myself for having worried about a nocturnal assault. He was benign enough, picking the raisins out of a sugared bun.

The white-painted iron tables had crisp cloths thrown over them and the little peak of a starched napkin stabbed the air under McCaughrean's chin. Grant Bradford's fork flashed and his *International Herald Tribune* crackled. He and the other tabloids had obviously stayed up drinking all night. Red-eyed and hungover, bravado was necessary. His laughter was forced.

A waiter buzzed about with a tall silver pot of bitter coffee, a fat jug of milk, and a tray of pastries and steaming rolls, mountains of bright fruit. Blinding light glared through the shade of the citrus trees. The French RTF correspondent had put her sunglasses on. It was already hot.

I pulled on a pair of scrumpled pants and went into the bathroom. While I was asleep, someone had drawn a big question mark on my mirror in black felt tip. What the hell was that supposed to mean? I was reminded of something my mum used to say: 'Someone walked over my grave.' Then, to completely knock the lovely calm of the diazepam out of me, I dropped the sodding tooth glass, stupidly perched on the edge of the sink. 'Shit!' I shouted, as it smashed to the floor. A tiny shard lodged itself in my calf and a trickle of blood ran down to my ankle. I tweezed the sliver of glass out and washed it down the sink, picking up the bigger pieces from the floor with my fingers. When I finished I noticed I'd made a bloody footprint on the tiles.

'Fucking hell,' I sighed and left it for the chambermaid. I'd have to tip her properly when I checked out. I pulled my hair back, put on a shirt, jeans and boots and stomped outside for some breakfast.

'Hey, Don,' I said, sitting down next to him.

'Hey, Zanetti. Sleep well?' he asked. 'Hot as an A-rab's armpit already.'

I laughed. 'You always say that, McCaughrean.'

CHAPTER TWO

I drank some coffee and squinted at the newspaper while McCaughrean played with his pile of raisins. Another Israeli soldier killed, more night raids on Palestinian suspects. Boring now, and all the more bleak for that.

'You still going out to Ramallah, Grant?' I asked, holding a hand up over my eyes.

'Mmmm.' He nodded, pulling a piece of tobacco off the end of his tongue and exhaling grimly. His face is so covered in freckles it looks as though someone has thrown a huge handful of sesame seeds at it and they've stuck there. His hair almost glows. The colour unnatural.

'Near there. Shiv's coming. Get your arse in gear though, driver's in reception already,' he said, looking down at his watch and standing up.

Then, holding his cigarette between his lips and wincing to keep the smoke out of his eyes, he pulled some crumpled notes from the back pocket of his jeans and tossed them on to the table where the crumbs of his breakfast were scattered. 'Don't spend it all at once, Ihsan,' he shouted to the waiter. I wondered if Ihsan thought he was a tosser or was just grateful for the big tip.

'OK. Let me call the desk. Give me ten seconds,' I yelled over. I think it's one of the things people like about this job. Having to tell someone where you are every second of every day. Never out of touch, never alone. Someone has always booked you a room, hired you a car. People think it involves being all grown-up and brave and independent, but actually we are happily infantilised by it all. This is where I'm going to be today, Mummy. Of course, it's really so that you can write what they want you to when they want you to if they hear the news first, but it's also so that if you get lost or hurt or kidnapped they have the beginnings of how to find you. I bet none of us were properly looked after as children. That's why we like the attention. Or perhaps I'm just speaking for myself.

'McCaughrean?' I asked, getting up. I like going on trips with McCaughrean. Makes me feel agile.

'Naaah. Might hang around downtown. Wait for a car bomb. You never know your luck,' he said, shaking his head and holding his hand up in farewell.

'You never do,' I agreed and skipped back into my room. It was cooler in there. Easier to breathe.

'Yup. Couple of hundred words,' Martin Glover crackled idly into his London receiver. 'Why are they killing our sons, type of thing. Be nice if you could get us a suicide-bomber who's having doubts about his vocation.'

I mean, did he want me just to harangue someone until they said something like: 'Well, when I was little I wanted to be a vet', so that the subs could then twist it into some kind of headline about how Hamas was dragging boys out of vet school and forcing them to kill themselves? Or did Martin Glover honestly believe that a terrorist was going to meander up to me, offer me a drink and pour his soul out?

'I don't know why I'm doing this. I love Israelis,' he'd say, crying into his empty cup.

I did once interview the wife of a martyr. One of the Saturday specials they used to send me over for. McCaughrean did the pictures for it, actually. He's good. Annoying, but good. Anyway, she'd met him at university and hadn't been particularly religious until then. She said his fervour was completely captivating. He had always told her he was going to kill himself for God and for Palestine and she had spent years almost expecting it. They had two children and after a while she stopped thinking about it. The day it happened, he said goodbye to them all and he was crying when he hugged the children. That was when she knew. She said she was breathless and panicking all day and then she heard the news on the radio. He was gone. He told his sons he wanted them to be martyrs too, but she now tries to convince them that fighting with your education is fighting too. Fat chance she's got, poor woman. She said that not crying was the hardest thing. They are supposed to be proud and not mourn. She's married to her husband's brother now, but she says she'll miss him until they meet again in paradise.

Glover appeared to be doing foreign today. I'd only dealt with the real foreign editor twice and now Glover had taken over while the new girl had been relegated to doing some silly column about abroad (Martin's opinion, not mine). Before I could say anything else, he was shouting over the receiver about an orangutan in St Petersburg zoo who was addicted to *EastEnders*. 'Talk to you later, then,' I said. I would make my own decision about his story idea I supposed.

'Yeah. Don't let my Shivvy get up to no good, will you, Zanetti?' he laughed, hanging up. At least I'd got him before lunch – sober, and therefore with an outside chance of remembering he'd commissioned me.

It's difficult, Israel. Obviously the papers have to cover it pretty comprehensively and we all love being here (always a good story plus hot and beautiful), but most people at home aren't that interested. Nobody without some kind of racial or religious link at any rate and they, as we know, don't count. It's middle England we're aiming for. As Martin so loves to tell us all with a swill of his claret – 'Nobody Reads Foreign News.'

The American media have tried to do away with it altogether, despite the fact that they spend most of the time killing people abroad. We just try to grab people's attention with orangutans. That or a diagram of a tank or something. You know, big pieces written by the diplomatic editor and featuring weaponry for boys.

I remember once the office manager telling me back in London that she'd taken her three-year-old son to the Science Museum, and despite the fact that he had never seen a space rocket before and they hadn't looked at any of the space stuff in the museum, he'd chosen a rocket out of everything in the gift shop. He'd just pointed his little finger at the ten-inch penis thing with the American flag on the side. Without even knowing why. Thirty years from now, he'll be scrutinizing some newspaper diagram of a supergun and reading political biographies, God save him.

'*Ahlan, habibti,*' I said, hopping into the back seat of the car next to Shiv. '*Kief halek?*' It was hot. It's almost not worth a comment because it's always hot, but somehow every time you feel it, it's all you can think about. 'God, I'm hot' . . . 'Jesus, it's hot' . . . or, as McCaughrean will tell you, 'Hot as an A-rab's armpit out here.'

Shiv shoved up to make room for me.

'Not too bad, actually.' She smiled. 'Misha was rather lovely once I'd shaken him back to life. Weird, though. I haven't slept with anyone uncircumcised for ages.' I'm sure that had to be a lie. She seemed to sleep with pretty much anyone she could lay her hands on. Maybe she had Martin set up as some sort of father figure and was taunting him with her conquests, rebelling. Maybe it was an agreement they had. She once told me, in a gushingly sincere moment (we didn't tend to do American soap conversations as a rule), that he made her feel safe. She liked having someone to go home to.

'Oh rubbish,' I said.

'No, really.'

Grant lurched round from the front to look at us, slouching his face over the back of his seat. The pale watery-blue of his eyes was even paler in the sunshine, his eyebrows orange crescents of hair above them. A little girl came up to the car window and tried to sell the driver a box of tissues. She was about five or six in a filthy pink cotton dress once made for someone to go to a party in. She was shooed away with a couple of shekels.

'God. I don't know how come you notice these things,' I said, rooting around in my pocket for some chewing gum. You don't lie there in bed taking notes like some genito-urinary nurse. Not that I had done too much lying there in bed with anyone lately. Suddenly, I couldn't remember whether or not Eden was circumcised. No, I didn't think he was.

'*Wallahi!* What are you talking about? How could you not notice when someone's got this whole thing of skin hanging off the end of his dick?' Shiv asked, incredulous, holding her hand out for a piece of gum.

'Hey. It doesn't hang, thank you very much, and we're much more sensitive.' Grant coughed, reaching over to poke Shiv in the shoulder.

'Yeah, you come quicker.' Shiv unwrapped the gum I'd passed her, glancing up as the driver started the engine. She put her shades on with a smile. I wondered about Martin, but was too repulsed to ask.

'Just spoke to Martin,' I said. 'He asked me to keep an eye on you.'

The driver asked Grant in Arabic if we were ready to go and Grant leant out of the window to see if the bloke from the *Mail* was anywhere around. He wasn't, but McCaughrean was. He took up most of around.

He was running towards us, his belly shaking, his face streaming with sweat. He looked as though he might actually melt.

'Changed my mind,' he told me, squeezing in so that Shiv was pressed up against the door in great discomfort and I had his enormous legs spilling into my lap. He smelt of nasty aftershave and I noticed he had a bloody scrap of tissue over a cut on his face. Why can't men shave without cutting themselves? Women seem to manage to shave their legs without cutting themselves. Surely, after twenty years of practice, it must be possible. It's like tennis players serving out. You'd think they'd have mastered the serve early on in their training, it being such a key element of the game.

'Fuck me, McCaughrean. Lose some weight,' Shiv told him.

'I've lost about a fucking stone trying to catch you guys up,' he moaned, gasping. 'What are we waiting for?'

'Nothing,' said Grant. 'Let's go.' He nodded at the driver and we skidded off in a cloud of dust towards Ramallah.

'FBI forecast for the Israeli occupied West Bank today . . .' Grant began in an American newsreadery voice.

'Reoccupied,' Shiv corrected him.

'Reoccupied West Bank today,' he went on. 'Hot. Sunny. Seasonably dangerous.'

'Great,' said Shiv. She was being ironic, but she meant it too. If it wasn't dangerous we wouldn't be going. We'd be doing stories about the decline of British seaside resorts for the features pages. We knew we were lucky, but to say so would shatter the illusion.

The radio was playing 'She Drives Me Crazy' by The Fine Young Cannibals and we all sang along as the desert whizzed past: '. . . and aaaaaaah caaaaaan't heyyylp mahseeyeyelf . . .'

They're nice, these trips where you just go off as a pack, all doing the same daily story. Most of the time it's obvious what the story is and you all have to file it whether you like it or not. You don't get a big bomb going off and a couple of papers covering something else. Half the time, everyone's copying it off Reuters. It makes for camaraderie, anyway. Investigations, where people are being cagey about their contacts and what they've got, tend to sour an atmosphere. I'd do the daily stuff with the others today and try to keep as quiet as possible about my mole.

McCaughrean handed Grant a piece of paper with 'Press – Don't Shoot' written on it in Arabic and Hebrew and Grant propped it up in the car window. The driver snorted.

By the time we pulled up at the first Israeli checkpoint, I had had just about enough of being engulfed by the spread of McCaughrean. There was a biblical-looking shepherd up on the hillside and olive trees speckled about beneath him. The sky was a livid blue.

'Come on, lardy. Let me out,' I begged, reaching across him to open the door while a soldier with an M16 and a skull cap fiddled around with our documents. McCaughrean hauled himself out, leaning breathlessly against the car. He dragged a camera from his bag and put it to his face. Suddenly he looked healthier, professional, whole.

I stood in the dust at the side of the road and touched my toes, rolled my head from shoulder to shoulder and lit a cigarette. The desert rippled gold into the distance, but near us the landscape was rocky and grey, olive and palm trees bafflingly alive in the barrenness. Likewise people who haven't much changed since someone did the illustrations for *Children's Stories From The Old Testament* in 1934. A shepherd with a crooked stick and no teeth. A mother breastfeeding a baby while she walks along carrying a bundle of sticks on her back.

'Boucherat?' the soldier asked in a very English accent. He leant into the window, screwing his face up at the cloud of acrid smoke.

'That's me, gorgeous.' Shiv winked. ''Sup?'

'Up, Ms Boucherat, is that I can't see any accreditation here,' he told her, flicking her passport and various bits of press plastic into her face.

I looked again at the back of his head. Something familiar. Or maybe just the sneer of north London in his voice.

I moved closer, aware that this was a man who could be seriously useful. And someone I could get on with, by the sounds of him. I'd grown up with hundreds of these types. He looked a bit like Simon Albert. I could easily picture this boy in a UCS uniform.

It could be Simon Albert, come to think of it, though I didn't remember him as the devout synagogue-going type, so it was unlikely he'd be here, policing an Israeli checkpoint. In fact, he was a left-wing atheist. The only person in the world who called people 'Trotskyites', meaning that they were disgustingly right-wing. On the other hand, he did do quite a good impression of someone called Rabbi Goldberg who was always telling his congregation that there were more important things in the world than being Jewish and believing in God. I can't remember what they were, though.

'What are you doing not in Hampstead?' I asked him, smirking. Worth a try, I thought.

He laughed.

'You remind me of someone. You don't know Simon Albert, do you?' I tried again.

He stood up to face me and he smiled.

'He was the year below me at school,' he said. 'Why?'

We stood there laughing for a bit, reminiscing. His name, he said, was Yo. Yoram. We'd both been at a party in Simon's parents' house on Frognal in 1985. Dan Lucas was sick on a glass table and somebody put a terrapin in the toaster.

'Hey!' Shiv shouted from inside the car. 'Can you stop chatting up the military and get back in?' I was cramping her style.

'Are you going to let me past or not, darling?' she asked Yo. Most people wouldn't have dared refuse.

He looked at me and raised one eyebrow. 'Sorry. Closed Military Area.'

The whole car swore in unison. I listened to the pitch of their bickering about what to do next. As insistent and belligerent as the background whine of the *Today* programme and at least half as annoying.

'What's the deal with the raid? Can you get me on it?' I wanted to know. I smiled pleadingly. No point in messing around with these things. Sometimes asking works. Quite apart from the fact that you usually only have a couple of minutes to get the right answer. It's the tone of your voice and the look on your face. This time, I'd got it right.

'Should think so. Captain's my dad's cousin. You'll have to hang around here a bit, though. Pretend you're still planning to go back to Jerusalem,' Yo told me, shooting a glance over towards his superiors who were standing by a corrugated iron hut. He didn't do checkpoint patrol, he told me, but they had stopped here to get ready, and a guy he knew had wanted to go on a fag break.

There was a big armoured-looking van with blacked-out windows parked next to the hut and what seemed to be a whole battalion of blokes in flak jackets loafing about waiting to get in. It was, he said, his unit. The kind of unit, I thought, that you wouldn't want raiding your house of an evening. Nothing slap-dash here. And one of them could even be killing off his own comrades, impossible though it seemed. Or not impossible. Even the slickest armies, and this is one of the slickest, has its corruption, its own personal psychopaths. Shame. I always really like these boys.

I said waiting was fine and I made Shiv and the others bugger off back where they came from without me.

'Shit,' Shiv said. 'When I flirt all I ever get is laid.'

'Suicide bomber watch it is, then,' McCaughrean sighed. It was a fair cop and they knew it. I was better at the flirt than they were. Shiv made a snarling face at me, the suggestion being that if she'd managed to get out of the car and confront him she could have beaten me to it. Into his trousers, maybe. To the story, no chance. I threw up my hands in a 'tough shit' gesture and blew them a kiss.

'I'll see you back at the hotel tonight,' I said, patting the side of the car like a horse and watching them cruise off into the distance. 'Be careful!' I shouted after them and Grant waved his hand from the window. I kicked some of the dust off my boots and squinted at Yo.

'It's surreal to meet you,' I smiled, still disbelieving, and he waved at a friend to come and relieve him as another car pulled up. 'Did you know Becky Kaufman?'

'Know her? I went out with her for three years,' he said, grinning.

'No!' I laughed.

Actually, the vehicle that had slowed for inspection was a truck driven by a young Arab boy. His mum was sitting next to him with a basket of stuff in her lap. Bread, lemons, a bottle of Coke. Yo's colleague waved them through as we walked away from the roadside. I saw that they had an ox's head lying in a pool of blood in the back. Supper, I suppose.

I smacked my lips. 'Mmmmm.'

Yo laughed and introduced his captain to me as Moshe. I had butterflies in my stomach at my success in getting him to let me stay. A flirt victory was always satisfying and he'd already got me a story. If I could keep him going, he might even help me with the mole thing, juniorish though he was. As well as being a dream source of daily violence to fill the pages with. It's the weirdest thing about this job. Every single day (if you're lucky) you see something that for the poor fuckers involved is the biggest thing that will ever happen to them – that will inform their lives for ever: being shot, losing a relative or friend, witnessing some personal horror, watching their own house explode or whatever. Unimaginable drama that we go back to the hotel, digest, rehash and, for the most part, forget. A blank slate for tomorrow.

Moshe looked tough. He was about forty, broad-shouldered, slightly scarred, very tanned with a short grey crew cut. He had hands like huge hams and thick dark hair on his arms. He sat on a stool with his legs splayed apart as though he had a big black boot stomped down on the heads of two of his adversaries.

'Faith Zanetti. Old friend of mine. Come to tell the world what evil oppressors we are,' Yo explained. That wasn't precisely my mission, but mention that Palestinians have children or go shopping and Zionists pounce on you as the enemy. And, of course, vice versa.

Moshe laughed mirthlessly. If I wasn't mistaken, he was actually polishing his gun.

'You hang out with us – I don't know about you. Clear?' he told me, scowling from the shade of the hut. That was fine. The less he knew about me, frankly, the better.

You see, they put on this fuck-you act, but actually they're dying for some decent coverage. They like it when the press describes them as militarily superior. The government PR people might not like it, which is why you can never get official permission for these things, but the actual army loves it as long they don't get any personal blame for our presence.

I nodded and felt around for the comforting shape of my cigarette packet in my pocket.

'Raid to arrest a Hamas operative,' Yo told me quietly. 'Karim Rakhmani.'

'Right,' I answered. An F16 flew low over us and a few of the blokes waved up at it.

'A busy day,' Moshe stated, standing up with a sigh.

'He's quite . . .' I muttered to Yo when Moshe had moved away a bit.

'Yeah,' Yo agreed. 'Just a touch.'

We waited all day. We played chess. I got stung by a black and white butterfly/dragonfly thing the size of my hand. We ate a whole jar of pickled gherkins. We smoked. We sat in the sand. We talked about being teenagers in London. Some of the boys taught me dirty words in Hebrew. We played charades. Yo did *Everything You Always Wanted to*

Know About Sex But Were Too Afraid to Ask. I did *Gulag Archipelago*. Eventually the sky tinged orange around the edges, the traffic on the dirt road thinned out from a car every fifteen minutes to one every half-hour and there was very nearly a breeze. It was time to go.

Moshe called his men together and I kept close to Yo for immediate translations of the Hebrew.

'OK, everyone black up,' Moshe shouted, and the men started drawing black stripes on their faces with thick, greasy crayons of stage make-up. It was odd to think that a soldier just like them, or maybe even one of them, was a traitor, a double agent with his head full of fear and bravado. Made me edgy. The grease paint smelt familiar. Weird to be reminded of school plays out here in the sweltering sand. I was once Gwendolen in *The Importance of Being Earnest*. Not that I had to black up for it, obviously.

'Mmmm. Those Arabs'll never spot you now,' I whispered.

'Fuck off,' Yo told me.

The Captain was doing some more shouting so I shut up.

'I don't want to see anyone firing unless you see a weapon. We want to bring this fucker in alive. You!' he pointed, apparently at the unit's Arabic speaker. 'Tell them to let the women and children leave before we go in. Explain to everyone exactly what is happening. I don't want anyone saying there was no warning. OK, boys. We're moving.'

With a dark clatter of weaponry the soldiers leapt into the van and sat down against the sides, facing each other on thin benches.

I crept in after them, helped by huge arms proffered from within.

My leather jacket creaked against Yo's sleeve. It was very very hot and everyone's breath seemed loud.

'Hup you go, Pippi,' I heard someone say and a colossal Alsatian jumped in, panting, her head patted by each in turn, her claws clanking on the metal floor.

I raised my eyebrows at Yo.

'To chase if he runs,' he told me.

'Uh-huh,' I understood. I felt a bit sorry for this bloke already. I

36

mean, I know he was in a fairly risky line of work and all that, but . . .

Yo fiddled with his night-vision glasses.

'You!' I heard Moshe shout from the front. 'You!' he said again. I looked up. 'Me?' I asked.

'You. You are responsible for your own safety. I don't want my men to die for you,' he said.

'No problem.' I smiled. Great. Thanks.

'I just want you to know,' I whispered to Yo, 'that I am fully expecting you to save me even if you die doing it.'

'Same to you.' He grinned. 'This is my first operation.'

'Oh, superb,' I sighed and leant back against the van. I would have to assume he was joking.

Rakhmani, our quarry, was a bloke who produced munitions for suicide bombers – those belts full of explosives that they wear. He had some sort of makeshift factory in one of the villages. The Israelis had been tipped off. Shin Bet's 'intelligence' was that he would definitely be there tonight. I was reminded of the Groucho Marx thing about military intelligence being a contradiction in terms. Laughing to myself, however, seemed out of place in the circumstances.

I like these stories. You can lose yourself in the pace of it. In the lack of responsibility. We bumped along and I watched Yo and the boys getting their weapons ready, checking their grenades. But I wasn't really there. Just looking in at them from outside. It sounds stupid, but it's comforting.

When I was little, before it happened, I used to sit in front of the television with Evie, watching the news. Sometimes we saw Dad in the shot, standing there with his notebook in front of some blazing building. I would lie awake at night hoping that he was safe and would come home to us. I felt as though everywhere he went he was surrounded by fire and the sound of gunshot. I didn't know then that he actively went out to find all that and that he then returned to his hotel for a Martini up with a twist.

At home, in the grey gloom of 1970s London, I felt responsible for him, for the whole chaotic world. I fell in love with Elvis Presley. I thought if I counted enough magpies we might stay safe tonight. And now I am here myself, watching, waiting, witnessing the terror, and then slipping back to the nursery safety of the hotel and all the people who are expecting me. Let Evie worry, let Eden miss me (I wonder if he does), let Londoners get worked up about tube overcrowding. I am a long way away, safe in my shell of anonymity, like Don behind his camera. It's not my war and they are not my people. I will be drinking vodka tonight when Karim Rakhmani lies defeated in his cell. He doesn't yet know that he has made his last explosive belt.

Moshe held his hand up.

'Cut the engine,' he said. Pippi pricked up her ears. The driver opened the back doors and she leapt out into the dust, wagging her tail. We followed her, silent now, the men creeping in their big boots. We were on an ordinary street, surrounded by a maze of houses and alleys, satellite dishes on the balconies, dirt roads, a few roaming dogs alert to Pippi's presence. There were a couple of shops with their corrugated iron blinds down. The kind of place that sells fizzy drinks, plastic combs and cigarettes. Some of the houses had been inhabited half-built when the money ran out; others made an effort at sedateness – pots of flowers on the steps, a painted door. It was quiet. The kind of quiet that seems suspicious: Too quiet. I felt, and I imagine the soldiers did too, that we were expected. No blinds up, no net curtains twitching.

The night was thick and black. You don't get street lighting in these places and the moon makes everything metallic. A billion stars pricked the sky.

The soldiers shuffled slowly towards Rakhmani's house, backs to the wall, weapons cocked. I followed, tiptoeing in my cowboy boots, holding my pockets quiet. Yo looked like a real soldier now, grim-faced with sharp edges, chiselled like an action man.

The dust made me want to cough. When Moshe knocked on the iron door with the butt of his gun, we all flinched. It was a deliberate insult to the silence, an act of seemingly unwarranted aggression. And this was just the beginning. Not all that surprisingly, there was no answer and Moshe knocked again. He beckoned to the Arabic speaker he had been shouting at earlier and the boy raised his megaphone to his lips. His instructions echoed into the night. He repeated them. A cat yowled and we all span round to see it crouched in the middle of the street, fur on end, hissing at Pippi. She snarled and strained at the leash.

I didn't catch anyone giving the order, but after a breath of a pause there was an explosion of action. The first few men, just three or four, dashed forwards at a crouch, weapons thrust in front of them. Somebody bashed the front door down and a woman screamed from inside. A baby started crying and the sky filled with smoke. A machine gun flashed and crackled and the air was dense with fear and noise and running. From a cellar door a terrified woman appeared with three or four children and a bundle of stuff, shading her face from the assault. An empty Sprite can rolled in front of my feet. One of the soldiers, not Yo, shunted the family quickly and gracelessly away from the scene towards the van. The night was bright now from our floodlights and the gunfire.

When my eyes adjusted enough to squint through the chaos, I spotted Yo hurtling into Rakhmani's house through the front door and, ducking my head down more out of instinct than any real belief that this might somehow be safer than standing up straight, I ran up the steps to follow him. He flicked his gaze back to register me but he didn't speak. Every nerve in his face was taut with purpose.

Inside, the hallway was narrow and filled with smoke. Everyone was shouting in Hebrew and somebody was obviously returning fire from somewhere, but I couldn't tell where yet. Yo edged along, breathing hard. I copied him and shut my eyes against the stinging smoke, feeling the coarse cotton of Yo's uniform brushing against me. Small comfort, really.

We were edging down some stairs in the screaming darkness when Yo tripped and fell.

'Shit,' I whispered and crouched down to help him up. I stumbled over his boots to find a hand. I pulled hard at it.

'Get the fuck up,' I hissed. 'Yo?'

He groaned ominously.

'Get up!' I told him. There was a crackle of automatic fire just beneath us.

'My hand. My fucking hand,' he said.

'Yo! I've got your fucking hand. Get up!' I was shouting now. Mustn't stay in one place too long.

'Not that one, you silly cow,' he spat. 'The other one. I've been shot in the fucking hand!'

'Oh God,' I said as he vomited.

I knelt down and put my arms around him, dragging him up by the shoulders. He leant on me hard and we staggered, coughing, back up the steps and out of the front door to petrify in front of a bank of eager gun nozzles. Blinded by lights, I put my hand over my eyes and screamed in English.

'Yoram's been shot. Help!' There was a kerfuffle as orders were given and a boy with a gun ran up to take Yo back to the van while a paramedic with his tools in a briefcase followed them.

I stood alone for a second on the doorstep of Rakhmani's house in the intense stage lighting with smoke spewing out behind me like dry ice. I was just about to move when an enormous force bashed into my back. For a second I was flying through the dark air, not sure how far it was to the floor. Like the feeling of leaping off a high diving board. But I soon felt the sharp edge of a stone step in my thigh and rolled off it to find myself face down and winded in the dust. I had been hit by a gang of four breathless soldiers. They were carrying a skinny, struggling man by his arms and legs. They threw him to the ground next to me, a Britney Spears T-shirt billowing surreally out as he fell. A soldier sat on him and tied his arms behind his back. The prisoner spat out a mouthful of dirt, and wriggled to get his green bandana out of his eyes. He was yelling in Arabic, but he stopped, stunned, when he saw my face on the floor less than a foot from his own.

'Hi,' I said, stupidly. Well, it just came out.

The fear and hatred skittered about in his eyes and he seemed almost to soften. Raising his eyebrows in acknowledgement of the bizarreness of the situation and perhaps of our common humanity (is that possible?), he looked at me.

'Hi,' he said. It was that thing again. Here I was at his crisis. Watching. This was it for him. For me, what? Nothing really. The whole interlude must have taken less than three seconds, but it seemed far longer. I stood up and wiped my cheek as a few other, seemingly less important, captives were dragged out, one of them bleeding dramatically from the head. A stream of blood already stained the route to the armoured van – Yo's hand, I suppose.

Now that the mission seemed over, and the quiet was beginning to return, I could hear his muffled shouts of pain. Rakhmani, apparently, had been silenced.

Moshe shouted an order to evacuate the area and I followed Pippi. Her tail wagging, her nose thrust forward, she was dragging her trainer behind her. A rifle cracked in the distance.

'Hey! Hey! Wait for me!' a familiar voice sounded from inside the house we'd all just left. I knew immediately who it was. I turned back.

'McCaughrean?'

'Zanetti. Help me, for fuck's sake.'

He stumbled down the front steps through the lingering wisps of smoke, his bag banging against his side.

'God. Don, did you get hit?'

I ran towards him, terrified I'd have to turn him wound-down and dredge up other first-aid memories. ABC. Airway, breathing and c . . . c . . . can't remember. I'd have to have a glance at *The Bad News Bible* next time I was in London. It's what we'd called some booklet from a course the desk once made me go on. Something to do with the foreign insurance expenditure being cut if we could all do battleground first aid. We spent three days mostly in the bar, as I remember. I think the name had something to do with the *Good News* bibles we'd all found by our hotel bedsides. Shiv thought it up. Not me.

I could see a dark patch of liquid on Don's khaki jacket.

'I think I've sprained my sodding foot,' he complained.

'Oh Jesus Christ. Come on,' I said, as he leant his stupendous weight on me, his arm round my shoulders. We staggered up to the doors of the van.

'Fuck are you doing here? I thought you'd gone to find a car bomb?' I asked him, throwing his bag to someone just ahead of me, sinking under his bulk. His underarms smelt strongly of goat's cheese.

'Yeah, I was, but the checkpoint bloke told me I could . . . shit . . . get here the back way down the hill. No patrol there,' he said. 'Found a kid who knew Rakhmani's place and I've been stuck in his festering bloody cellar all day. He's a total nutter. Obsessed with Britney Spears.' McCaughrean was sweating so much he looked as though someone had tipped a bucket of water over his head.

'Happened to your chest?' I asked him, inclining my head, which was trapped between his armpit and his elbow, towards the worrying stain on his jacket. He looked down.

'Oh. Spilt my coffee.'

'Bloody hell,' I muttered, heaving him with real difficulty now through the last few feet of dirt.

But just before we got to the open doors of the van, he seemed to stop moving and his head lolled forwards. His shoulders shook. It took me a bewildered moment to realize that he was crying.

'Don? Don? What is it?' I asked, peering into his crumpled face in the black night.

'Oh shit, Zanetti. I miss them. I really miss them,' he sobbed.

His kids. He misses his kids. I almost burst into tears myself. This guy was an emotional wreck.

'I know, Don. I know,' I said quietly. 'Come on. Hup.'

I patted him uselessly on the back and clambered up to sit on a bench with the victorious unit. They were slumped in total exhaustion. McCaughrean was wiping his face with his sleeve.

'Sorry,' he muttered.

'Shit, Don. I'm sorry,' I said. 'I can't imagine . . .'

And I can't. I could once. I nearly could. When I first met Eden I had this picture of myself standing over some stove making cookies or something, looking out of a kitchen window at children playing in the garden. Love can do that to a person. I thought it was love, anyway. Lust, maybe. Desperation. Proximity to thirty. Who knows. Thank God I never told him. It embarrassed me even to think of it and I slapped my hand to the cigarette packet in my jacket pocket. Could hardly wait the journey. It flickered into my mind that I ought to have asked Yo about the double agent, not that he was really in a position to know stuff. But I had enough story for now and I wasn't going to let him get away from me.

The prisoners were all at the front end, hessian bags over their heads. (Is it hessian? Rough, hay-coloured stuff. Must be itchy. I mean, apart from everything else.) Rakhmani, I noticed, had thin, bare feet. I didn't think he would appeal much to Britney should the moment ever arise. Yo was still having his hand seen to. He was biting his lip hard and groaning.

'Seriously. My foot really hurts, Faithy,' Don complained, shuffling around to get comfy.

'Don,' I whispered loudly, pushing my hair out of my face. 'On a scale of one to ten, crucifixion is ten. Childbirth is one. Some tortures come in between. Your foot does not hurt.'

'Hurts,' he mumbled, wriggling it back and forth and wincing.

Back in the bar after a long and uncomfortable journey home, Grant Bradford was shouting.

'You must be joking!' he said, slamming his empty glass down on the counter. Salim snatched it up, wiped underneath it, and replaced it with another Jack Daniels on a slightly padded doily in one elegant movement. 'She's an emaciated corpse. Doesn't even get in the top thirty. I would rather eat my own shit than fuck Posh Spice.' He wore Timberlands and armyish khaki trousers. He always did. None of us seemed to have more than one outfit.

'OK, then who?' McCaughrean demanded, shifting awkwardly on his chair, his injured foot balanced ostentatiously on another.

He had insisted on calling a doctor to get it bandaged and was showing it off like a battle injury, telling the story of the Rakhmani raid as though he had played some heroic part in the proceedings: 'Then I spotted bloody Zanetti hobbling around in her high heels and holding hands with a bloody Israeli marksman. Had to carry her handbag back to the van for her afterwards so she didn't break a nail,' he'd said. I kicked his foot and he yowled.

'Dunno. Robin Givens, maybe,' Grant conceded. I don't think he even noticed that he'd finished one drink and that Salim had poured him another.

'Jesus. If you're on to your top ten fucks I'm going to bed,' I told them, sinking the rest of my vodka and slipping off my stool. I still had red Ramallah dirt behind my fingernails and in my hair. 'Where's Shiv?' I asked.

'I left her here at lunch,' Grant said. 'She didn't want to come on bomb-watch. Haven't clapped eyes on her since.'

'I'll check her room. How was it, though?'

'Nothing,' Grant admitted. 'You know how it is. Nothing for days and then three come at once.'

I raised my eyebrows.

''Night, 'night, darlings,' I said.

'Aaaaw, Faithy. You're always in at number one,' McCaughrean assured me, and I bent down to kiss his pudgy cheek. I think we'd bonded in our own little way.

'Thanks, Don.' I smiled, and took the stairs two at a time to get out of the bar.

I trundled up to Shiv's room and knocked on the door. No answer. The crickets were singing and the stars out of the window seemed close and low. I knocked again.

'Shiv? You in there?' I asked.

Nothing. Must be in some sort of drunken coma, I thought, and started to walk off.

But then I heard something. A glass breaking.

'Shiv?' I put my ear to the door. Someone was definitely moving around.

I tried the handle and pushed the door open slowly. The lights were all on and there was a weird smell.

'You OK?' I asked, walking in, my boots somehow too loud on the tiles. She had one of the Pasha's wife's rooms with a big domed ceiling. The whole place had once been a palace. There was a copy of *Crime and Punishment* on the floor and a picture of the Mount of Olives, the frame broken, pieces of glass scattered about. Shiv sat naked on the bed, her legs hugged into her chest. She was rocking backwards and forwards and shivering. Her hair was wet with sweat. Her painted toenails looked oddly incongruous.

'Shiv, what is it?' I asked, sitting down on the bed next to her, pulling a sheet round her shoulders. My first thought, insane now I consider it, was that she had opened the hotel sewing kit thinking it was a book of matches and seen the four unattached buttons sitting there, menacing in their slip of cellophane. Well, she had the fear.

She'd scattered pieces of paper from her wallet all over the place. Receipts, press cards, stamps, a photo of Martin, some letters.

'Is it Misha?' I tried another tack, stupidly hoping for some kind of lovelorn excuse that a different kind of woman might have given for a breakdown. I must admit, it did look like a breakdown. Had Misha maybe done something to hurt her? I wondered ridiculously. For really, of course, the danger had definitely been the other way round. I think if I were to be honest, though, even back then I knew it was Misha's story. She'd been frightened last night when she'd told me about it. More than I especially wanted to admit.

And yes, the mention of him jolted her, and she rolled her eyes and rocked more energetically. It was getting scary. It was like the time we'd taken acid after a party with some bloke Shiv was seeing. He walked out and left us to come down on our own, only Shiv didn't. Not for three days. I stayed in this horrible squat somewhere in Stoke Newington and brought her packets of crisps and cans of Fanta. Afterwards, she said she had no memory of it whatsoever.

'Shall I phone a doctor or something?' No response. I sat on the bed and held her hand. Isn't that the sort of thing you're supposed to do? I'm rubbish at sympathy.

'A drink? Do you fancy a drink?' That was more my area. She nodded. Looking back I suppose I should have known. But the world was bad enough without Shiv succumbing to it. She was the best at laughing it off and I had to hope – for my own sanity, never mind hers – that she'd be better in the morning. After a drink. After a fag. After a coffee. It had always done the trick in the past.

It was a relief anyway to have got at least something out of her, and I ran back down to the bar, clomping across the courtyard, the heat hitting me in the face. I got a bottle of white wine off Salim and the boys started up a great chorus of shouting.

'Who've you got up there, Zanetti?' . . . 'Didn't your mother tell you not to drink alone?' . . . 'Need any help with that, Faithy?'

I ignored them and rushed back up to Shiv. She hadn't moved except to shake the sheet off her back. I poured the wine into tooth glasses and sat beside her. She drank the whole lot in one go and held her glass out for more.

'Shiv, please tell me what happened,' I said, wiping wriggles of hair away from my face. She didn't even seem to hear me.

Four glasses later, all of them slammed back like the first, she lay down with her eyes shut. At this stage I gave up. I stroked her cheek. It was freezing cold, so I put her sheet back on but she pushed it off and stared at me, like someone I'd never met before and frankly never want to meet again.

'Tell Father Bryan – runs an orphanage in Bethlehem,' she said and shut her eyes. I spent ten minutes trying to get more out of her, but she had completely clammed up. Tell him what? This must be the General's guy. This was seriously weird. I had enough on my plate with a mole and a raid and I didn't want to start taking over the investigations of self-serious Russians. Even if Shiv wanted me to. I went downstairs feeling detached and light-headed. I could feel myself pulling back from reality, putting my armour on.

I tried to phone Evie before I went to sleep, so things must have been bad. She is mother substitute enough. Has been since I was small. Still, the more I reach out for comfort, the edgier I feel, so I keep it to a desperate minimum. But she was out and I got the machine. I went to bed, too tired to worry about last night's intruder. Thoughts of Shiv swimming around in my head. I dreamt Eden was having an affair with Britney Spears . . .

CHAPTER THREE

When the ringing smashed into my nightmare, I could hardly remember where I was. My first thought, as I reached out for the receiver, was that nobody calls you at four in the morning with good news. It was already starting to get light outside and a bird was singing from one of the trees in the courtyard. Dawn prayer had begun. Did people seriously get up and do this? I wondered. Probably the kind of thought that in itself brands one an infidel doomed to die a thousand deaths for all eternity.

'Yup?' I asked the telephone, rubbing my hair which spirals completely out of control in the night.

'Hey, pumpkin,' Evie said. 'I was worried about you. How's Israel?' No bad news. Just Evie in London.

'I hate it. It's a sweltering slime pit and my friend Shiv's gone off her rocker. Apart from that it's great,' I said, leaning off the edge of the bed for my cigarettes. 'Beautiful anyway.'

'Shivvy Boucherat?'

'She'll probably be fine. Don't say anything to anyone. Just a harrowing day, I should think. Better in the morning.' I nearly believed it as I said it.

'Well, sugar, be careful. Listen, baby, I gotta go. Just wanted to say hi. I have to be at the airport in an hour,' Evie told me, slurping at some coffee. She was going to New York to do a Gap advert. The ones with beautiful old people.

'Have fun,' I yawned.

'Sure I will, honey. You be careful now. Don't try to be like your father. He was an idiot,' she advised and we both laughed.

Evie is the nearest thing I have to home. I stayed with her and Dad most of the time when I was little. She was the first girlfriend he ever had who didn't buy me any presents. 'Honey,' she said, 'if you don't like me, a Barbie doll ain't gonna help.' Actually, it might have done, but I liked her anyway. Dad had met her on a story and fallen madly in love with her because her picture was in magazines and she had a maths degree. His dream woman. Really, though, I think she could have got away without the degree. Not without the looks, though. She was still a real model then. Doing her best to put Pittsburgh, Pennsylvania behind her. She called it Shitsburgh. Ha ha.

It was Dad who really put it behind her though. Hooking up with an English man. And Mum was already a lost cause. You get a lot of Americans like that. People who feel that being with someone British will give them a feeling of permanence. I bet it doesn't work. Dad, at any rate, can't have been much comfort to anyone. Symbolic comfort, perhaps, I thought. After all, you couldn't ever have anything but a little scrap of Dad. I felt, as she probably did, as though I spent half my life clinging to what I could get of him, collecting the pieces he gave me, little presents from around the rumbling world, and desperately trying to scrabble back the pieces I felt should have been mine – some that he had given to Evie, to his work, his friends. Bits I thought they didn't deserve since I didn't have enough myself. I knew he was slipping through my fingers all the time, like sand through an hourglass, and that one day, when I was least expecting it, it would run out, slip away, and that would be that. And it was.

I must have been about two or three when I spent a whole day trying to wake Mum up. I remember the dark room and the feeling of horror. Dad and Evie came to get me and Evie was wearing a silk nightie the colour of dark chocolate with creamy lace around the edges. Or, at least, that's how I remember it. The older you get, the more you realize how selective and inventive memory is. We use it like Soviet historians, cutting and shaping it to support our interpretation of events. Or all historians, perhaps.

I sat on the edge of the bed to finish my cigarette, cooling my feet on the tiles. My computer lurked accusingly on the desk next to the water carafe, so I paid it its dues and filed the piece about the raid, fiddling with a tangled nest of black wires to get the connection to London.

I decided not to check on Shiv again until morning. Give her time to be fine again. To have forgotten all about it, like the acid. When I made it to the bathroom, my mind was so full of my piece about Yo and the intention to find out how his hand was that I forgot to expect my message on the mirror. There it was, though. A heart, this time. I smiled. That was not so bad. A whole hell of a lot less menacing than the question mark, at any rate. A crush. But who? McCaughrean? The General? It was hard to take seriously the idea of either of them creeping around my hotel room once I had gone to sleep. And how would they know I'd gone to sleep?

Now if Janet Fischer had been around, I'd have suspected her immediately. Fischer is the gritty, hard-faced CNN correspondent with a reputation for lechery. Among her colleagues, that is. Her public would never suspect her of anything but righteousness. She's everywhere they wouldn't want to be, bullets flying around behind her, explosions lighting up the corner of the shot. We, however, know her as the one who turns up pissed at two o'clock in the morning, banging on the doors of the female members of the press pack, her dressing gown slung low enough to reveal her wares. I wonder how often she's successful. Certainly I haven't succumbed. Yet. I rubbed the heart off the mirror with a wet flannel and cleaned my teeth.

Dashing Dr Ahmed was at the door twenty minutes after my 6 a.m. call, and I walked him up to Shiv's room. I pulled at my hair and strode too purposefully. I hoped she would be in there getting dressed, baffled to see me with the men in white coats. Well, one man in a maroon leather jacket and a glistening moustache.

Dr Ahmed was used to being called out to the hacks at the American Colony. Indeed, he had bandaged McCaughrean's silly foot only yesterday. He was effectively the hotel doctor and he made a great living out of it. Vaguely comical though he was. A lizard flashed in front of us just as we got to Shiv's door.

'A good omen,' Dr Ahmed commented, uselessly.

'Good.' I smiled. 'It had better be.'

It wasn't though. She was exactly where I had left her, except awake. She acknowledged us in the sense that she could clearly see that we were there, but she wouldn't speak or move. The doctor took her temperature, pulse and blood pressure, felt her glands, peered into her eyes, and tutted a lot. He had white socks on and a lot of something or other shiny in his hair.

'I think your friend is suffering from nervous exhaustion, Miss Zanetti,' he concluded, rolling his R's and pouring himself a glass of water with an unnecessary 'May I?'

He put a few Valium down on Shiv's bedside table and told me that the best thing she could do was sleep for a day or two. I thanked him. I didn't believe it though. I mean, we could all lie there and claim to be suffering from nervous exhaustion. She didn't have the kind of nerves that got racked. Nonetheless, she seemed to perk up a bit at the sight of the pills, sitting up naked in bed, popping them expertly out of their foil and crunching them enthusiastically between her teeth like an old horse with a sugar lump.

'Better?' I asked and she met my eye and nodded before lying back down and pulling the sheet up over her head. A sign, I assumed, that I should leave. I didn't want to. Frankly, if we'd been in London I probably would have dragged her off to be sectioned. There was though, I think, still a bit of me that thought she'd bounce back. That later on I'd find her laughing and apologetic.

'Be well,' I said. 'I'll come back later.' I put my mask on in the corridor. Faith Zanetti. Unflinching.

When I got down to the courtyard, it was breakfast time.

Coffee seemed like a good plan before what was becoming an unavoidable trip to see the Jesuit priest. It seemed the least I could do for her. In fact, Father Bryan was indeed the same man the General had mentioned at dinner in the context of being a friend to humanity. These kinds of things, mutual friends and contacts, always seem like an enormous coincidence when you first start working. Or to people who arrive somewhere in a non-journalistic capacity. In fact, of course, the world inhabited by ex-pats is minuscule and they all know not only each other but all the same locals as well.

I pretended to myself that I was really going out there for the story, which was in any case a nice one. The desk would love it. Human interest, Palestinian kids, an English bloke, an Israeli military benfactor. All the ingredients. They liked to do that at the weekend – make people see that the country they have been reading about all week has peacetime too. It isn't all bombs and booby traps. Real people live there. People with feelings, just like you and me. Ugh. Still, you never knew, he might even have a dog – a reliable-companion-in-an-unreliable-world-type of thing. Perfect.

I sat down with Grant Bradford who was doing the word jumble in the *Herald Tribune*. He had chewed the top off his biro and was getting blue ink on his lips. I took one of his cigarettes and was just about to wave for some coffee when Zahir from the desk psychically brought me some, seeing what I needed before I had a chance to open my mouth. Coffee – steaming, thick, and black as oil. He put a fat slice of dripping watermelon down next to it on a gleaming plate which was the same turquoise as the mosaics on our table.

'Fuck it. I hate this thing,' Grant sighed, pushing the paper round to face me. 'Help.' He poked his finger at the offending word.

'Canary,' I said, smiling triumphantly. 'It's canary.'

'Cafuckingnary. Yup,' he admitted, throwing his head back in defeat and squinting in the blazing sunlight. The lemon above his head looked as though it might drop off on to him at any moment.

We smiled at each other, forgetting for less than a second the conspiracy of silence about how lucky we are. It was a childish open smile about the lemon and the loveliness of the place. We banished it as quickly as it had snuck in and coughed awkwardly. I drank my coffee, burning the roof of my mouth.

'Shivvy not about?' he wondered, and I almost considered telling him the truth. Almost.

'On a story,' I lied.

When McCaughrean stumbled out, unshaven and bleary, I stood up to give him my seat.

'Where you off to, tarted up like that, Faithy?' he asked, bewildered by the suddenness of my movement. Something he'd be hard pushed to imitate. He was limping dramatically.

'Is this joke going to be a permanent fixture?' I asked, my hair tied back off my face, a crumpled T-shirt and the same jeans and cowboy boots on as yesterday. McCaughrean himself probably had more make-up on than I did. Does aftershave count as make-up? Well, it will have to.

'It'll run and run, baby,' he said in a silly American accent.

'Got to see a priest,' I told him, putting one of Grant's cigarettes behind my ear.

'Haven't we all,' he said, and slumped guiltily into a chair, scraping it along the tiles. 'I haven't told Mum about the fucking divorce yet. It would polish her off.'

'No emotional outbursts at breakfast. Punishable by red-hot poker up the arse under Sharia law,' Grant insisted, lighting his next cigarette off the butt of his last. He wasn't much of a one for oxygen, Bradford.

'Sorry. Didn't know,' McCaughrean apologized and I went to my room to get my jacket.

I sat down on a pillow and phoned the General. I had to get into character first. Pretending to like him was a stupendous effort. Much worse than Gadaffi or Arafat or someone. When you meet Arafat, he gives you three huge slobbering kisses like a St Bernard or a bloodhound. He smells like festering camel dung. But in fact he's great – funny and fascinating. Exciting to meet him. And the Colonel. They always do this thing of letting you be an honorary man, one of the gang. It's invariably flattering even though what it ought to do is make you feel sorry for the women (their wives, sisters, daughters, cousins) who don't get awarded this status. No Jack Daniels and a ride in a helicopter for them, I shouldn't think. The General, on the other hand (and he could do with another one), is pure sleaze.

'Miss Zanetti. I have been waiting for you to telephone. Did you receive my letter?' he oozed.

'It was delightful, as ever, to hear from you General. Who let you into my room?' I asked, flicking specks of dust off my pillow.

'Your room, Miss Zanetti? I would not enter a lady's room without her permission. I left my message with the young gentleman at reception. Mohammed? Abdullah?'

'Zahir,' I sighed.

'Whatever,' he laughed. 'What can I do for you, my darling?'

I told him I was hoping to do a piece about his wonderful munificence and the Jesuit priest today. He was, predictably, helpful as pie, not only giving me the address and phone number, but promising to call the priest himself to smooth the way. The price, of course, was another dinner. But it wasn't tonight, and I don't like to look ahead much further than that. Anything can happen. Especially to him. His life was one of the most precarious I could think of.

I borrowed a car from the hotel manager, a decrepit maroon Volvo, and put my sunglasses on. Crunching into gear, my map fluttering about in the passenger seat, I pulled away into the pounding traffic.

Father Bryan was based just outside Bethlehem. I wondered if he found any comfort in that. I know it's a war-torn hell-hole, but if you actually believed in God you might well be glad to be as close as possible to the site of Jesus' birth. If that's where it really was.

I love being in Israel. Palestine. Going to places with biblical names. I can't help it. It must have rubbed off at school. Seeing a road sign to Bethlehem sets my brain off singing straight away – 'Above thy deep and dreamless sleep, the silent stars go by . . .' I remember singing it in assembly one cold, dark day, the papier mâché nativity scene propped proudly up in a corner under some tinsel, while notices were read out about the end-of-term disco and the parents' carol service (chances of mine turning up – negligible to negative). It's a song that goes with Christmas cards of robins and holly and snowy country scenes.

And then there's the actual road to Bethlehem. Not lying very still at all. Hot, dusty, clogged full of choking traffic and threatening road blocks, a driver in reflector shades leaning out of his window swearing in hissing Arabic, the corpse of a stray dog, one of many strewn by the roadside, a gun waved by an edgy checkpoint soldier, a coach full of worried tourists, pink with big sunglasses and yellow T-shirts, and a little band of pathetically poor children searching through heaps of steaming, rotting rubbish. I leant my elbow out of the window.

Galilee, Jericho, Nazareth. Places with a McDonald's, a Dunkin' Donuts and a breath of hostility in the air. But huge with historical resonance and an enormous nostalgia that makes your head swim with a kind of biblical grief.

✳   ✳   ✳

Realizing I had arrived, I lurched into life in the sand outside one of those West Bank concrete slab buildings with an olive grove and a downstairs for keeping goats. The handbrake was almost too hot to touch. When the skidding cloud of dust cleared I saw a teenaged boy dash out of sight. He had been glowering at me as I approached. Red shorts and a blue T-shirt.

The priest was raking over what looked like a patch of vegetables just by the front door. He stood in the shade, adjusting his thick glasses every few seconds and stooping to scrutinize his plants. He had messy grey hair falling over his face. He was wearing an old black suit, frayed at the cuffs and thick with dust. Even at this distance he exuded goodness. He shaded his eyes from the sun and nodded over to me. My clothes were sticking to me and my hair was at its silliest.

'Hello,' I said, reaching out my hand and striding towards him.

'Did you find us all right? I'm afraid we're a bit out of the way, but it serves its purpose,' he coughed, nodding his acknowledgement of the area's not inconsiderable troubles. Well, OK, the war. Intifada is too pretty a word for the blowing off of limbs and stuff.

'Yes,' I answered, looking around. I wouldn't have been surprised to see some youths slouching about with machine guns. His land went all the way down to the bottom of the hill in the near distance, crowded with spiky, grey olive trees showing their fruit off and an orange grove closer to the house. I smiled as a dog ran forward barking and swinging its tail madly. Some sort of a spaniel, I thought. In any case not a mangy stray waiting to get flattened by an armoured personnel carrier. 'Fantastic place,' I said.

The priest lifted his twinkly old eyes happily, fiddling with his glasses and displaying his lack of various important teeth. 'We're rather proud of it,' he said. He was tanned as dark as an old ski instructor, skin turned to wrinkly leather in the sun and wind.

'Come in, Faith. Come in. Faith. A rare name these days, I suppose,' he said, almost in awe, wandering off vaguely. 'Faith,' he repeated.

I was terrified he might ask if I had any, but he seemed to be one of those people so sure of his own that it barely occurred to him others might lack it. I had to duck to get through the concrete doorway into the dark house.

These kind of places are usually crammed full of stuff that try to make a few concrete slabs look like home – rugs on the walls, a television proudly blaring above all conversation, an old velour sofa protected by a plastic sheet and used only for the most important guests. Family photographs on a fake-wood table and a bizarrely opulent tea-set displayed as an ornament. You always have to perch on the special sofa while the women of the house fuss around deferentially, smiling lots of gold teeth and bringing you amoeba-infested delicacies. I know that as soon as they get back to the kitchen they sneer at my hair and my crumply clothes. Western women, they think, have the money to be well-turned out, so why is this person wearing rags? I couldn't answer that.

Here, though, none of that kind of effort had been made. The odd crucifix, a wooden chair, an iron bed. A lot of books.

'Where do the children . . . ?' I wondered.

'Oh, no no,' he said, embarrassed, flustered. 'The children don't sleep here. They are next door. Not here, no.'

I asked something tediously pat about how he came to be in a place like this and he coughed thoughtfully, staring out to an imaginary horizon, and started telling me about his seminary and how difficult the idea of celibacy had been, but how important. He seemed to ruminate like a cow.

There was a long pause before he said: 'I'm not gay.'

I could hear a bit of Irish in his voice and imagined he was thinking of a Molly Malone he had once been in love with and her cockles and mussels and whatnot. It was a romantic idea – giving her up for God. Or perhaps she dumped him for Paddy O'Leary from the butcher's shop down the road and that's why he was so vague and bumbling – fundamentally unwanted.

'It would change my relationship with all the women and men I deal with. The sexual element,' he said, not to me at all. He emphasized the word 'sexual'. He spoke, in fact, to a picture of the Virgin Mary and Jesus. A tacky affair with the blues too bright and the eyes too mad.

Before I met Bill Clinton, I always thought Jesus must have been a bit mad. What can he have done to make people believe him and follow him (this is from the point of view that he wasn't actually the living God)? But then I shook hands with the former US President and I realized that some people do have the kind of overwhelming charisma that makes you want to do whatever they tell you to. I heard him give a lecture at the London School of Economics (Clinton, not Christ). Then I went up for the drinks and dinner afterwards. I was standing in a queue talking to a lady in pearls. I thought we were waiting for a devil on horseback or something, but then this marine with a neck thicker than his head, a crew cut and a gun at his waist, said: 'Introduce yourself to Bill Clinton and look at the camera.'

So I did. He is inhumanly magnetic. 'Hi. I'm Faith Zanetti,' I said. 'We have a friend in common. You remember Tod Brenman?'

Clinton laughed. Brenman was the FBC Washington correspondent for the whole of Clinton's presidency and had made himself a determined enemy of the White House administration. Laughing too, I realized that this here is what Hitler and Christ and people must have been like. People who meet Clinton would do anything for him. Jesus didn't say: 'Put down your fishing tackle and follow me' (or whatever it was), in the kind of English vicarish voice you get in a village church in Oxfordshire. He said it like Bill Clinton would say it. He said it in a way that made you know you had to do it.

'It would be like a paedophile being a school teacher,' the priest muttered.

'Sorry. What?' I asked, crashing back into the moment at the word paedophile.

'Not being celibate. In itself it would be an abuse of trust. For a priest. You see?' he asked earnestly.

I did, actually, and said so.

'Speaking of paedophiles, where are the kids?' I asked, laughing. Apparently, Father Bryan edits out the unsavoury. Ignoring my question, he got up off his wooden stool and showed me out through a different door towards another scruffy building with a rusty watering can outside it. He smiled broadly towards the horizon. The boy I had seen earlier was now lurking about in the trees.

We walked in slow motion through the blanket of heat. I was thinking about celibacy. After all, I practised it until I was fifteen. Not that I had given it much thought ever, but I think I basically assumed that the vow of celibacy was one of the things which made Catholic priests sinister. This one though took it seriously as part of his devotion to others. It had never occurred to me that it might have a positive side.

'Do you miss it?' I asked. A bead of sweat dripped down my forehead.

He knew what I was talking about. He had had this conversation before. I took my cigarettes out of my jacket pocket and held them out to him. He took one and stood still in the dust, waiting for a light, the sun smashing down on him.

'Sex? No. I don't. You can find a greater intimacy outside of it,' he said, sage-like. His voice was slow and flat. The way he said 'intimacy' made it sound as though it actually might be important.

'Do you feel sex to be the most fulfilling part of your life?' he asked me.

At this, his interest seemed enlivened. His eyes glittered.

The suggestion was so insane that I choked on my smoke and spluttered forward, laughing, as he looked down at me through the glare of light. Bryan flicked an enormous insect off his sleeve. He broke the filter off his cigarette and put it in his pocket, drawing deeply on the Western tobacco which, I saw, he could not normally afford. He ruffled his hair. He knew he had won the argument before it had begun.

'No,' I said. 'Not the most fulfilling part, no.' I thought about the boys at school and all the embarrassment. My husband, the Russian, who had loved me. I thought about the men on assignment and all the baggage that came afterwards. The sort of man who smokes sadly by the window, gazing out at the snow/rain/morning sunshine, imagining the children he barely sees. Or the wife he had loved before she turned against him (i.e. discovered his affairs). Maybe the guerrilla girl from Nicaragua, killed the day after he proposed (or, more tragically, the day before). And my own void. There's that moment just before. I'm drunk, he's pretty, there is something we both need. But afterwards I realize it wasn't that. Of all things, not that . . .

'I did once think I was doing it right,' I said, quietly, moving forward in step with Father Bryan. I wasn't telling him, exactly. I don't think he was interested, anyway. But his lack of concern allowed me to be honest. If he'd cared, I would have kept my guard up. As it was, disarmed by what might even have been the priest's moral purity or something, I let my mind show me the freckled shoulder of Eden Jones leaning off the edge of a bed, a flop of hair tumbling over his face. The time when I had said something I really meant. What I said was this. I said: 'There is nowhere else I would rather be.' Doesn't sound that much, but it was. To me it was the sort of truth you feel when you read a great poem or hear some devastating piece of music. An acknowledgement of what is left – after all the vodkas and the jokes and the hangovers. Of course, the slim second of epiphany fled into another glass of wine and some professional cynicism in no time. A breath, and we were colleagues again, about to sling our clothes back on and go and get on a plane to find some mutilated corpses. But it had been real. Perhaps in the way that God is to a priest.

Watching me think, Father Bryan touched my face and looked at me a bit like parents look at children who have misunderstood an adult joke. Fond but condescending. Real parents, that is – the kind who pack lunch boxes and iron gym kits. Not my parents – the kind who can sink a bottle of whisky in forty minutes and fire a Makarov 20.

Disturbing my self-indulgence, a little girl ran out of a door in front of us. Actually, it wasn't really a door. More a sort of door-shaped piece of corrugated iron. She was about four – I'm terrible at children's ages – and wore a pair of denim dungarees and nothing else. Her skin was brown as a conker, her eyes shiny Minstrels in her head. She had bare feet, but she was clean and fat. And crying.

Hurtling towards Father Bryan she mumbled in Arabic, choking back sobs. She tripped in the dust just near us, her hands reaching out hopelessly to break her fall.

It was some sort of reflex. I had scooped her up before I knew it and I held her to my chest, stroking her hair and kissing her pudgy cheek.

'It's all right, sweetheart,' I told her. 'It's all right.'

Rather than struggle away and scream louder she wrapped her arms and legs around me and laid her head on my shoulder, smearing snot on to my jacket.

'Someone took her rabbit,' the priest told me, translating, stamping his sandal on the very last of his cigarette. 'She's called Bushra. Her parents were killed in the 2002 fighting. She's only just started to speak.' He said it as though it in some way reflected well on him. You often get that with people on a mission. Especially a mission from God.

'She's lovely,' I said, coughing loudly. Fuck, but I'd rather be doing a proper war story. I hate all this. Emotional spreads for a Saturday paper held for a weekend when there's no news. Not only is it far more traumatic than counting tanks and naming the type of bullet used, but it is also relegated to features and dismissed as women's stuff.

A cat with no tail meandered across our path and the little girl cheered up.

'Look, there's Ariel,' the priest said.

'Ariel?' I laughed, putting the girl down to stroke the beast.

'If you don't laugh . . .' The priest smiled, for the first time.

'Yes,' I agreed.

It seemed like the moment to mention Misha.

'I wondered . . .' I began. 'I'd heard you had a Russian connection of some kind. That you maybe take in Russian children, or perhaps have a Russian benefactor?'

Father Bryan stopped in his tracks. But it was to scratch at an insect bite on the back of his wrist.

'Russians . . . ?' he murmured, as though he was saying something unfathomable. 'No. Not that I can think of. No. Where did you hear that, Faith dear? Perhaps you might ask Adam. Adam will know. My right-hand man. We'll see him anon.'

Taking Bushra's hand, he led me through the clanking door and up some concrete stairs to a small dormitory where lots of kids were fighting. Or were they playing? It's so hard to tell.

I squatted down on the floor. My Arabic peters out after what's your name, how old are you, and could I have a slice of lemon in that please, so Father Bryan beckoned a few kids over to talk while he translated. I was sure I wouldn't have gone near him when I was their age. Utterly benign he may be, but he looked so corpse-like in his dusty black suit. Something someone's found in the attic. They giggled and nudged each other and couldn't take their eyes off my hair.

'OK,' I said, leaning towards them and gesturing invitingly. 'You can touch it.' They all reached forward for a pat and then fell about laughing.

The stories the children told me through Father Bryan's faltering translation were uniformly grim. You could fill in the gaps yourself. 'Now an ordinary seven-year-old, Kamal has already experienced a lifetime of tragedy. When he was just three, he witnessed his whole village . . .' Well, he did. One little girl had a Benetton T-shirt on. United colours. The girls had pierced ears and a lot of the boys had scars on their faces or the black speckles of shrapnel.

The children mentioned Adam a lot as they spoke. They were obviously fond of him. Father Bryan seemed proud of this, since apparently traumatized children find it hard to form attachments. He always chose his helpers very carefully, he explained. People from UNRWA, usually. The United Nations relief for something something.

Now that's the kind of acronym that really puts you off a person. 'What do you do?' 'I work for UNRWA.' Not only can nobody say it without sounding as though they have a speech impediment, but you just know that someone from UNRWA is not going to be telling you many jokes. Sincerity and fervour are so often used as a personality substitute. All very worthy, of course. I can almost hear Evie telling me not to be mean.

When I got used to the noise level, I could see that this was a dormitory. Fluorescent strip-lighting above our heads, about twenty beds close together against the sides of the room, and four glassless windows, square holes in the deep concrete looking out on to the hillside. Children's drawings were sellotaped to the paint above the beds and neat piles of clothes sat stacked on the pillows. That looked to be about it for belongings.

Another good source of workers is the International Solidarity Movement. I wrote 'ISM' in my pad as Bryan mumbled his asides to me while the children spoke. I've met people claiming affiliation to this thing before. It's basically a kind of pacifist organization – students and actors who come over to proclaim their liberal views. Then they fall in love with the place as people who've hardly been anywhere always do, and they end up tending olive groves and working in Father Bryan's children's home. You can spot those ones no problem, because they all wear the Arab keffiyah. The Arafat tea towel. Call them pretentious, but at least they're doing something and not sitting at home over a bottle of Chablis talking about the concept of pretension. There we are, you see, my meanness isn't confined to the voluntary sector.

My stomach twisted into knots of sorrow listening to these tiny people telling me unspeakable things. I took it all down, feeling sad already that, of the few people who would actually read my feature to the end, more would send in a surreal letter about how I had misrepresented the Catholic Church (the very mention of a priest gets the nutters on alert) than would make a donation to Father Bryan's home.

'Actually, your friend the General is our most generous donor,' Bryan told me quietly.

'I wonder why,' I said. There was no question in my mind of this man's being a genuine philanthropist, though I could see that Bryan was at pains to think the best of everyone. I've never known how people manage that. Personally, I tend to find it hard to see past the obvious vileness. Perhaps Meier just uses this place to somehow excuse his hard-line Zionist views. 'I don't hate the Palestinians – I even fund an orphanage for Palestinian children – I just think they should get out of the following areas . . .' That kind of thing.

'He finds new homes for them very often,' Bryan said, getting up now to indicate the conclusion of the interview. He had removed his jacket and had big sweat patches under his arms and down his back. 'That's the problem, you see. What to do with them as they grow up.'

'He finds Palestinian families to take them?' I wondered, looking up at him, surprised. There were dated-looking posters on the walls with pictures of children brushing their hair and cleaning their teeth. Educational things with their slogans in a swirling flourish of Arabic underneath, the lips painted too red, the hair a solid wedge of black.

'Not always.' Bryan smiled. I found it hard to take seriously the idea of our General as a friend to humanity.

'Israelis? Really?'

'It happens.' He smiled. I felt another feature coming on. You have to have a vast backlog of featurey stuff ready to offer as well as the daily news and the more investigative things. The features are what they really want. That's what they take most seriously. Sending photographers over from home, faffing about with the layout forever.

I thanked the children for talking to me. They could sense I wasn't a mother myself. I had none of that ease. I gave out the chocolate bars I'd brought with me and stood up, looking out of the window at a playground fenced off from the olive trees. There was a blue plastic slide almost melting under the sun, some swings, a wooden see-saw. A young Western man in sandals was supervising a few kids.

'That's Adam,' the priest told me. 'He might join us for a cup of tea in a minute.'

The teenager who had been watching me since I got out of the car was still skulking around, staring angrily. It seemed ludicrous, later, that I hadn't had any sort of inkling. His shorts, I could see now, were actually baggy swimming trunks. He shuffled his flip-flopped feet and slumped his shoulders. And it was on the word 'minute' that he lunged at me. In retrospect, I suppose I knew he was potentially dangerous. I had not imagined, however, that he might try to hack me up with a pair of paper scissors. He seemed almost to fly across the room towards me, his face contorted with hatred. He landed on top of me, throwing me backwards to the floor. Then he raised his hand to plunge his weapon into me, not aiming or seeming to care where the scissors fell. He smelled of apricots.

As it happened, some of the smaller children were fighting to restrain him, so when Adam appeared in my range of vision, the boy had already been rolled on to his back on the lino which, I noticed, was orange with an ancient Felix the Cat motif. I was winded and gasping. Adam helped the boy he called Hassan to his feet and, it appeared, asked him for the scissors. Bowing his head, and spitting on to the floor by a flip-flop thrown off in the scuffle, Hassan handed them over in shame. Adam put his arm round the boy's shoulders and walked him away, having not once met my eye.

Bryan's reserve was gone. He was shaking with sorrow. He held out a hand to help me up, but he was weak and old. More of a hindrance than a help. One boy was screaming now, horrified, staring at my face. Older girls comforted the littlest ones and Bryan gestured apologetically towards my right cheek. I put my hand up to my face and brought it down covered in blood.

'Oh fuck,' I said.

I wiped myself with my T-shirt, exposing my stomach and bra in the process. Those children that were still watching gasped.

'How bad is it?' I asked Bryan.

'Just a scratch, I think. I'm awfully sorry, Faith,' he said, cringing in apology, wanting to defend Hassan, wanting to persuade me that it was an unusual event. 'You must understand that so many of my children have a pretty dim view of the West.'

'Of course,' I said. 'Is there somewhere I can clean up?'

He sorried and this-wayed me out of the room. Some of the braver kids waved and said, 'Bye-bye.' They laughed at the silly sound of the words.

'Bye,' I waved back, half smiling. There seemed to be a lot of blood.

'Hassan punched the General in the jaw last week. The poor man is not popular here, despite his generosity,' Bryan sighed.

'No,' I said. We walked in silence back to his living quarters. His bathroom was a shower attachment on the wall of a flaking concrete cubicle. I held the nozzle to my face and watched my blood disappear down the grate in the floor. When the water ran clear, I dressed and went back into the main room. Bryan handed me a dishcloth to press on the wound.

'We'd like to find some work for Hassan. Something apart from growing vegetables, that is. I think the boredom feeds his anger. He's a very bright lad,' the priest said thoughtfully.

I wondered if he might be willing to befriend Westerners in return for their money. He seemed like the type who might be good for getting us into places and showing us things. Stringer material. I decided to give Bryan a call next time one of us needed someone.

A fat lady in a headscarf and apron brought us some mint tea. As she leant down to put everything on the table she put her hand on the priest's shoulder and looked at me with a big smile.

'This is a very good man,' she told me, and waddled off, her huge bum swinging the folds in her big red skirt.

Bryan humphed angrily and looked at my cigarette packet.

'Khuloud. Came here looking for her children and stayed,' he said, lighting up. I would have to come back and bring him a carton.

'Did she find them?' I wondered.

'No,' he said, shaking his head.

Someone once told me that you ought to be able to describe a room by picking out a single detail. I was usually so busy looking for this one salient object that I completely forgot to interview whoever it was about the nuclear weapon he was planning to put into a suitcase. There I'd be, looking at the flower arrangement, while he'd be saying: 'If you had any idea how much illegally produced plutonium I am able to cram into this tiny . . .'

Anyway, I was finding it a difficult thing to do here. The mad picture of the madonna and child? The book on 'meaningful prayer'? Or the *New Yorker* cartoon next to the crucifix above the iron bed. It was framed and dedicated to Bryan and it had two parts to it: the first was a drowning boy shouting to his dog, 'Lassie get help!' The second was Lassie lying on his psychoanalyst's couch saying, 'My mother gave me away when I was only six weeks old . . .'

I was laughing when Adam walked in.

'I gave him that,' he announced. 'Good, eh?' Was he not going to mention the Hassan incident?

Bryan put his hands up in meek surrender. He was a trained

Freudian analyst, he explained, and was notorious for asking his staff about their childhoods. Adam looked to me like someone who was still experiencing his. When I asked him how he had ended up here, he told me he had come to clear his mind after a bad acid trip.

'In the evenings, I sing big band numbers at the bar in the King David hotel,' he said.

'You do not!' I laughed.

'Yup.' He nodded.

Shiv would love Adam. He was proud of the fact that he hadn't been laid off in all the sackings that came with the death of the tourism industry in Israel. There are some things people just won't risk for a week by the pool.

'Sorry about your face,' he said, at last.

'It's fine.' I smiled, my T-shirt drenched in blood, my face smeared with it. 'I don't expect to be popular.'

Adam shrugged. 'Hassan is . . . he has had a difficult time.'

'Sure,' I acknowledged.

There was a long pause while the three of us thought our own thoughts. Mine were about Shiv. My fantasy was that I'd rush back to find that there had been nothing to worry about. True, Martin, whom I had summoned from London to deal with her, wouldn't be too impressed if that were the case, but that was the kind of problem I would happily have confronted.

My mind flicked briefly away from the scene in front of me and back to the conversation I'd had with Martin.

'Happened before,' he barked when I told him.

'Has it?' I was almost pleased.

'Gets very het up under pressure,' he said, not explaining further.

I couldn't ever remember Shiv being 'het up' under anything. I'd told him about Misha. No, not about her having sex with him, but about the child-trafficking story she'd mentioned when she was still faintly sane.

Glover guffawed. 'Red herring, Faithy,' he said and started hassling me about the mole. Bloody hell, I'd only been here twenty-four hours I pointed out but he'd laughed some more and promised to hop on the next plane. I entertained Glover's theory for a billionth of a second. It was true her editor did put a lot of pressure on her. Barbara-Ann. No, honestly, it's her name. Nobody ever believes you when you tell them. She was nice, really. She's been the foreign editor of the *Correspondent* for years and doesn't take herself too seriously – unlike a lot of the women on Fleet Street. (I know, I know, it's not there any more, just banks, but it still means something.) Most of them think that you have to be the most horrible person in the office in order to succeed amongst the boys, or that you have to somehow prove how clever you are to everyone every day, usually by being unimaginably rude. Barbara-Ann, though, tells jokes and is normal. At the same time as insisting that her correspondents wipe the floor with the competition every single day.

I needed to get back to Shiv.

'I have to get back to Jerusalem. My friend is ill,' I said, perhaps too suddenly.

'Can I have a lift?' Adam asked, raising his eyebrows flirtatiously high. A Londoner, I thought. Twenty-three. Oxbridge. Type of bloke who is impressed with himself just for being abroad. Longish, shaggyish mousy hair, friendship bracelets, tan.

'Hop in,' I said.

So he did.

The hot afternoon sang past the car – a big neon sign advertising Coca Cola, music blaring from a makeshift kiosk selling sizzling meat, a waving palm, a wandering shepherd, a blur of other people's lives.

We were held up at a routine checkpoint when I asked him about the Russians. We'd been talking about the kind of stories I do, in that way you have to when people are 'interested in journalism' and asking advice on how to get into it. I always find it embarrassing. But then it occurred to me I could weave something I wanted to know in without too much trouble.

'Trying to get a child-trafficking story going at the moment, actually. Russians. Someone said Bryan might have a lead, but he didn't . . .' I opened, leaning my arm out of the window and exhaling.

'Who told you that?' he asked.

'Can't say,' I told him. I don't know why I was being cagey, but Shiv had been scared and now bloody look at her.

'It's weird you mention Russians, though. Hassan was housed with someone Russian – friend of General Meier's – and he came back. Refused to stay with them. It was last week sometime.'

'Did he say why?' I asked, waving my accreditation and passport out of the car window in the sickening heat. A soldier nodded us through, sweat dripping down his face.

'Won't speak about it. He's definitely been screwy since, though. I fucking hate Meier. Don't trust him,' Adam said, scrounging a fag off me to close the subject.

I dropped Adam at the flashy multi-storey hotel. It's a vast white tower – modern, but built out of Jerusalem stone. You occasionally get the odd journalist checking in there by mistake. They always move to the Colony once they've seen it. Now the only hotel in East Jerusalem that hasn't gone bust. Only just in East Jerusalem, it's true. A uniformed doorman swept down to help Adam out and the lobby glittered marble and gold. A woman with glossy black hair and sequined shoes tottered through the revolving doors.

When I got back to the Colony, the blood on my face and clothes had dried. 'Faith Zanetti, war correspondent,' said Eden Jones as I walked in, my sunglasses on my head. There was a twitch of irony in his voice.

CHAPTER FOUR

'Fuck off, Jones. What are you doing here?' I asked. 'Aren't you supposed to be infiltrating Al-Qaeda somewhere?'

Eden took his key from Zahir and picked his suitcase up. It looked like a hired prop with all its stickers and tags. Zahir nodded at me as to a princess, his eyes low, his bow gracious. I wiped some sweat and blood in a smear across my forehead.

'That's right. I have at last uncovered the true identity of the evil Osama bin Laden. Anything you say or do may be taken down and used in evidence against you,' he told me, grabbing my arm. I shook him off.

'See you in the bar in ten minutes. Don't wash, Josephine,' he laughed as Martin Glover waddled out of the lobby loo.

I kissed my boss on both cheeks.

'Thanks for coming. There is something really wrong with her,' I told him. 'I think you should take her home.' I might have sounded vaguely composed, but I think my panic about her was blazing in my eyes. Martin held my shoulders to show he was now in control and I wasn't to worry my pretty little head about it or something.

'Number twelve again, sir.' Zahir smiled, handing Martin his key. He let go of me to take it.

'Do me a favour, Zanetti,' Martin burbled. 'You will keep schtum, won't you? Eden's covering for her, but I don't want the girls in the bar . . . you know.' Martin always called the boys the girls, like some Las Vegas drag queen.

'Yes.' I nodded. 'I know.' I did. I hadn't said a word to anyone.

I stood under the shower and wriggled my toes. I thought about Shiv's painted toenails. Is that some sort of psychological escape mechanism? Huge problem, but you focus on some completely silly and irrelevant aspect of it. I had a friend in London who was getting married to a woman his mum hated and all his mum could do, from the moment they decided to get married to the end of the reception, was to go on and on about the potential parking difficulties. How odd it would be, I thought, to colour my own toenails in. How did one choose the right colour, or is it always red? Why is it nails one has to colour? Being a woman is a bafflement to me.

Anything but think about Eden Jones. He's a mess. He's a drunk. He's promiscuous to the point of insanity. He's lonely. His twin brother is dead. He wants me because I don't want anyone. Or at least he says he wants me. Enthusiasm always makes me suspicious. It's that Groucho Marx thing about not wanting to be the member of a club that would have you as a member. Really, I think Eden is just intrigued – because I know his tragic stories, and they don't touch me. Let the grief of others touch you, and you've had it. I just put it in a knot in my stomach and ignore it. Like falling in love. It goes away after a while. We had a thing once. A couple of years ago now. He said I wouldn't let him in. 'How can you sleep with me and spend all your time with me and be blanking me at the same time?' he asked me. I told him he sounded like someone who had just read a copy of *Just*

Seventeen. You see, usually Eden tells people about his brother and they cry. They reach out and take his hand. They vow to look after him for ever. They bare themselves to him and he despises them. Not me. Intimacy is my sarcasm trigger.

It's a trip switch. All systems down.

'How bleak,' I said when he told me his story. His brother. His mother. The horror. I just winked at him and ordered another drink. It was a transparent attempt to melt me, to hurdle the distance between us. He was expecting me to fall for it.

If I ever do find that I actually give a toss about this guy's problems, I thought, I will be in trouble. And I nearly was. Not then. Years later. I had been up for forty-eight hours and my defences were down. It passed. And he became just the raddled, cynical, brain-fried, emotionally damaged and permanently lost foreign correspondent I'd always known. Too long in the direct sunlight, too much time plumbing the depths of humanity, too much to drink. Maybe the only person in the world who can see how unstable I am.

'Hello,' I said. I sat down next to him in a clean white T-shirt, clean jeans and bare feet. My hair was wet. I was going to have a scar across my cheek. 'How are you?'

Salim held the vodka bottle up and I nodded, smiling. I noticed that his eyebrows meet in the middle. A big gold crucifix swings at his neck. Coptic, I suppose. He clanked around behind the bar.

Outside by the pool, some American children were playing. They had an enormous inflatable shark.

Eden slashed my jollity down with a glance. His eyes told me not to bother pretending the world was all right. 'Don't give me your "How are you?" crap,' they said. 'Let's be honest, shall we?'

There was no way I was going to crumble.

He lit a cigarette. His shirtsleeves were rolled up, the hairs on his forearms golden, his Rolex unpretentious with age. Anyway, he had no idea that a watch might be used as a status symbol in the real world. He had bought the most expensive watch available in Abu Dhabi airport in 1982 in the sincere belief that the woman behind the counter was selling him the most reliable one they had. Certainly she had given a reliable fuck. I was guessing.

His clothes were crumpled by the plane, his stubble a couple of days old. The wrinkles round his eyes made him look sad, though they were all laugh lines. I decided not to look long enough to see the flecks of gold in the green of his irises. So he'd won some kind of genetic lottery. Did that mean I had to fall at his feet? He would never go bald. His hair was thick and dry and dark and disorderly, but he was beginning to go grey. At thirty-nine. He wore, he always wore, jeans and ancient trainers. Nobody believed he owned a suit because even wearing it he gave the impression of jeans and trainers. There were often-told stories about this. King Hussein of Jordan had been offended to be interviewed by a man not wearing a suit. When Eden complained that he *had* been wearing a suit, the King was more outraged than ever. 'Am I being accused of lying?' he asked.

Eden is six-foot-four and stoops to disguise it. And that is absolutely enough about him.

'No, really. How's it going, Jonesy?' I smirked, thanking Salim and swigging my drink, the ice clunking against the side of my glass.

'Please,' he said slowly, almost stuttering. He often did it, but nobody else seemed to notice. Sometimes it makes my heart ache. When that happens I tend to get up and leave. I don't do heartache. What am I? A schoolgirl?

'Please,' he repeated, not looking at me. 'Please don't call me that. I like to hear you say my name.'

He screwed his empty cigarette packet up in his fist.

'God, this place is a shit-hole,' he said. 'I fucking hate Israelis. And Palestinians.'

'And Brits?' I wondered.

'The English are insufferable.' He nodded.

'And we'll all be dead soon,' I sighed. 'In the meantime, though, perhaps we could all have a nice cup of tea and cheer up a bit.' I was joking. Eden smiled.

'A nice cup of tea,' he laughed to himself.

'Soon set you straight.' I nodded.

He rested his elbows on the table and leaned forward, rubbing his hair as though drying it. He stared at me and took my hand, turning it palm-up in his and scrutinizing it before returning to my face.

'Faith,' he said. 'How are you, Faith?'

'Fine.'

I paused.

'Lovely weather,' I added.

I pulled my hand away and gestured out to the blazing day.

We each took a sip of our drink in silence. I looked at the scar above his right eyebrow.

'Do you think I should buy an orange shirt?' he asked me at last.

'I think that would be a good idea,' I told him, already exhausted by the whole thing of him. The emotional intensity. Why couldn't we just sit down and have a chat? Everything was so loaded and tragic and God knows what.

'I might buy you one too, Faith,' he said, looking at me almost imploringly.

I finished my drink and stood up.

'You do that,' I said, touching him briefly on the shoulder and walking slowly out of the bar and up the stairs.

He watched me go and then, as I was almost out of sight, he called after me.

'Don't go.'

I pretended not to have heard. If I'd sat there with him, told him how I was, begged to hear about his life, gazed into the agony of his soul and felt his pain, all that kind of thing, he'd soon have got bored. He hacks people open and then treads in the wounds he has made. Emotionally speaking, of course. I bore myself thinking about it.

✳   ✳   ✳

Martin Glover had his head and both his hands against the white-washed wall outside Shiv's room when I got there. He had ignored the approaching pad of my feet along the tiled corridor. There were window slits down to the courtyard and sunlight dappled the walls. I could see Zahir putting nightlights into the blue glass globes on each table. Martin's eyes were shut and he was grey as wallpaper paste. Not just office-grey – that exhausted, dry, computer-screen look that the London staff have. Worse.

'Glover?' I said, quietly, touching the sleeve of his blue shirt. His breath was short and droplets of sweat were forming on his temples. He looked at me and I could see he was afraid. Behind the closed door Shiv screamed as though she were being tortured. Before Martin could answer, Dr Ahmed came running towards us, like a character in a farce, his black bag in his hand. As he got near he scrabbled around for a syringe and loaded it, knocking the metal cap off the vial with his teeth, and nudging the door open with his shoulder. A chair was knocked over inside, Shiv's screams grew louder, then softer and then died away. The silence was worse than the noise.

'It's all right, Martin. She'll be all right,' I said, putting my arm around him. He stank of booze. His teeth were stained black from El Al's first-class claret.

'She'd have killed me. She just went for me,' he said, his chins wobbling, the skin a livid pink beneath the white stubble. I had never believed that this was the best lay she'd ever had though it was sometimes possible to see the remains of his beauty in the ruins. Shiv said it was that crumbling grandeur that attracted her. 'You know, the Colosseum. There's a Cole Porter song, I think. "You're the tops, you're the Colosseum, you're the tops, you're the Louvre Museum." Or something. He's incredible,' she insisted. I didn't much want to think about whatever kinky thing they might be into that would make Martin seem in some way attractive. You know – he's the only man I ever met who was willing to smear avocado over his . . . or whatever.

It was easy to see how Shiv's loveliness was attractive to him. It was attractive to everyone.

I could imagine the features pages doing some kind of spread about old being the new young. 'Fat old drunks can be good in bed too.' That sort of thing. I doubted it was true, though. Father Bryan could probably have asked Shiv a few salient questions about her dad.

'I need a drink,' Martin sighed, pulling himself up to standing and shaking his head. He set off down the corridor with real determination. Now if there's anything he really knows how to do . . .

'Eden's down there,' I told him.

I ignored the Do Not Disturb sign that had been up since Martin got here. By the time I had Siobhan's door fully open, Dr Ahmed was already putting his equipment back in his bag and was looking more like someone in a Cairo nightclub again. For a moment outside, he had had a touch of *ER* about him, with the running and the deftness of syringe-handling. Shiv was on the bed, sheets pulled up around her, face peaceful and serene. There were plenty of signs, though, that things were not well. For a start, nearly all the furniture was overturned. She had been using the floor for a toilet and the place stank in the heat. Flies swirled around the green glass lantern forty feet above our heads. Her hair was filthy and had made grease marks on her pillow. A bruise was forming around the needle puncture in her arm. I used the phone to ask maid service to come and see to the room while she slept.

'I recommend that Miss Boucherat sees a psychiatrist at her earliest possible convenience,' Dr Ahmed said. The man's a diagnostic genius.

'Thank you,' I answered. 'I think her boyfriend is going to take her home. If physically possible.'

When I got back to my room, the phone was ringing. I hoped it wasn't the desk with moron queries about my piece. I once wrote an article from Moscow for one of those American magazines that always have glossy photos of burning buildings on the front and open with a page of supposedly satirical political cartoons. Their fact checkers called me every half an hour for twenty-four hours. 'Is that Yeltsin, Y-E-L-T-S-I-N?' . . . 'Is ten minutes for the journey from Belorusskiy Voksal to the Kremlin an estimate, because we make that a fifteen-minute journey?'

The London desk wasn't that bad, but they always had something insane to say for themselves. Usually, 'Are you sure it's true?'

Hey. What's truth?

'Yup,' I said, shaking a cigarette out of the packet with my spare hand and standing by the phone. I swivelled on the heel of a boot to look for some matches and lunged for them as someone said: 'Faith Zanetti?'

'Mmmmhmmm,' I confirmed, inhaling and flicking the match out. There were fresh flowers in a white vase on the table. Orchids, perhaps. I'm not very good on flowers.

'Faith. It's Mikhail. Siobhan's friend? We met in your hotel bar two nights ago.' He was calling from the street. I could hear traffic and a siren. He sounded urgent and breathless.

'Yes. I remember you. What is it?'

'Meet me in the Old City, by the second station of the cross as soon as you can. Please come quickly. I need to speak with you. Now.' It certainly sounded that way.

'Where's the second—' I began, but he'd hung up.

'Christ,' I said. Well, it couldn't be far. I knew you could walk the route Jesus was supposed to have taken to his crucifixion. They tell you about it on the plane; a booming voice over some mystical music. I had no idea where all the various sites were though. I'd need a tour guide to find anything in the Old City. You get lost the second you go in. I had to assume that Misha thought it would be convenient.

'Bollocks, bollocks, bollocks,' I said to myself, slinging my jacket on and scanning the room. 'Keys, fags, money,' I said to myself. 'Keys, fags, money.' Check. I ran across the courtyard and out through the main entrance into the street. Having failed to get anything much out of Father Bryan or Adam, I was hoping Misha himself was going to be more forthcoming.

The sun was just starting to go down and the white stone glowed golden in the evening light. Jerusalem is the colour of warm sand. I went into the Old City at the Damascus gate, the high battlements imposing, even now that the place is more of a tourist attraction than a fortress. Not that many tourists dare to come these days. I bought a guidebook at the first kiosk, a kind of hole in the wall, and walked quickly along the cobbled alleys. A boy as young as six cycled past me on a creaking bike, a vast plate of couscous balanced on his head, a chicken, trussed but alive, in his basket. An old man in Arab headdress, his face a grey-stubbled prune, clopped past on an emaciated donkey. A woman swathed in dirty black robes, old greenish tattoos on her dark face, sat in the filth at the side of the alley, peeling ugli fruit and offering them up to passers-by in her fingers. The air was dense with spices and in the covered section men shouted out to me in English, Russian and German to come into their shops. They sold gold plates and coffee sets, 'I heart Jerusalem' T-shirts, hubble-bubble pipes, carpets, Aladdin lamps and olive-wood camels.

'Deeeeeess way, beautiful laydeee,' said a fat bloke with a bushy moustache, grabbing my arm. He had Saudi-in-a-lift aftershave on and wore a lot of gold.

'*Lah. Shukran*,' I told him, hurrying on, towards, according to this book, the second station of the cross. I was already tired by this bloody journey and I wasn't carrying some enormous scaffold on my back. And I was younger than Christ had been. Just. These thoughts and others about Shiv and Misha and Martin swam around in the mush of my head. From the sound of Misha's voice, he knew, if anyone did, what had sent Shiv over the edge and he was going to tell me. It was hard to imagine anything awful enough to have done that to someone so tough. She'd been scared that night and it was something to do with Misha's story.

It was getting darker now and people were packing up. The narrow lanes, littered with bits of vegetable and animal, were now seething with people going home from work. Home, presumably, a tent or a hut somewhere. A woman emptied a bucket from a window just above me, and two naked babies sat playing on a six-hundred-year-old doorstep. Well, the dating is a guess. I don't actually have any formal archaeological training but they looked, in my view, old. The further I went, the fewer people I saw.

Here, the empty frames of stalls stood silent by the immense walls and my footsteps got louder on the stones. I was startled enough to cry out when two boys hurtled round the corner at a gallop, riding their horses bareback; the wooden carts they pulled clattering terrifyingly behind them. They whooped, racing, as they passed me, their white robes billowing out behind them. I flattened myself against the wall, feeling the mildew of the millennia beneath my shaking fingers.

'Fuck,' I gasped when they had gone. 'Where the fuck is this place?' I find swearing brings me to my senses.

By the time my map told me I was nearly there, it was almost completely dark. The sun sets early here, and quickly. The market noises had disappeared and all I could hear was the distant murmur of traffic from the new city outside and the sounds of families somewhere within the walls. That is, until an appalling screech echoed out just up ahead. I ran towards the sound, already knowing that this was going to have something to do with Misha. I don't mean in some psychic sense – 'I just knew' type of thing – I just mean I was nearly at the place where I was supposed to meet an agitated man, and an agitated-sounding person was screaming. The first thing I saw was the woman in black who was making the noise and waving her arms in the other direction, after an invisible assailant. The second thing I saw was Misha, lying face-up on the ground. Blood poured from his mouth and gushed from his slit throat, soaking a thin short-sleeved shirt and some grey nylony trousers. There seemed to be more of it than could possibly be contained in one body. I rememberd that from the boy in El Salvador.

'Holy shit,' I said. 'Holy shit.'

The woman continued to scream. 'Wallahiiiiiiiiiiii,' she wailed, kneeling down and taking Misha's head in her hands. I knelt down next to him, tipping up the contents of my bag on to the cobbles to find my phone. He knew it was me, I could see that, hardly daring to watch him die as I shouted into my phone. 'Ambulance! Ambulance!' It is lucky, I thought later, that so many people in Jerusalem speak English.

This is a resonant place to die. And that is what Misha was doing. I reached out and touched his forehead. The stomping ground of living gods. They do, I suppose, stomp. Gods. One of the most sacred sites of all three of the world's major religions – drenched in bloody historical and religious significance. I wasn't in any kind of doubt that Misha's murder – could it be murder before he had actually gone? – had something to do with the state of Siobhan. It was obvious without even having to let the thought form. If I hadn't had to stop for the guidebook, I'd have seen the whole thing. I would have come round the cobbled corner and seen the knife at Misha's throat. Seen his glasses fall to the ground and smash. It must have been his spare pair. But the fact that I was seconds away from being a witness meant that whoever did it didn't know I was coming. Looking at the state of Shiv and Misha that was definitely a good thing.

Then here they were. Just the presence of the paramedics, their equipment, their new trainers, young arms and shining needles, made the situation seem less apocalyptic. An awful thing that happens. Not a portent of further doom. Though that's what it turned out to be – a portent of further doom.

*   *   *

I remember thinking when the Twin Towers collapsed – if only the news channels could scramble some coherent coverage together it won't seem like the end of the world. And later that evening, when panels of experts had been assembled, the accused had been named, the dead counted (well, almost), it did seem like another catastrophe rather than a verse of Revelation.

'You family?' a young woman with cow eyes and a pierced nose asked me, straining with the effort of lifting Misha, who was gurgling frothy pink bubbles from his mouth and neck now, on to a stretcher with her colleague.

I shook my head and looked into Misha's face. He met my gaze, fearlessly. 'Svetlana,' he said. 'Svyeta.' I nodded as though I understood and the paramedics heaved the stretcher up to their shoulders. His girlfriend? Wife? Daughter?

'Might he survive?' I asked, surprised at myself for letting the hope lurch out.

The girl shrugged.

'Who knows,' she said, and they ran off, a team on either side with drip bags and tubes and boxes of bleeping monitors running in time.

I was picking my stuff up off the ground – a notebook, some chewing gum, cigarettes, my lighter and a broken watch – when a squad of policemen thundered up the pathway, walkie-talkies crackling, black boots creaking. I stood up to face them, putting the things into my bag and pushing my hair back off my face. I noticed now that I had blood on my hand.

A man with a darkly stubbled harelip took down my details. Another couple took samples from the blood on the cobbles and a woman with a completely shaven head interviewed the Arab lady who had been with Misha when I arrived. She was still screaming.

The police weren't all that gripped by the murder of a young Russian. They had enough on their plates and I didn't think I could honestly tell them anything helpful. When they asked why I thought he had called me, I said: 'Why does any man call a woman?' They went for it. They always do.

Zohar, for that was his name, took a bleeped message while we spoke and announced, to nobody's surprise, that Misha had been pronounced dead.

'No ID. No personal effects. Did you take them?' Zohar asked me.

I scowled at him in reply. Of course I didn't bloody take stuff out of this guy's pockets while he was bleeding from the throat. Somebody did, though.

There wasn't really room for me in the police car and I felt dizzy as we swept through the black night to the hospital. The team shouted and joked in Hebrew, ignoring me, squashing me into the tinted, and presumably bullet-proof, window. The case, for them, was already over and they had that bravado that comes with a job in the emergency services. If you don't laugh you cry and all that sort of thing. I once asked a paediatric heart surgeon (depressing investigation about murderous children's ward nurses) how she coped with the grief and she said that you just develop a really bleak sense of humour. A bit like being Russian, basically.

When I lived in Ryazan, my husband got me to have rat poison sent over from England to deal with our horrific infestation (they lived between the walls and we could hear them gnawing through all night long. In one corner of our shabby room there was a metal grate in the floor and I used to crouch over it watching them grip their teeth round the little bars). There was a shortage of absolutely everything in those days and some of the rats succumbed to their desperate hunger and ate the poison. They went mad with thirst and would often die in the bath fighting each other for a drop of water. I had lived there long enough to find this funny. When we told Russians about it they started laughing at the very mention of rat infestation.

I identified Misha's waxy body (though to be fair, it had been waxy

85

when he was alive) in the sterile stench of the hospital morgue and was left to wander out and into a taxi by myself. I thought about the kinds of jokes pathologists must tell. Laugh a minute, they probably are. Really.

It was late when I got back to the hotel. The only person I wanted to talk to was Shiv. It was a big effort trying to pretend to everyone, and to myself, that she was fine. Just a little episode. The kind of thing that happens to women. You know, nerves. Hysteria. Something very Restoration. I almost wished Martin wasn't here. I felt like I was treading on his toes trying to see her. He was the closest thing she had to next of kin, not me. Next of kin. That's what they say about dead people's relatives. And she wasn't dead yet.

'Puny bloke with the glasses?' Grant Bradford asked, the only one with so much as the dimmest memory of Misha's presence in the bar the other night.

'That's him,' I said. 'Was him.'

We leant over the zinc together while I told him what had happened.

'He must have been on to something huge,' Grant said, looking at the melting ice in his whisky glass. He spoke ruefully, obviously wishing he could one day be on to something big, instead of filing trite sensationalist stuff that tabloid readers would flick over on the way to the football results and sex scandals. The fact that Misha was now dead didn't seem to diminish Grant's jealousy. It never does with journalists. The deader the cooler. 'Any ideas?'

'None,' I lied. 'I think he said he was doing Russian underworld stuff. You know, drugs, prostitution.' I sipped at my vodka. The bar was filling up behind us, the noise level rising, the air thickening with alcohol and smoke.

Grant's eyes misted over with envy at the words 'drugs' and 'prostitution'. If only there were Brits involved he could do those stories too.

Martin, I noticed, was sitting with Eden over in the corner, drowning what was left to drown of his brain cells. He has told me a lot of times that it's the drink that keeps him healthy.

Russians always claim that having a sweltering sauna followed by a swim in an ice floe is the secret of their good health. The fact is that if you weren't already in the peak of fitness, it would kill you. Martin survives only because he has the constitution of an ox. Normal humans would have been long dead after a lifetime of that kind of alcohol abuse.

'Come and meet my boss.'

I took Grant over to Martin and Eden's table.

'Joining us, Zanetti?' Eden asked, looking at me as though to translate his banal question into: 'Please sit down. I love you.' It was a lie, though. He just always looks at women that way.

I put my drink down and told them about Misha.

'This Russian journalist Shiv knew had his throat cut in the Old City just now. Three seconds before I arrived to meet him,' I said.

'You're bad news, Faith,' Eden smiled, uninterested. Russians didn't count as proper members of the press pack. For some reason they came under local hire. People whose stories and contacts you can steal in return for a drink.

'What do you mean "knew"?' Martin asked, chortling as though he shared the joke of his girlfriend's promiscuity. It's open knowledge that it kills him.

Before I was forced to answer, McCaughrean stumbled in, red, unshowered, unshaven, his camera bag on his shoulder.

'Hear about that poor Russian cunt in the Old City?' he asked us, collapsing on to a stool that was, as ever, far too small for him. Salim brought him a pint of beer and he smiled as though to an angel. Grant and Eden both groaned.

'Zanetti got the scoop,' Grant grumbled and McCaughrean looked at me, baffled.

'Why am I always the last . . . ?' he smiled, a foam moustache on his refreshed upper lip.

Martin, who was failing to be one of the lads, began to stand up.

'I think I might . . .' he burbled, looking at me significantly. He was almost too drunk to focus.

'Would you rather I went, Martin?' I asked.

He nodded enthusiastically and slumped back down, banging his fists on the table like an old politician at his club. He was incapable of speech though, let alone coherence.

I left the heat and noise of the bar for the cool white space of the rest of the hotel. We just needed her to agree to go home, or to take enough drugs so that she couldn't refuse. Her room was quiet from the outside and I was glad. The muezzin at the mosque down the road started to sing.

Smiling to myself, I pushed open the door to Shiv's room. I had prepared my approach. I decided I hadn't been firm enough. I'd been all kind and sincere when she probably needed someone to laugh and tell her to pull herself together for fuck's sake.

What I wasn't ready for was her naked body hanging from the hinge of the bathroom door. Not really the hinge. I don't know what it's called. The contraption at the top that makes it close slowly and quietly instead of slamming. Isn't this what that Australian pop star did? I looked up at her. She had looped her leather belt round her neck. I looked at the furniture. She had kicked a wooden chair away from under her. Jumped maybe. Not within the past couple of hours either.

Her swollen tongue lolled from her mouth and her head was bloated and blue, her eyeballs looking as though they might burst out of the sockets. The rest of her was stiff and getting the yellow tinge of a corpse. Her painted red nails gleamed on the end of bluish toes.

I put my hand over my mouth and tears came to my eyes. If only I hadn't gone to meet Misha. I sat down on the chair she had used and looked up at her.

'You silly cow,' I said to her, letting myself sob into my hands. The only person I would like to have talked to about a friend of mine who went mad and committed suicide in the American Colony was Shiv. She would probably have made a joke out of it. Made it seem safe – the death of some psychotic tart who couldn't handle the sight of blown-off body parts. Or leaves. There was an Italian bloke, a newspaper guy, who had become obsessed with the leaves that fill the air after a car bomb. Naked trees and a sky full of leaves fluttering down on to all the bodies. He's still in hospital in Italy, I think. Anyway, Shiv would have made her own suicide ridiculous, not something that affected us. Death on the streets near the hotel was one thing. But once it had crept inside and taken our bravest, funniest and most untouchable member, then our immunity was affected. We weren't watching any more. We were being watched. And I had loved her.

CHAPTER FIVE

I lay in the dark listening to Eden breathing. He was calm, motionless. The windows were open and the night poured in.

'Something's going on,' I said, leaning up on one elbow to flick my ash. It was about 3 a.m. We were both fully clothed and awake.

'You'd have to get up pretty early in the morning to get one over on you, Zanetti,' Eden laughed.

'No, I mean it. Shiv was scared out of her wits. Literally,' I said, lying back and moving closer to him.

He took a spiral of my hair in his hand and twisted it round his finger.

'You know why you're so tough, Faith Zanetti?' he asked. I feared he might be going to tell me. 'You've never really been loved.'

I slapped his hand down. I mean, for God's sake.

'Eden,' I said firmly. 'Fuck off.'

'See? Defences up. You're like a porcupine.' He laughed to himself at the idea of a porcupine and lit himself a cigarette. He poured the

last of some wine into a glass and took a swig before passing it to me.
Warm white. I didn't want to spend the night alone.

I had walked slowly down to the bar from Shiv's room. I suppose I was
allowing Martin another few minutes of the life he had known before
his girlfriend of six years committed suicide. I suppose I was saying
goodbye to her myself, composing myself for my grim announcement,
collecting my thoughts.

Every step that brought me closer to the cellar where Martin sat,
drunk, but not for long, seemed to echo through the old palace walls
with the bad news I was bringing. I felt myself move through the
seething crowds of the bar in slow motion, the only person in there
with a purpose. Like the lead character in a film, followed by the
camera; everybody an extra except me and Martin Glover – the man
who was waiting for me without knowing it. I could see him sitting,
talking, dribbling, at Eden. Ten seconds. Nine seconds. Eight. Seven.
Six. Five. Four. Three. Two. One.

'Shiv has hanged herself, Martin. She's dead.'

He looked at me, bleary-eyed, pissed, red and puffy. I watched as the
colour drained from his face, his cheeks seemed to cave in, the wine
was turned to water by the adrenalin gushing into his bloodstream,
and his eyes regained their ability to focus and show fear. He stood
up, solid and steady on his feet. A few people around us said 'Fucking
hell', and Eden closed his eyes.

'Thank you,' Martin said to me, walking straight up the stairs, across
the dark courtyard where a few couples sat cooing, and along the
corridor to Shiv's room. He was purposeful and precise, his bumbling
buffoon act dispensed with.

'Zanetti. Get Reception to call the police, would you?' he said,
bracing himself beneath her feet. She swung sickeningly, perhaps the
force of the opened door.

I don't know what we did while we waited. I couldn't tell whether
it was five minutes or an hour before they arrived. Glover and I

were suspended in grief and horror, unable to function, sitting there, standing there with Shiv's body, the air in the room sweet and barely breathable.

The officer who climbed up to get her (or was it one of the forensics team?) had trouble undoing the belt. I could smell her unwashed hair and her death as he fiddled with the buckle, groaning on his tiptoes to free her.

When he had done it, she fell hard and one of the others, there must have been six or seven of them, caught her, grunting with the weight. She was stiff as a shop dummy, but too strangely contorted to be anything but a human corpse.

He lay her down on the bed, leaving the belt round her strangled neck, and covered her with a sheet, oddly touching her purple cheek as he did so.

Martin coughed. He was from a military family. He wasn't going to cry.

'Martin. Somebody made her do this. It's got to do with a child-trafficking story the dead Russian bloke was doing. I'm going to get on to it,' I said, quietly, so that the police would think I was comforting Martin rather than shouting about taking over their investigation. Presumably they would investigate. Nothing is accepted as clear suicide without some cursory questions being asked, is it?

'Sounds a bit far-fetched,' he muttered. 'She's been depressed on and off for years.'

Had she?

'I'll take it from here, Zanetti,' he said, moving towards the phone. For the first time, I quite admired the composure of Martin Glover.

I shuffled around a bit, looking for something personal of hers to take away with me before this team of white-coated officials tidied my friend's life away into a steel drawer. I went into the bathroom where her washbag stood next to the sink. Her Filofax was balanced precariously on the glass shelf under the mirror. I picked it up, stuffed it not that easily into my jacket pocket, and

left. And you never know, it might have an answer in it somewhere.

I went back to the bar and sat down in Martin's seat, grabbing the
nearest glass and draining it. Eden, Grant and McCaughrean looked
at me, silent. It seemed that all eighty or so people in the room already
knew about Shiv. The atmosphere had changed. There was an urgency
to the hum and people were quieter, more intimate.

'Faith, you're shaking,' Eden said. He took my hand in his. 'You're
freezing.'

I pulled away and held my palms up on the table. They were
shivering and twitching. I clasped them together, but then my
shoulders shook.

'Come on,' Eden said. 'I'll take you upstairs.'

I went with him. Sorrow is Eden's forte. I think he is almost relieved
to see other people enduring it. He always says he has nothing to say
to anyone who has not experienced suffering. Perhaps he doesn't put
it quite as pompously as that. He says he can't stand their bright, naïve
eyes and inane smiles, 'like a puppy that's shat on the carpet'. He says
they have no sense of proportion. I think that must be why he does the
job he does. A suicide-bomber, a mutilated shell casualty, an AIDS
orphan, a teenaged sniper – these are people he can understand.
People who have experienced the agonizing extremes of human
emotion. With them he is calm.

And he was calm now. Escorting me back to my room like a patient
lover. His hand in the small of my back said, 'It will pass. You will
feel like this for a while and then you won't. Everything will pass.'
I understood his touch. Even his own grief, after all, had passed.
The searing pain of it, anyway. It was a dull ache now. Constant
but endurable. When Eden and I were . . .

A few years ago, I was watching television in a hotel room in Beirut
with Eden. There was a tedious documentary on BBC World – old
men airing their memories. But then it became clear that one man

was talking about having fought in Korea. His chin began to tremble
and he stopped speaking, unable to go on. There was a long pause
which wasn't edited out and then, instead of telling his story, he
just said: 'You see, we went to hell. And we only came halfway
back.' At this, Eden burst into tears and sat sobbing on the edge
of the bed for twenty minutes, his head in his hands, inconsolable.
He didn't need to tell me what he was crying about. He had seen
his brother murdered and a part of him had died too. 'I have only
come halfway back,' he said as he began to recover. 'I have only come
halfway back.'

Shiv had not even been able to face trying to come back from
whatever she had seen. That's what I thought. I suppose she knew
she would never get there.

I stood under the bright moon with my key in the door while Eden
waited. Asking for help is not something I am good at. I shuffled from
foot to foot and cleared my throat.

'Actually, my . . . er . . . my shower's broken,' I said to Eden's left
ear. He looked uncomprehending for a moment, and then his eyes
lit up and he laughed.

'You can stay in my room tonight,' he said, pushing his shirtsleeves
back up to his elbows.

'Oh, well, if you're sure . . .' I raised my eyebrows at him in a
question. A siren wailed far away on the street.

'No sex,' he offered.

'Thank you,' I said, breathing out with relief, and I followed him
through the night. I hadn't wanted to say it myself. It wasn't the actual
sex I didn't want, of course. In fact, I felt so shaky that if someone else
had been offering I might well have taken him up. But the last thing
I fancied was a huge emotional love-making type of deal. The kind
of experience where you both cry afterwards because of the intensity
of all that has so long been unsaid. No thank you very much. And I
certainly didn't want to start finding myself wondering when I was
going to see him again, what our relationship meant to us, whether or

not we wanted children. I laughed grimly to myself at the thought and walked into his room. The idea of children somehow coming into our battered lives was sweetly ludicrous.

We had lain there now for three hours, talking quietly. Even in a situation like this, it was nice to talk to Eden as though we had all the time in the world. No rush, no phone calls, not too much irony. It was like being on a plane, or lying in hospital. I remember after I was shot, blurred by the painkillers and exhaustion, I couldn't tell five minutes from five hours. It was like that now.

I told him I wanted to find out what story Misha had been on.

'If someone's going to start coming after me, then I want to know what I'm dealing with,' I said, reaching out for a cigarette. 'I nicked her Filofax. Got to be something in there. Even if it's only Misha's work numbers.'

'Tampering with evidence at a crime scene!' He couldn't even pretend to be shocked. 'Faith. Nobody's coming after you,' Eden said to the dark, taking my hand.

'It's not that I'm paranoid,' I smiled. 'It's just that everybody's out to get me.'

We both watched the fan whir on the ceiling, flashing slightly in the dark.

'Seriously, though. I was with Misha for ages while he died. Whoever it is could easily have seen me. And look at Shiv, for fuck's sake.'

'Yes,' he said, drawing the word out like a barrister doubtful about the truthfulness of his witness.

I got up to find my jacket and bring out Shiv's Filofax. I flicked a light on and riffled through the pages.

A page fluttered to the floor, loose, and I picked it up. It wasn't exactly a surprise. People don't get involved in scary stuff without leaving pages of phone numbers and scrawls behind. Not in my experience. And I hadn't taken the book as a souvenir. After all, I could have grabbed her bottle of perfume or a sock or something.

It was torn out of one of those cheap notepads where the paper looks badly recycled, like Russian loo paper. Not that they had loo paper in my day. Little pieces of torn-up newspaper tied together with string for presentation's sake. The writing was Russian. Blue biro. A list of names. It didn't take a genius to see that this must be Misha's list of contacts. Russian names, Jerusalem addresses.

'Hey. Look,' I squealed, and bounced on to the bed next to Eden. I do love a clue.

'It's in Greek,' he sighed.

'Russian. It's Misha's. His story. It must be his story. Look, Petr Kolbasov, Flat 23, blah blah blah, East Jerusalem.'

I looked around for my boots.

'Zanetti. We are not going now,' Eden said, sitting up, trying to calm me down.

'Jones, Siobhan is dead. They're all just going to think she was a suicidal nutter unless we do this!' I shouted it, but I sat back down. It was true that now might not be the best time.

'Faithy. Maybe she was,' he said, reaching out to touch my hair.

'Well, if she was, it's because somebody did something to her. Maybe Petr Kolbasov himself.'

I already felt silly. I lay back down. We must have gone to sleep quite soon after that. And a good job too. Just before I dropped off I nearly kissed him.

McCaughrean grieved as though Shiv had been his own daughter. In his photographer's weird schizophrenia he begged to be allowed to photograph the body and the scene of the suicide and he did so completely impassively, crouching to the floor with his sausage thighs to get a better shot, leaping about the room, peering through his lens, changing filters, setting up lights. Then, leaving the room, he collapsed into a sludge of tearful emotion, mumbling to himself about what a bad friend he'd been to her. I'd never been aware of him knowing her particularly well and would have preferred he shut up.

I shared a look with Eden as Don snivelled into his coffee cup at breakfast. We all sat together for a change and pretended not to notice when Martin tipped a whisky miniature into his hot milk.

'Get a fucking grip on yourself, McCaughrean,' Grant Bradford hissed, gesturing with a music-hall glance at Martin, still and desolate.

'Sorry,' McCaughrean sniffed. 'Hot as a fucking A-rab's armpit, isn't it?'

Nobody answered him.

'Is it just me?' he wondered, mopping his brow.

'I think I'll . . .' I said, getting up and going into my room. In fact, I hadn't showered in Eden's room and wanted to wash the world out of my hair. I also wanted to get away from Eden's glares of open malice towards Martin Glover. He had what was, if you asked me, an almost obsessive hatred of the guy. To make up for it, he always made sure he was ultra pally, but it was transparent, if only to me. I mean, OK, so he'd sacked him a decade ago. It didn't make him Pol Pot.

I'd had a feeling of being not quite alone enough in my room a few times since I'd been here, but it didn't occur to me to be wary this morning. The hotel bustle was going on around me and the sun, as ever, was out in a big way.

'Jesus,' I said, opening the door and going in.

''Sup?' Grant asked me, spinning his chair round. Everyone was on edge today.

'Look at this,' I beckoned to him, and all four of them got out of their seats to come and see, leaning farcically in through the door from both sides.

Everything had been trashed. My bed had been stripped and the mattress sliced open. The chairs were upturned, the table on its back like a cockroach. There was paper everywhere. Someone had emptied every last scrap from my overflowing Filofax. I trod quickly on an old passport photo of Eden. There were computer disks all over the floor and my computer itself was, bizarrely, on. It was where I had left it on the bedside table, but someone had been sifting through the files. I picked up the picture from the sole of my boot and went carefully into the bathroom. The bathrobe had been chucked into the bath. I didn't really have toiletries to tamper with. There were three crosses drawn on the mirror. No, not crosses. Kisses.

'What were you two up to in here last night?' Grant said, and we all did him the courtesy of laughing a bit.

McCaughrean heaved his way in to have a better look.

'Have they taken all your jewellery, Faithy?' he asked, sweating.

A lizard dashed across the floor in front of his feet.

'Little buggers,' he muttered to himself.

'Ha. Ha.' I said.

I did once have a pair of earrings actually, but I lost them on the beach in Split. They were my mum's. I looked down at my hands and thought how strange they would be if I did wear hundreds of rings. I would have to grow my nails a bit longer. At the moment they were cropped down like a cellist's. When they get long and scratchy, I bite them off. Eden once told me I was like a little girl with older brothers, trying to be like them. 'One day I'm going to brush your hair and buy you a pretty dress,' he said, and kissed my nose. It was a long time ago.

Now he glanced around, businesslike as one of the policeman last night. Inspection complete, they went back out to their table and ordered more coffee. I stood briefly in the doorway, stunned.

I picked the ringing phone up without thinking. Technically, I expect that's a bad idea. That after this sort of thing there ought to be some kind of police phone tap or something?

'Vera?' she asked.

'Da,' I said, confused. I hadn't spoken to anyone who called me that since I left my Russian husband. It's Russian for Faith. Too hard for them to get 'th' right and it sounds horrible and masculine to their ears, so I let them translate it. Mostly I was Verochka.

She told me her name was Svetlana and that she was a friend of Mikhail's. She had been trying to get in touch with him. Had come over from Moscow to find him. His hotel room, she said, was empty. She had phoned all the Jerusalem numbers in his diary and this was the first one she'd got an answer for. He'd written me down as Vera. It was odd, because I was sure he'd called me Faith when he phoned me from the Old City before he died.

I would break it to her face to face when I'd got work cleared up for the day. Off the top of my head, I agreed to meet her later in Pizza Piazza. She started to describe herself.

'Don't worry,' I said. 'You're Russian. I'd know you from a thousand miles.' It's a look in their eyes, a set of the features. I don't know. It used to be the strange Soviet shoes, but they don't wear them any more.

It was all go. My room. Svyeta. Jesus, I had assumed that Misha was saying a mental farewell to his girlfriend when he'd said her name. Now I realized that he was telling me something.

I stumbled outside to join the boys. A drink would have been nice. Martin was leaving today with Shiv's poor body if the British Embassy would release it. He handed out information to us in militaristic factual bursts. There was some Scotland Yard team here helping with a big investigation into some particularly brutal attacks on settlers and so Shiv's case, such as it was, had been handed over to a Commander Whitehorn. When foreign nationals die, the local police leap at any opportunity not to have to deal with it themselves.

The paperwork for shipping the body was being worked on now and they'd booked Shiv into the hold of the BA flight later on.

We all knew we might one day be going home like that. From the blood and dust and bullets to some English country churchyard with mossy shade, tangled ivy and bluebells in the spring. I wondered where Shiv would be buried, but Martin didn't seem up to discussing it. He preferred not to discuss Misha either. That, though, I could understand. The last thing he can have wanted to talk about was his dead girlfriend's extra-relationship love life.

'Coming to the briefing, Zanetti?' McCaughrean asked at last, deafening us with a change of subject. The French woman and her crew had already left and a bunch of German sound engineers were standing up under the lemon trees looking purposeful.

I glanced over at Martin. It was strange to have my boss here, pale and hungover. I don't suppose he had slept all night. He had managed to bring a whiff of East London to Jerusalem with him. The rest of us were so deeply tanned that in an office we always seem foreign and transient.

'Should go if you can face it,' he told me. I wondered if he would have gone when he was out in the field. He'd written a book called something like *I've Been to a Lot of Wars*, in which he describes eschewing press conferences for more 'real' experiences like creeping about in morgues. It's full of sentences that start: 'As I stood atop the mountain and surveyed the devastation around me . . .' etc. You can make it all up for yourself. The language is manly to a syllable and dense with army phrases, like 'a big push', 'a major offensive'. Still, you have to admire his honesty writing a book about himself, and how cool he thinks he is. Most foreign journalists do this, but pretend they're not doing it by going for titles like: *Whither Russia?*

My favourite bit of Martin's book is when he goes out with some soldiers and says: 'I stripped an Uzi just to kill the time.' I'm always teasing Shiv about this. Was always teasing Shiv about this. God. I feel as though I am always losing people whose loss makes the world a less funny place. My dad, Shiv.

I wondered if he stripped weapons as some sort of macho foreplay or if she lay beside him asking him admiringly how he got all his scars. Acne, if you ask me.

'Sure.' I nodded and stood up.

'Don't forget about the mole, Zanetti,' he shouted after me. Sure,

sure. I'm on to it, I thought to myself, holding up my hand in acknowledgement.

I found my jacket under my bed. My cigarettes and matches had been taken out of the pocket and thrown on the floor. What the fuck had they been looking for? Not a light obviously. I was always getting into trouble using people's torches to look for my matches in blackouts.

'You're going to get someone shot, Zanetti,' McCaughrean had once told me in Beirut. He didn't try to stop me looking though and he took a light from me when I found them. Nobody got shot that night either. Well, nobody we knew.

I hate Israeli government briefings. They are always the same. The announcement is invariably that they have decided to take a harder line, and you have to be there to take it down because that's the story the papers tend to want to splash on. Somehow, they manage to take an hour and a half to actually say this and the security is insane. You spend at least another hour standing in an overlit corridor being poked and prodded by people with guns looking for your guns which aren't there. Of course. Then there is all the business with accreditation and somebody or other doesn't have it.

'Fucking bureaucratic fucking quagmire,' McCaughrean gasped as someone flicked through his documentation. The security man had reflector shades and a short-sleeved shirt on. He looked pityingly up at McCaughrean.

We bundled in with everyone else and all the camera crews set up at the back as noisily as they possibly could. The air-conditioning wasn't up to much. There must have been ten bodyguards in here already, glancing around the room, flinching towards me every time I put my hand up to my hair. It would get me into serious trouble one day. They have to play out every possible scenario in their heads as they watch us. What if he pulled out a gun? What if she runs at him with a knife? What if that whole row there gets up and starts firing? What if? What if? What if? That's what they think. All the time. It must be exhausting. I bet they can't help doing it at home: What if my daughter hurls a grenade at me?

They were all extremely handsome. I wasn't lying when I told Martin back in London that I find the men in this area of the world pretty uniformly attractive. Uniformly in a good way. I wondered if Shiv had slept with any of them.

'Good piece about the Rakhmani raid,' the *Economist* correspondent shouted over at me with a wave. It was true. I had made a nice start here. Usually you had to scrabble around trying to find all the violence and drama. In this case Yo had kindly brought it right to me.

The *Economist* bloke's wife ran off with their driver last year. A Palestinian boy. Left her husband in Jerusalem with three kids.

'Thanks,' I said, sitting down on a grey plastic school chair.

'Did you get a line about Britney in?' McCaughrean asked me, wedging himself into the seat next to me, whispering as the important guy walked in, flanked by security.

'Yes.' I smiled. I glanced up to see that the speaker, who was supposed to be the Government Spokesman for Death, had been replaced by the Grim Reaper himself, General Meier. He caught my eye immediately and leered. Gripping the rostrum to reinforce his sincerity, he began to lie. He lied for what seemed like a hundred years.

The whole atmosphere of gravity and reverence made me want to throw paper aeroplanes or something. The *Economist* bloke – is it Tom? – cried out in surprise when my plane hit him on the ear. I looked away innocently. Three of the secret agent dudes had taken a step forward when I raised it in my hand. I winked at one of them and he very nearly smiled when he realized what I was doing.

'Zanetti, you freak,' McCaughrean mouthed, nudging me hard in the ribs.

I suppose it was an hour and a half and a lot of doodles of camels, I always draw camels, later we had learnt that Israel intended to take a harder line.

'Well, that was illuminating,' I said, joining the crush to get out.

'Coming back for a drink, Tom?' McCaughrean asked the *Economist* man. It was Tom.

'Can't. Got a lunch,' he said, making it sound as though his lunch was a contact too important even to name.

'Are you ducking The Duck?' McCaughrean asked and Tom laughed.

We stood on the steps of the briefings building, smoking in the shade of a palm tree. There were lots of them in terracotta pots all over the place. Obviously somebody thought that the pots lent gravitas.

'The Duck?' I asked.

'Tom's a schoolmate,' he explained. 'Don. Donald. The Duck.'

I laughed genuinely for the first time since I'd found Shiv yesterday evening. I think it's the worst thing about death, life going on. People say it to bereaved people as though it's a comfort, but it's not. It is precisely the problem.

I would tell Eden that life goes on later. He'd think it was funny. Where the fuck was he, anyway?

'Where the fuck's Jones?' I asked, as we lurched forward for a taxi with the other stragglers. Smokers, that is.

'Dunno. He's working on a story about an army mole who's suicide-bombing his own side. Can you imagine?'

I got butterflies of disappointment in my stomach. I hadn't got any further since I'd filed the first piece with only Glover's contact cited, and now Eden was on it too. I had the unpleasant thought that Glover might have told him by accident. Boasting in a drunken rant on the plane over. Damn it.

I shrugged as though it sounded an unlikely tale.

'Any idea who did your room over?' McCaughrean asked.

'Maybe. The General's trying to bully a blow-job out of me,' I lied. It was a reflex. I was keeping what I thought about Shiv and

Misha and my list of Russian names to myself. Or rather, to myself and Eden.

As if to help me out with my lie, General Meier himself burst out of the building in the middle of a crowd of jittery security men and made his way over to where we were smoking. He pushed his guards aside to come and kiss me.

'I have something that might interest you. Dinner soon. I will call,' he said, not making it clear by his tone whether this something was something of journalist or erotic interest. And he was swept away into his purring fleet of cars.

'Thought you'd have supplied him with one of them ages ago, Zanetti,' McCaughrean said, and I kicked him hard in the shin.

'Hey, fuck off!' he yelped. 'That's my injured foot.'

'Injured, my arse,' I laughed and we got into a car.

CHAPTER SIX

The Duck said he needed a drink and sloped off down to the bar. I was fishing around for my key when I noticed Yo slurping coffee on an ornate lobby armchair. His hand was bandaged and his boots looked ostentatiously military against the flagging. Just the man.

He smiled and raised an eyebrow when he saw me. Bringing me a story, I hoped.

I went up and kissed him, sitting down opposite with a sigh. I wiped the sweat off my face with my hand and Zahir brought an extra cup. Craning round to see if there was a table in the courtyard, I saw all the university students having tea and we moved out there, Yo hobbling as though it were his leg not his hand that had been hurt. Must be some kind of reflex.

'I've been meaning to phone you. Did they mend it?' I asked, pleased to see him.

'Minus a finger, yeah,' he said.

'Could have been worse,' I smiled, lighting a cigarette and offering. We both shrugged.

We sat silently for a bit, smoking and looking at each other and at the kids who waved their arms around passionately as they argued.

'Colin Powell this . . .', 'Sharon that . . .', 'Hanan Ashwari the other . . .' It wasn't a bourgeois debate about foreign affairs, an opportunity for those who'd read *The Economist* to shout louder than those who'd only managed the *Guardian*. It mattered. They knew people who'd been blown to bits in nightclubs, who'd come here from Kazakhstan, Ethiopia, India, Iran only to find themselves unsafe in their own homes. Again.

'Did you know,' Yo asked me, breaking the silence, 'that they have power points in the House of Lords where you can charge your wheelchair up?'

I grinned. 'I didn't,' I admitted, looking at his hand again.

'Thanks, Zanetti. I came to say thanks for getting me out,' Yo said, embarrassing me with his sincerity, looking me right in the eye. He wore a Star of David round his neck.

'Don't be stupid,' I told him, leaning my elbows on the table. I hate this. It's not as though I performed any emergency first aid or anything. I was hardly going to leave him there, bleeding to death. Almost just to change the subject, I told him.

'My friend Shiv – Boucherat? Remember? From the car? – she hanged herself the other night. She was sleeping with a Russian journalist. He had his throat cut.' I looked him straight in the eye as I told him. I was asking for help and he knew it.

'In the Old City? I heard about that. *Moskovsky Komsomolets* reporter, right?' Yo asked. Responsible. Capable. Mature.

I beamed at him. He had helped already. I hadn't known that Misha worked for *MK*. He didn't have his cards on him. Or anything much else. They'd taken everything. Had it maybe been a simple robbery? That's obviously what the police had thought. No. Of course it hadn't. When they went through his pockets at the morgue, it had been a shekel or two, a watch, a wedding ring (oops) and a gold Orthodox cross on a chain.

'Yeah,' I said. 'I was there when he died. Nearly. I think someone might have seen me because my hotel room got trashed.'

'Well, if you were there, how come you didn't see who did it, and if you were there and didn't see who did it, why aren't you under suspicion?' Yo wanted to know, smirking.

'Ha ha. I just missed them and I'm a woman without a knife. Can I tell you something?'

He looked down, allowing me to get on with it.

'Misha was doing a story about child-trafficking,' I said, leaning forwards to properly register his reaction.

Not that I had to lean forwards. His whole face looked like something they could use to teach aliens about human expression. Look everyone, this is what happens when they are very, very surprised.

But he plainly wasn't about to tell me anything. He managed to get a handle on his facial features almost immediately, and I started pouring information at him in the hope that there'd be something he wouldn't be able to resist. It's quite a good technique usually. When people go quiet on you, just talk and talk and talk and they can't help joining in when you hit something that presses the right button.

'I saw General Meier today,' I tried. 'He said he had something to tell me. He's been really helpful to me in the past. Set me up on an orphanage feature the other day and he gave me a major clue about a traitor in the army,' I lied. Pausing, I looked up to see if by some miracle he knew something.

His lips opened a bit and he coughed.

'I've heard the rumours,' he said. Nothing. Blank.

I lit a cigarette and gave up.

Now suddenly grave and formal, Yo said if I got any further he might be able to help out. If I could be specific about the information I needed.

'Actually—' his brain chugged round visibly. 'Would you like to come out to Gesher Haziv? Your friend Meier will be there . . .'

Was that supposed to make the invitation more inviting?

I do love contacts like this. Usually so hard to come by. Of course, like the General they always want something back in the end. With Yo it wasn't clear yet what it would be. I knew what I wanted though – apart from some decent access for the daily stuff. I wanted the mole. And now, pathetically competitive, I wanted to get the story before Eden.

'You can't say fairer than that,' I nodded. He was offering to take me to a kibbutz which had essentially been requisitioned by the army and was being used as a base from which to launch what seemed to have become known as 'anti-terror' operations. Doubtless this was not what the Palestinians call them.

You have to be insanely careful with this sort of thing in the British papers. How the hell we ever got into a situation where criticizing the Israeli army is considered by middle-class Hampstead Jews to be anti-Semitic and criticizing crazed Islamic fundamentalists is considered by middle-class Hampstead Arabs to be anti-Muslim, I have no idea. That, however, seems to be religion for you. Not that most of these London-based types are remotely religious. It's all just somehow become such a taboo that anything you say is taken down and used in evidence against you. Plus which, it's true that British Muslims say things in private about Jews that Jews would never get away with saying about Arabs.

I've got a friend who is always sending me text messages by accident. They are meant for a friend of his who used to be in Hizbollah. The last one said: 'Massacre in Jenin and the Yids are releasing doves in Trafalgar Square.' It's just that the Arabs have been given the licence of the oppressed and the Jews have lost it. That they managed to lose it is pretty phenomenal.

Not that this has anything to do with me in any case. My job, I suppose, is to describe what I see, but I can't pretend it's objective. Even seeing is subject to preconceptions, like the cameramen choosing what to shoot. Then the editor chooses from what the cameraman has chosen, and the producer chooses from that, and the executive producer runs the piece or not, pretty much according to her whim. Inevitably, the extent of the horror and gore is minimized to the point where it can only be described as deception. 'Here are some pictures of what happened, only they're not really pictures of what happened because we have decided that would be too horrible for you, so here are some pictures of the scene just before and just after something horrible happened.' Ludicrous.

Luckily for Yo, I spared him my opinions about press objectivity and racism in general and said I'd love to go. I was dying to meet the rest of his unit properly and make my guess as to who, if anyone, had switched sides. A waiter I'd never seen before tripped up with a tray of tea and all the little silver spoons, white china cups, starched napkins and sugar cubes crashed to the floor, bouncing on the cobbles, glancing in the sunlight. The table of students nearest leapt to its feet, one girl with long dark hair wiping splashes of tea off her jeans with a tissue. 'So, I'll pick you up here in the jeep at five?' Yo said as he left, the atmosphere between us tense now, crackling with unsaid things. On his part, not mine. He waved his bandaged hand like a mummy.

I waved back and set off to meet Svyeta.

It was mid-afternoon by the time I got there, but the city was quiet. The perpetual fear. A few cars cruising along, a group of well-dressed teenagers drinking milk shakes out of paper cups, a stray cat with half a tail scavenging in the gutter. It was still terribly hot. I had my jacket over my shoulder and a dirty T-shirt on.

Svyeta sat nervously by herself. Her hair was dry and frizzy from perming and dyeing. At the moment it was white-blond, but her dark brown roots were showing. She wore a satin-effect blouse with puffy sleeves and bobbly buttons down the front. Her shoes were worn down at the high heel. She had cheap jewellery on and her hands clasped round a Coke. She stood up awkwardly when I came towards her, but she didn't smile. She was about thirty-five, I thought, but looked older. She shook slightly and she spoke quickly and breathlessly. She was smoking very thin cigarettes with a flower on the packet – designed for women. For Christ's sake.

'I am looking for my son,' she said as soon as I'd sat down.

I held my hand up to stop her. I thought I'd better get in first.

'Misha's dead,' I told her. 'He was murdered in front of me. Practically.'

I waited for a scream, tears, at least a gasp and a horrified hand to the mouth. But she barely reacted.

'Yes. I thought so,' she nodded, apparently completely uninterested. 'These people are dangerous.'

'Yes. I had gathered that,' I said. 'But what people?'

I was so close. I could taste the truth, could feel things unravelling around me. I pulled at a coil of hair that had bounced down in front of my face. When I was little, I used to suck them. Evie said I might swallow one and choke.

'I don't know,' she said. Oh great. Well, nor do I, so where are we? I put my head in my hands.

'Vera,' she said. 'I am looking for my son. He is six years old.'

I raised my eyes to hers in apology. She was right. I had barely registered the enormity of this. It must have gone into the dead bit of my brain that Eden complains about. I ignore anything genuinely painful, he says. I can do physical suffering, I can do gore and horror, but personal? I shut down. That's what he says, anyway. What is he? My shrink?

I reached over and put my hand on hers.

'We will find him,' I said, despite the fact that I had no idea what I was talking about. I didn't exactly feel overwhelmed with determination either. What with everything else – Shiv and Misha and moles. There's a Garfield cartoon where the cat is looking glumly ahead with his eyelids hooded wearily over his eyes and the caption reads, 'I've never even been whelmed'. Well, I was barely whelmed with tenacity for this story. It would have been nice if the goal had been clear.

If it was more like: 'This wasn't a story I was investigating for some kind of journalism award. This wasn't a war I had to describe so that politicians and scumbag arms dealers could see what they were doing. This was about Svyeta's little boy. This, to make myself sound like a film with Arnold Schwarzenegger, was personal. I could hear the voice-over for the trailer, 'one woman on a personal revolution of her own', in that gravelly voice like he smokes sixty papirosochki a day.

But really I was just shattered. I could hardly even take Svyeta in.

And then she burst into tears.

'That's what Misha said,' she sobbed. '"We will find him." He lied.'

I lit a cigarette with the matches from the King David.

'He wasn't a friend, then?' I wondered, leaning forward on to the Formica.

'No. I went to the offices of *Moskovsky Komsomolets*. I wanted to find someone who would help me. He was their best investigator, they said. He promised me he would keep it all a secret until Sashenka was found,' Svyeta snivelled. She had a white handkerchief with daisies embroidered on to it.

'Svyeta,' I said. 'Keep what a secret?' The waitress put two plastic menus in front of us with lurid pictures of ice-cream sundaes on the back of them. Really stomach-churning food porn.

Please, please, please don't say I don't know, I thought.

'I don't know exactly,' she said and I wanted to burst into tears myself.

'Sasha's father drinks,' she explained. Earth-shattering news. 'Russian Man An Alcoholic' – not a classic headline.

I nodded understandingly. I was desperate for a vodka but it perhaps wasn't the best moment. I ordered a beer instead. She was turning a photo of her son over and over in her fingers. The quality even of very recent Russian photos always makes them look forty years old.

A glimpse of our parents' childhoods. That kind of thing. It's the graininess, the crap colour, the kind of wartime eyes Russians have. You know, when children have the gaze of adults?

'He took Sashenka for the weekend. Sasha forgot his crocodile. He sleeps with this furry crocodile—' she broke off to wipe her eyes with the back of her hand. 'When I went to pick him up, they had gone. The man in his communalka said they went to Jerusalem. He told me Nikolai, that's my ex-husband, had gone to Jerusalem before. Always with a child. When I asked what child, this guy said he thought they were street-children. You know, the ones who take orders for McDonald's?'

I said I knew the ones. Little four- and five-year-olds who stand in the middle of six-lane roads offering to fetch takeaways for drivers in the jams. You give them the money and they come running back victorious to you through the snow and fumes with your order. They usually get a tiny commission. And very proud we all are to have provided them with such a fine opportunity to set themselves up in capitalist enterprise under the golden arches themselves. They are all on glue. If they live long enough, they usually start to fuck the truck drivers under the bridges by the time they are eight or nine. It is the sort of thing that proves Eden's point about the world. And who can argue with him?

I drew in my breath, with understanding of what Svyeta was saying. The only thing that I could feel positive about was that her little boy was almost certainly still alive. Who knew what this prick of an ex-husband of hers had sold his own son into, but it probably required him to continue to breathe. I felt sick.

'He hates to sleep with all the lights off,' she said, her hand to her mouth. 'I hope they are leaving him a light on.'

'We will find him,' I told her again, my stomach twisted with disgust, my feet firm on the floor with absolute certainty. And this time I meant it. She'd got me. It had got me. I was going to find this boy. This suddenly became the first thing I'd worked on for ages that I sincerely cared about.

'Where are you staying?' I asked her. A siren wailed past outside, and I wondered, almost idly, if it was a bomb. One's reaction to sirens is strange when you do a job like this. When I hear them in London, it's hard to rearrange my mind to understand that it's probably a fight outside a pub.

'With a friend in the Russian quarter,' she told me, pulling herself together. She gave me her number and I said I'd call her tomorrow.

When I got back to the hotel, I didn't even try to stop myself running to Eden.

'Lovely day,' I said, putting my hand on his shoulder. I couldn't stand to tell him about Svyeta straight away. It was hard enough dealing with it myself. He was leaning over a little table, his arm around his bottle of beer. He flinched at the unexpected touch. People are always jumpy out here. Especially since Commander Whitehorn started interviewing everyone about Shiv. He had yet to get to me. I had a lot I wanted to tell him. But nothing that couldn't wait. Eden Jones, admittedly, is jumpy everywhere. We were in some restaurant in Mostar once and this bloke, a war tourist, took a photo with a flash and I thought Eden was going to kill him. He doesn't like fireworks either.

'What were you doing with Yoram Jakobs earlier?' he snapped. 'Looked very pally.'

'How do you know him?' I asked.

Eden raised his eyebrows.

'Everyone knows Yoram Jakobs!' he laughed. I was disappointed. Often happens that you think you've made a good contact, but he's everyone else's as well. It's a certain type of person who gets pally with the press corps.

'He didn't help with our mole thing,' I sighed.

'Our?' Eden wondered.

'McCaughrean grassed you up,' I told him.

*   *   *

McCaughrean sat across from Eden, red, breathing heavily. Out by the pool I could see Grant Bradford, his *Herald Tribune* over his face, a Walkman on the tiles by his lounger. Even the hair on his legs was bright orange.

'Do you think his pubes are ginger?' I wondered aloud.

'Glow in the dark,' Don nodded, seriously, puffing his cheeks out in awe.

'Do you think we could just drop this ironic tone for a change, Faith?' Eden asked, with a stare.

'Dunno what you mean,' I replied, smiling.

He breathed out slowly, visibly rearranging himself, putting his armour on for yet another day of insincerity, of pretending to be someone else. Someone alive. Someone functioning – eating, breathing, bathing, chatting. Eden Jones, war correspondent. Just what he'd accused me of being when I walked in that evening he arrived. He is so sure I'm a fake too that, underneath, we are both desolate souls, flailing in the darkness. He can fuck off.

'All right, Faith. All right,' he said, glancing up at a new waitress who was visibly trembling with the force of his sex appeal.

I told him about Svyeta now, edging up close to him to make the conversation private.

'She wasn't a friend of Misha's at all. She'd basically hired him to find her son. The dad had kidnapped him and brought him over. Apparently, he'd done it before with street-children. Looks like he's sold his own son,' I told him. He took it grimly. Well, you would. Smoking, occasionally closing his eyes. I suggested I cancel my trip to the kibbutz with Yo.

'No, don't do that. We'll have time later. We'll do the rounds of those addresses tomorrow night. The Russians. Should turn something up,' he said.

Eden, I thought, didn't quite understand what this might mean. I know our jobs are dangerous, or at least potentially dangerous, but we have a huge amount of control over that. There are some people, like that cameraman who just carried on walking towards the podium filming when Anwar Sadat was assassinated, who love to walk through a blaze of bullets, and there are others who just cower behind the nearest pillar and ask people what it was like. Not that I use the word 'cower' in any negative sense, of course. Nothing wrong with cowering and nothing clever about getting shot. The thing is, though, the people on Shiv's list – Misha's list, we had to assume – are Russian. Maybe it's just a list of his mates, people to look up while he's in Jerusalem. But maybe it's a list of child-traffickers. In that case they'd be those enormous scarred blokes with shaven heads and mobile phones that you see leaning out of the windows of speeding Mercedes in every backwater of the former Soviet Union. These blokes are brutalized by their ghastly upbringing, years in the army, and the general view (not altogether unfounded) that human life is worth nothing. Neither theirs nor anyone else's. Dropping round on them is a dicey business. If I were saying that to a Russian, they'd say: 'Life is a dicey business.' Sometimes they seem sage and almost moving. Sometimes they seem glib and stupid.

It's always annoying when you have to file a nothing story when there is so much going on. I had to drag myself upstairs to crouch in my room, curtains shut, ashtray full, and file a few hundred miserable words about the briefing – basic information in the intro, bit of colour about menacing speaker followed by ever-regurgitated background to conflict.

My new room, my night room, is circular, up in the minaret. Sort of up in the attic, if Pasha's palaces have attics. It's at the top of a long, winding flight of stone steps and down a narrow corridor. It is the only room up here – hardly ever used. Occasionally for a child or a nanny, apparently. It has the feel of servants' quarters with its sloping ceilings and narrow slit of a window. I can see the mosque out of the slit and hear its noise above the traffic and the insects. It would almost feel appropriate to get out a prayer mat and kneel down in my garret. I didn't, of course. I got out a cigarette and lay on the bed with my boots on.

Zahir had been very understanding. I told him to move me, and on no account to tell anyone that I had been moved. I would continue to pay for my original room and I would leave my stuff there and work there during the day. I gave him a hundred dollars which he took with a wince of displeasure. I gazed out at the stars and wondered if I'd brought my washbag up.

It was another diazepam dream. This time my mum telling me that she had killed me and then killed herself. That we were both dead. This was heaven.

In the morning, there was a crescent moon drawn in black felt-tip on my bathroom mirror.

CHAPTER SEVEN

'Looking delectable,' Yo grinned, running into the lobby like someone who's been up for hours, showered, shaved, given a few orders. I put my cigarette out and stood up, shuffling my jacket on.

'It's the middle of the night,' I said. It was four-thirty in the morning.

'Your pumpkin awaits,' he bowed, and I followed him into the street. We both span round when we heard something behind us.

McCaughrean was huffing and puffing after us in the dark.

'Oh God,' I murmured to Yo. 'Sorry.'

'A little birdie tells me you're off to Galilee,' he gasped, throwing his camera bag into the back of Yo's military jeep, the canvas awning flapping like a groom's tailcoat behind it. Normally a dozen soldiers would peer out from the cell, but today it was ours. It was a wrench leaving the city when I knew little Sasha was in it somewhere, that the answer to Shiv's death was here. On the other hand, if I didn't file something tonight, I might end up back in London writing features about different types of yoga. It was only a day. He would have to wait a day.

'Near there,' Yo nodded, scowling at me.

'Great,' Don said, climbing in with great difficulty.

'How's the foot?' Yo asked, without a touch of sympathy. He put his reflector shades on slowly, despite the black night about us. He was pissed off and I couldn't blame him. I hadn't said anything about the trip to McCaughrean. Eden must have told him after I went to bed last night. Or he's psychic. Either way, annoying.

'On the mend,' Don said. 'How's the hand?'

Yo walked round the jeep and opened the door.

'Fine, unless I'm driving or something,' he laughed, getting into the driver's seat.

I sat up front with Yo and peered out at the darkness. There was nobody around and almost nothing visible anywhere. The odd flicker of light from a house, and the silver splash of the moon. We were hurtling across the desert at high speed, throwing up sand all around us. The roads were sometimes tarmac, sometimes just dirt track. It was a bumpy ride and we rattled around in silence, Don and I still half asleep.

But then, at about half past six, without any kind of warning, the sky exploded in colour as though someone had lit it with a match. The sun, flaming orange and scarlet and huge enough to fill our field of vision, burst into view, and all around it pinks, oranges, yellows and reds blazed across the horizon.

Don said, 'Fuck.'

I said, 'Wow.'

Yo seemed barely to notice.

As suddenly as the sun had risen, the villages in the desert around us sprang into life. A woman in a toga-like robe with a large amphora on her head started out for the well or the river. A band of scraggy children with a herd of goats set off for some pasture and a man on a donkey began to look purposeful. The whole desert shone golden and the palm trees had an artificial look about them, spindly and abrupt as if taken by surprise, standing alone there like that.

The villagers and Bedouins barely spared us a glance and there certainly wasn't any of the animosity you'd get on the West Bank with Israeli number plates. Nobody, in fact, threw anything at us at all, let alone tried in any way to kill us.

By the time we drove through the gates of the kibbutz, the sun was searing down from high in the sky.

'You could fry an egg on the side of this thing,' Don shouted from the back. You couldn't, though. Last time I was on a job with him somewhere near the Dead Sea, about a year ago, he decided to try. He stopped and bought some eggs at a market stand and cracked one on to the admittedly extremely hot bonnet of our car. It went a tiny bit white round the edges as we stared enthusiastically, but that was it. Then we had to wipe it off, but a smear of it hardened there and stank.

'Don't you dare,' I said.

Actually, Gesher Haziv is a hotel. A kibbutz hotel, meaning that the work of the kibbutz is to run it. There are orange groves and a swimming pool, little cabana-style rooms and a big dining hall and vaguely flashy lobby area. I imagine it has lost some of its immediate charm since it was taken over as an army base. Don had done away with any pretence that he happened to want a lift to Galilee and his presence on the trip hadn't been commented on since we set off. What harm could he do? Well, that seemed to be Yo's approach at any rate.

Yo had been oddly quiet all the way, except to say: 'When Anne Boleyn was beheaded, her head carried on saying its prayers.'

'They what?' Don shouted, but neither of us told him.

We stopped outside the main hotel entrance, within some rickety wire gates and up a long drive. As well as a row of army jeeps waiting by the doors like taxis and a few little groups of military men with guns strapped around them, there was a band of hippies sitting on the rough grass near some fat fig trees.

'Deep cover?' I asked Yo, putting my sunglasses on and stretching my legs out. It was nice to be out of the city. It smelt different. I could hear the sea and there was a breeze.

'Rehab,' Yo said, walking in through revolving doors.

I chased after him while Don organized himself and got his bearings.

'Hello?' I asked, dumping my bag down on the tiles.

'Rehab. Seriously. It's a twelve-step centre. We couldn't exactly kick them out,' he said, and handed his ID to a soldier on reception. 'The kibbutzniks run it.'

'That's brilliant,' I said and span around to have a look at the place.

It was really more like a youth club or a modern town hall than a hotel. It has that slightly Soviet seventies thing going on, with big frosted ceiling lights like enormous staggered ice cubes, glass swing doors, and too much useless dark space. Reception is a tiny little desk in a vast empty hall, shadowed by a staircase leading to nowhere but a wide balcony with brown armchairs on it.

Yo slapped hands with a black man in khaki. Probably one of the Ethiopian Jews who came during Bob Geldof's famine. There is this cliché that women like a man in uniform, but personally I don't think it's the uniform. The point is that men in uniform are almost always very fit, under twenty-five and more than averagely brave. What's not to fancy?

I went back outside to find Don and my little daytime cabana while Yo organized our press clearance. McCaughrean was already taking pictures and neither the army nor the addicts looked particularly pleased about it. I was about to call out to him when an Apache helicopter landed behind us, blowing us out of its way with the force of its whirring propellers. They never look very efficient to me, helicopters. Even these big butch ones. You can see exactly why they're always crashing and there is something not very manly about flying them. Speaking of macho, it was General Meier who leapt out, ducking until he was well clear of the thing.

'Faith Zanetti,' he said as he passed me. It might have been a greeting or a statement of fact. He paused as though to speak to me, but was whisked away.

'And Donald 'The Duck' McCaughrean,' I added when he was out of earshot.

'Fuck's he doing here?' Don asked. He had been in full *Top Gun* shades, manly stride and broad shoulders mode.

'Search me,' I said. 'Yo said he'd be around.'

Don and I pottered off out the back to see the pool. It was empty and there was nobody but us about. I don't suppose it's seen much use since the tourists left. I couldn't resist it.

'This'll be good,' Don said, sitting on the end of a sun lounger. I kicked my boots off, threw my jacket over a plastic chair and pulled my T-shirt over my head. Then I hopped about tugging at my socks. When I stepped out of my jeans, McCaughrean's lounger tipped up with his weight and left him plonked on the searingly hot poolside tiles.

'It's an arse, Don. Just an arse,' I said.

I dived in naked and swam a length underwater. Popping up at the other end I shook my head like a wet dog and shouted out to McCaughrean.

'Freeeeeeeeeezing! Get in!' I yelled.

He looked sheepishly about him and then started grinning like a schoolboy. Stripping his sweat-stained shirt off, fiddling with his belt and snapping his Y-front elastic, Don McCaughrean got completely undressed. It was weird, but he actually looked more, rather than less, dignified with nothing on. I think it might be just that clothes don't fit fat people. Naked, he looked almost like a baby – pink, glowing and round, an enormous tummy hanging over completely dwarfed genitalia. Leaping into the air and pulling his knees in to his chest he shouted 'Geronimo!' and dive bombed into the pool, sending huge tidal waves slopping over the edges.

Screaming and splashing, we swam up and down a couple of times and then hauled ourselves out to dry in the baking sun. For this we were modest enough to put our underwear back on, but it wasn't sufficient to impress Yo and the General who had turned up (together of all things) with our accreditation.

'Mad dogs . . .' muttered Yo, and Meier flicked our passes, in their plastic casing, on to our bare tummies, staring without any pretence of modesty at my breasts. It was, he seemed to believe, his lucky day.

I sat up, my hair hanging down in soaking ringlets.

'Thank you,' I said. 'It's so hot—'

'Good to see someone enjoying it,' he said, getting an erection that was visible from his facial expression, and he stomped off to run his army. I wasn't aware he did anything hands-on these days. I couldn't imagine why he was here. I mean, some of us have deadlines to meet, pages of newspaper to pad.

'Wednesday evening, perhaps?' he asked me significantly.

'Lovely.' I beamed.

They walked away together, beauty and the beast.

Don and I giggled like children.

'Oh, God, that man is repulsive,' I said.

We basked for a while, smoking and breathing in the sunlight, hoping, perhaps, to be healed.

'Think Shivvles really killed herself?' Don asked me, an admission of what we were both thinking about, moving his big head to his left and squinting sweatily to look me in the eye from his lounger. I wanted to tell her about the way he said 'Shivvles' and hear her rail against him.

'As opposed to what?' I asked, not about to confide in him. Because, no. Of course I didn't think she killed herself. Well, maybe she did it, but not without persuasion. Not without being somehow tortured into thinking there wasn't an alternative.

'Don't be a spastic,' he said, his face wobbling redly.

'Sorry. I don't know what to think,' I said. And it was true, up to a point. Which is about as far as anything's ever true.

We were sitting on high red-leather stools at the lobby bar later, when a dead soldier was brought in on a stretcher, a blood-drenched towel over his face. He was surrounded by colleagues, one of whom was sobbing into his hands, unable to walk straight. Yo came in behind them and said a few words to the crying boy.

'Shot his mate by accident,' he told us, sitting down and ordering a beer from an old woman who had clearly worked there since long before the army turned up. She had a big red flower from one of the bushes outside in her hair.

'Jesus. How?' McCaughrean asked.

'I don't know. Safety catch not on, I suppose. They were in a car having a fag,' Yo said, shaking his head in disbelief. He reached into his pocket now and brought out a piece of paper folded in four.

'Do you mind?' he asked Don and he gave me a look that told me to slip down off my seat and move away a little.

'I've got something to show you,' he said. 'Look at it. Burn it.'

He handed me his document and watched while I read it.

It was incomprehensible at first. A typed list of names with numbers by their sides. All confusingly in English and in Hebrew. It was a photocopy and not a great one. I read down the sheet of paper for something familiar and I found it: Yidzak Meier, acquitted for the attempted rape of Rachel Meier, aged twelve years. I flashed my eyes around for a date and found it in the top right-hand corner. It was just a court record, the results of the day for that particular courtroom in Hebron. Courtroom 7B, 12 March 1958.

'Oh, you must be joking,' I said, softly. I took my lighter out and set fire to the corner of the copy. I walked outside with it burning in my hand and let it flutter down to the paving stone at my feet.

Yo had followed me.

'Where did you get that?' I asked him. But I knew he wouldn't answer. Obviously he had been conducting his own investigations at the most incredible risk to his own . . . well, life. But why?

Even from here, we could hear the boom of anti-aircraft missiles being fired from the Bekaa Valley and the roar of F16s flying low overhead. We joined Don back at the bar, the mood changed.

'All right, my little lovebirds?' he roared, slapping Yo hard on the back. It was typical of him to be so shockingly impervious to the reality of a situation. I adored him for it just now.

Slurping the last of his beer down, Yo led us through to the vast canteen, saying that he would take us as near to the front as he could after supper, which was eaten, strangely, at five-thirty. Breaded chicken, chips and tinned green beans. To drink, fizzy lemon vileness. Don was very obviously, and indeed vocally, looking forward to the mini-trifles lined up in red and yellow rows on the steel stand by the till, hundreds and thousands sprinkled festively on top of them. He was keeping a close eye on how many were left.

There were four televisions on stalks sticking out of the walls, and they were all playing Duran Duran's 'Rio' video. The soldiers stared blankly up at their nearest screen, fork to mouth, eyes to TV. I recognized a lot of men from Yo's unit. They were stuffing the tasteless food in without protest. None of them looked like a traitor at first glance. Whatever one might look like. Shifty eyes, treacherous sneer?

When Meier arrived, beads of sweat glistening on his domed forehead, Yo stood up with a scrape of his seat, black rubber on clean lino, and insisted it was time to go.

'Did you know that sodomy is still illegal between heterosexuals in Britain?'

He paused.

'Apparently helps with nailing rapists,' he added, leading the way.

Don and I shared a complicit glance.

'But my trifle . . .' Don complained, heaving himself out of his seat nonetheless.

'Schmrifle,' said Yo dismissively, turning back. 'Diet. It'll do you good.'

I think we were going out through the swing doors as the man was coming in. He was in fatigues, same as everyone else, but I noticed at the time, definitely not only in retrospect, that there was something crazed in his glance.

We all span round as he threw his jacket open and shouted, '*Allaaaaaaaaaaahu Akbar!*'

I met Don's eyes in a flash of horror and he had time to say, 'Oh holy fuck' before all three of us threw ourselves down the corridor and face down on to the floor. Lying there, feeling the heat above me, my eyes shut tight, I realized that my presence here wasn't an accident. I had been brought here especially to see this happen. Hadn't I?

The panes of glass in the swing door blew out on to us in an explosion that was so loud I thought my eardrums might have burst. The noise hurt all over and the heat was immense. As we staggered to our feet, soldiers came running out of the canteen, their faces bleeding, their uniforms stained with blood and food. One boy held up his arm, screaming in pain and shock as he looked at the hand that was no longer there.

In an attack of inexplicable idiocy, McCaughrean and I were unable to help ourselves from running in rather than out. The smell of burning flesh and plastic in the canteen was overpowering. I retched immediately. Two hundred men were shouting and screaming. There were pieces of flesh and bone and brain everywhere. Tiny little flecks of person spattered around the room. Some families would have nothing to bury. The ZAKA people were going to have a job on their hands. They are these volunteers, ultra religious, who find and identify body parts. Jews have to bury some part of their dead and the ZAKA people will find a part.

Most of the tables were on fire, the plastic smoking like mad. Don and I grabbed an alive person each and dragged them out. Mine was slipping in and out of consciousness and was bleeding from the side of the chest. My *Bad News Bible* had said to lie people wound-down, contrary to your instincts. Then the blood doesn't run into the lungs. I did it and the boy opened his eyes and mouth to scream. Then he passed out.

Yo – alive, thank God – was leaning against the canteen wall with his head bowed as though about to vomit. His bandaged hand suddenly the least of his problems. Meier, unscathed too, was shouting orders. In his element.

The minutes before the ambulances arrived went very slowly indeed. There was nothing any of us could do for the men bleeding quickly to death. I saw the woman who had served me my chicken walking slowly towards the outside door, swaying slightly, a big piece of glass sticking out of her cheek.

'Think it was one of Rakhmani's?' Don said.

Now that I thought about it, yes, it probably was one of Rakhmani's.

'I'd better phone the desk,' I said, and went, dazed, to my hut. I thought that the resident addicts on their twelve-step programme would probably be needing a drink pretty badly by now. Or a fix of whatever it was they fancied.

My little cabana was a couple of hundred yards from the main building of the hotel. If you walked a bit further along, you could see the blue of the Mediterranean. The carnage and its aftermath hadn't reached this far and it was odd to be walking across dusty grass and under palm trees in an apricot sunset while men who had lost a limb were screaming in agony so nearby. It is always the things that are not affected by horror that make the horror so powerful. The little banalities of life, like needing a wee when I got into the room, checking the battery on the sat-phone.

I filed an immediate piece to copy and told the desk that Don could wire some pictures over within half an hour. Quite a big scoop, really. A huge scoop. Suicide bomb in an Israeli army base. The reprisals would be swift and deadly, no doubt. I was the only journalist for miles. There wasn't a lot of satisfaction in that knowledge, unfortunately. Given the circumstances. While I was on the phone to London, I asked for Glover and told him about the tip-off Yo had given me about the rape. Should we publish it now or should we wait and get more, confront Meier? His reaction was depressing.

'Don't be an idiot, Zanetti. He was acquitted. Not guilty. Not a story. Get back on to the mole. Meier is organizing the fucking investigation. My info on that is reliable. Go and lick his wounds clean and he might give you something.' And he hung up. Sometimes, I hate this fucking job. I had just sold them thousands more copies of tomorrow's paper, wiped out the competition, and he was hassling me about my failure to produce on the mole thing.

And the whole thing stank. If some Israeli lunatic really was double-crossing his own army, you'd have thought people like Meier would go to the ends of the earth to cover it up. Not let some low-life like Glover find out. And how the hell did Yo know anything about Shiv and Misha? He was telling me that the General was a nearly convicted paedophile (the girl shared his surname, so you can imagine how come charges got dropped). He had made a link.

'The Zanetti curse. Wherever she is, people drop like flies,' Eden said when Don and I walked into the bar back at the Colony at one o'clock in the morning. We were still filthy and traumatized. Salim, who had heard where we'd been, slapped drinks down on the bar for us without a word. Was he pleased some Israeli soldiers were dead, or was he ashamed of his compatriots? He wouldn't be telling anyone around here, that was for sure. His job depended on it.

I drank my vodka in one and immediately felt a lot better. Yo had got some underling to take us back to Jerusalem and none of us had spoken the whole way. There was nothing to say.

'Thought we were going out to visit our Russian friends tonight,' Eden added, drunk and ratty. Everyone hates to miss a story.

'Yeah. Got a bit held up,' I snapped and collapsed on to the bar, head on my arms.

Softer suddenly, Eden looked at me kindly and put his hand on my back.

'Is Yo the traitor? Our mole?' I whispered.

'It looks like it. But too much like it. Too easy,' he said.

I nodded and Eden smiled at me.

'You should go to bed,' he said.

So I did.

CHAPTER EIGHT

The others cheered when I came down to breakfast. A German correspondent with one brown eye and one blue eye threw a congratulatory roll at me. Don had obviously been up late telling everyone about our scoop. Had we been invited to witness the whole thing by Yo? Don, at any rate, just thought we'd got lucky.

Fair enough, he'd taken some good pictures but they were all too gross to run. Dead people's feet you could get away with, or some other relatively inoffensive part of them poking out from under a white sheet or a body bag. If the person is still alive, you can allow for a lot more blood and gore, but severed limbs and incomplete heads don't sell papers. Unlike a nice picture of a found baby or a minor royal with fewer than average clothes on.

'What are you? Lord Lucan?' Grant Bradford wanted to know. 'Sneaking off so nobody could sodding find you.'

I sat down with him and waved for a coffee. He was smiling, but he was pissed off. It wouldn't have mattered if Don hadn't come but now he thought we'd scuttled away without him on purpose. Plus which he'd never actually seen a suicide-bomber exploding before.

'Yeah, well, you'd only have fainted or something, Grant,' I said, and patted his hand.

He refused to let me help him with the jumble today and just sat there scowling with his pen in hand and his tongue sticking out of his mouth like someone in a cartoon. Commander Whitehorn had interviewed him first. He was peeved. I smoked a cigarette and watched for lizards.

McCaughrean soon stumbled out to join us, giving me a wink of victory.

'Nothing,' he said, splurging himself out over a chair and shuffling to get into the shade. 'Not so much as a fucking scratch. I've checked all over.' He'd been wanting a battle scar for years. The most he'd managed was his sprained foot which, he had been forced to admit, was very much on the mend already.

'Never mind,' Grant said comfortingly. 'You might get your cellulite blown off next time.'

'Ha. Ha,' Don glowered. He mopped his brow. 'Fuck me. It's hot as an A—'

'Shut up, McCaughrean,' Grant and I said in unison.

'Well, it is,' he mumbled, fiddling in his trousers for a light.

I got up and went into my courtyard room.

In the cool gloom I listened to a message from Martin asking for a big colour piece about yesterday. No word about the funeral or anything. I felt as though I was the only person who actually missed her. I missed her so much I felt as though I'd had a limb lopped off. Not that we show it, of course.

'What was it like – were you scared?' Martin's voice crackled out. He had obviously been up drinking all night. 'Did your life flash before you?' he wondered, in explanation of the type of piece he was after. When I was injured in Salvador, he ran a picture of me in my sling on the front page with a couple of paragraphs about what had happened. Without my permission, of course. I suppose since the publication of his self-congratulatory aren't-I-hard book he's decided he's in a position to make other people do the same. Hey, I'm not going to be precious about it. I wrote the piece he asked for. 'The first thing that hit me was the noise. It was closely followed by a pane of glass.' That sort of deal.

I had just tapped 'send' when Eden knocked on the door.

'Sorry,' he said, grimly. 'I was a cunt last night. I hate waiting for people. I always think they must be dead.'

I smiled round at him from my desk in the corner. I would have been pleased that he'd worried about me if I could have admitted it to myself.

He sighed and lit a cigarette.

'Come on,' I said. 'Let's go and find Sasha.'

I was being glib and we both knew it. But you have to keep the goal in mind, I always think. If you start off saying to yourself: 'Right, let's begin this slow and painstaking investigation into child-trafficking which we may never get to the bottom of', it's easy to get downhearted. If you see what I mean.

The Russian ghetto is hilarious. The first wave of Soviet immigrants created their homes in the image of contemporary Moscow, a city that has changed beyond recognition over the past twenty years. Remember the refuseniks? Jews who weren't allowed out of the Soviet Union but who, for having asked to leave, lost their jobs, homes and rights. Well, in the 1980s, under Gorbachev, they became acceptniks and poured out into Israel. So much so that loads of Russians who were also desperate to get out went to enormous lengths to pretend Judaism and join in the exodus. The successful fakes mostly went on to America, but the genuine article is still here.

So, while Muscovites have delicatessens and sushi bars, the Israeli Russians are still shipping in scraps of repulsive sausage and tins of oily sardines in order to perfectly recreate the smells of home. It's like Indians in London. In Bombay, the girls go out all night in high heels and mini-skirts, but in London people are still living by the old rules and the teenagers are swathed in saris and home by nine-thirty.

I could tell by the look in his eyes that our cab driver was Russian. He had prison tattoos on his wrist and a scar from one corner of his mouth all the way to his ear. He'd done fifteen years in a psychiatric prison in Oryol for armed robbery, he said. When I asked him if he liked living in Israel, he shrugged.

'Like? What's like?' he said. This was a man past preferences. He smoked as though his life depended on it. Eden watched us talking, concentrating, trying to hear a familiar word or sound.

'Amazing,' he said, shaking his head. He touched my back. Nikolai had married a Kazakh Jew whom he met at Hebrew class. She works as a cleaner out in one of the settlements and they have two sons.

A watermelon from one of the roadside stands rolled into the road and Nikolai swerved hard to avoid it, tyres squealing, a cloud of sand exploding round the car.

'*Pizdyets!*' he spat, curling his fat fingers round the steering wheel.

The idyllic holy sites and loveliness were a long way behind us. We'd been careening round piles of rubble, bullet-spattered ruins and streets where all the shop signs are in Russian, for ages by the time Nikolai slammed the brakes on outside a nasty-looking tower block. There were a few old ladies sitting on foldaway chairs outside, wearing aprons and drinking tea, a stray dog lurking about, and an enormous thug of a youth mending his motorbike. It could have been a Moscow suburb in August.

The entrance way was dark and dank, the metal letter boxes swinging off their hinges and the lift buttons melted by a moron's lighter.

'What do you think?' Eden said in the pitch dark of the creaking lift. The bulb had gone.

'Dunno,' I said. 'Mafia?' I put my hand in my pocket to feel the crumple of Misha's piece of paper.

It was apartment number 23 we wanted. We stood in the gloom and rang the bell. A cigarette and a couple of silent minutes later, Eden turned the handle and opened the door.

'For Christ's sake,' he said to himself, walking in.

It just wasn't particularly surprising to find the whole place over-turned. Not, let's face it, that it can have been that nice to start with. Everything breakable was smashed on the floor, the dirty net curtains had been pulled from the windows, the plants uprooted and the earth from the pots smeared about the carpet. Food from the fridge stinking the whole flat out and a black cat, who was mewing wildly, had been ignoring its litter tray for days.

'So. No Petr Kolbasov,' I said. That had been the name of the first person on Misha's list. A silly name that basically translates as Peter Salami. Without having any idea what we were looking for, it seemed unhelpful to search the flat ourselves, but we peered about anyway. Cheap clothes, no books, action videos like *Die Hard II*, some photos of kids on the wall. A lot of kids, actually. One snub-nosed girl with a scar above her eyebrow. None of them the Sasha I'd seen in the blurred picture his mum had shown me. I couldn't tell whether these were innocent pictures of relatives or a sinister clue.

'Think these are family or victims? Could have been a serial father,' Eden commented.

'Why past tense?' I asked, realizing that Eden's immediate assump-tion was likely to be the right one.

'Well,' he said, turning round to look at me. 'It doesn't look great for Kolbasov, does it?'

'No,' I agreed, wanting to leave.

I asked the women downstairs if they knew Kolbasov, and they shared a glance before shrugging a denial. It didn't seem suspicious – just typical Soviet behaviour. Don't tell anyone anything unless you have to.

We got back into the hot car with Nikolai who had been looking at some kind of Russian soft porn magazine which he now shoved into the glove compartment.

The next flat was just up the road. Another shabby building dotted with satellite dishes and flapping with washing, gaping wounds in its side where the plaster was hanging off.

This time we didn't even have to turn the handle. The door had been kicked in and was lying in front of us, dangerous splinters slashing at our feet as we stepped over it.

Pavel Ivanchenkov was not at home. I picked up a souvenir samovar from Yasnaya Polyana, Tolstoy's house. It said 'Made in the USSR' on it.

'This is a waste of time,' I said, sighing. The curtains blew in a hot breeze and the bin smelt bad.

I leant against the wall and shut my eyes. 'So. Svyeta gets Misha to investigate the child-trafficking she suspects her own ex-husband of being involved in. Misha comes up with these addresses – either helpful contacts or actual suspects. Someone finds out he's on to them and kills him.'

We stood in our own private silence and thought.

'But what about Shiv?' I asked the empty flat.

Eden drew his breath in. 'Well, maybe the paedophiles – whoever Misha gets on to – know that Shiv's having a thing with him and torture her to get to him. Disturb her so much that—' I turned to face him.

'It's not enough,' I shook my head.

'I know,' Eden quickly agreed, and he ran both hands through his hair in exhaustion.

Neither of us wanted to sit down on the pieces of furniture that hadn't been upturned.

'Computer's gone,' Eden commented, nodding over to an empty socket near a table that had a computer-sized space on it between coffee cups, bits of paper and empty fag packets. I raised my eyebrows in interest.

'What the fuck are they after?' I wondered to myself. They'd been through my computer, assuming it was the same people, which I did.

'I expect they're just flogging them on a stall in the Old City,' Eden said.

'What, and murdering anyone who gets wind of their evil scheme?' I laughed. 'Anyway, they didn't nick mine.'

'Haven't killed you yet either,' he yawned, meandering out of the flat in a gesture of defeat. 'Come on, let's go and call the police,' he shouted back to me. I suppose we'd hoped to find some compelling piece of evidence by ourselves. If you call the police too early you get cut out of the investigation, but since we weren't going to get anywhere by ourselves, it seemed like the sensible thing to do in basic defeat. I wasn't doing Shiv any favours, flailing about like this. We needed something, or someone, a bit more concrete.

It took us four hours to get home to the hotel because some new roadblocks had been slapped up since we drove out and a lairy soldier forced Nikolai to take an insane detour out to the edge of the desert and back.

'What am I?' he spat. 'A fucking Arab?'

I didn't bother to translate this to Eden who had clicked his seat down and was lying, slumped into the ageing maroon plastic, with his eyes shut, oblivious to the heat and noise. It's true that the roadblocks appear to be a kind of ritual humiliation for Palestinians trying to get across a city that is their home. Israelis get pissed off if you comment on things like that, but it doesn't take a genius to see who has the power and who doesn't.

I put both arms out of the window and leant on my elbows, breathing in the smells of spicy cooking, petrol, garbage fires and sweet tobacco. We got stuck in a traffic jam outside a Palestinian school where soldiers were stopping parents from pulling up at the gates. The parents were having to drive round and round the block trying to spot their child from amongst the crowd of Barbie and Power Rangers rucksacks and the clouds of dust.

Nikolai leant his hand on the horn and left it there until we were back on the openish road. Getting across East Jerusalem is a nightmare.

When Eden opened his eyes, he glanced around him and said: 'All the fucking religious lunatics in the fucking world congregate here. And people take them seriously.' Then he shut them again.

Nikolai and I shrugged. It's a stressful place to be.

'You filing today?' I asked, nudging Eden in the ribs.

'No. You?' he wondered, opening just the one eye.

'Done it,' I said. My boots hurt.

Zahir was on the desk when we got in. He gave Eden some messages and then rummaged around for mine, seeming to take an inordinately long time. Eden wandered off and, when he was sure he'd gone, Zahir handed me a red rose and my messages. One of those ones in cellophane that illegal immigrants are reduced to selling in restaurants in London and Rome.

'Who's this from?' I asked him, suspicious. I hoped the General hadn't been creeping around.

'For you, Miss Zanetti,' Zahir whispered, smiling at me. 'From me.'

Laughing, I leant across the counter and kissed him on the cheek.

'Thank you. It's lovely,' I said, and caught Eden up on his way down to the bar.

He had to duck to avoid hitting his head on the archway.

'Heeeeeeeeeey!' McCaughrean shouted enthusiastically.

We sat down with him and watched his eyes sparkling and gleaming. He grinned.

'Suicide-bomber funeral in Gaza, anyone?' he asked.

Eden and I groaned. Gaza is synonymous with hell. Honestly. They say, 'Go to Gaza!' if you do something like, I don't know, offer them tickets to an avant-garde poetry reading.

138

'What? It'll be great. There's some Fatah meeting down there and sheik whatsisface – you know, the Hamas one in the wheelchair – might drop in . . .' he trailed off, sensing that he had failed to completely infect us with his excitement. He finished his beer and burped. It had not been his first, needless to say.

'Eyeless in Gaza,' Eden murmured.

'Legless, more like,' Don guffawed.

'Will there be teenagers with guns firing into the air and shouting "Allah!"?' I wondered.

'I think we can safely bet on that,' Eden smiled, lighting his cigarette and sighing.

'OK, fuck you. I'll go by myself,' McCaughrean said, deflated, spongeing a fag off Eden.

'Jaded fuckers,' he added, quietly.

'Who's the rose from?' Eden smiled.

'Guy on reception.'

I drank a vodka and glanced at the messages Zahir had handed me upstairs. A note from Yo, 'Check Meier's orphanage links.' Why was he risking this assault on the General, for God's sake? Not that I would doubt Meier's connection to anything underhand, but for a reasonably low-level soldier to be implicating someone like Meier in this kind of stuff was brave to the point of real insanity.

Then, no surprises here, a note from Meier himself reminding me of our impending dinner. I flashed Yo's message up in front of Eden's face.

'Dodgy, though isn't it?' I said.

'Very,' Eden agreed. 'Just offering too fucking much information. Normally, you'd have to sleep with people to get this level of honesty. Faith?'

'Oh, sod off. Of course not. It's weird, though, don't you think?'

'I do,' he thought, bringing his cheek close to mine so that I could feel his breath. It was hard, irritatingly, not to lean into him.

''Sup?' McCaughrean wanted to know. He hates being left out. I flicked one of the other messages up. It was from Martin Glover.

It said, 'Suicide-bomber funeral in Gaza tonight. Five hundred words, please.'

I smiled.

'Ha!' McCaughrean beamed, delighted. 'You know we're a team, baby!'

Worried now, Eden fished his own messages out of his jeans and read them.

'Oh bollocks,' he said, laughing. 'Have you ordered a car?'

McCaughrean didn't show quite the same enthusiasm for Eden's company as he had for mine, and his face sort of wobbled a bit as he nodded his affirmation.

'Seven-thirty,' he said.

'OK, I'm going for a bath,' I said, getting up, waving my money at Salim to show that I was going to leave it for him on the table. He waved back.

'*Elf shukran*,' he said.

'Pleasure,' I shouted behind me, taking the stairs two at a time. I went to my courtyard room, not that there was much point in having two rooms any more, since someone was still leaving love tokens in my bathroom. I had some calls to make. First Svyeta, to tell her I was working on it (she sounded faint and resigned). She said she hadn't heard of either of Misha's contacts, they of the empty apartments, and nor had she heard of Father Bryan. 'Please. Just find him for me. Please,' she kept saying. I had no answer to that.

Then I called Bryan himself to arrange to go out and see him (I didn't want to talk about Meier over the phone) and to book Hassan as our stringer for the Gaza trip. 'We will be delighted to see you again, dear Faith,' he said.

As I hung up, Eden walked in without knocking.

'C'I use your computer?' he asked, sitting down at it and snapping the lid open.

'Why? What's wrong with your own bloody computer?' I asked.

'Don't know. 'S'fucked,' he said. 'How do you make a new document?'

I came out of the bathroom in my T-shirt and pants to show him, leaning over and getting him a blank sheet to work on without the vaguest hint of eroticism or awkwardness. It struck me as weird that there was sometimes such tension with us and sometimes he was more like a brother or something. Not that I had a brother, but you know.

It was nice to hear him tapping outside the door while I wriggled my toes in the hot water and went under to see how long I can hold my breath. Ages. When I came gasping up to the surface Eden was standing there above me with his Dictaphone in one hand and a pumice stone in the other. He hit play and smirked.

'No! No! Fuck off! No!' I squealed, hiding my face with my hands. On the tape the wail of a mosque muezzin could be heard, but above the music was the boom of anti-aircraft fire. With each boom Eden threw something into the bath at me. Boom! Pumice stone. Boom! Soap. Boom! Shampoo. Boom! Bottle of diazepam.

'Stop it!' I yelled and sat up, splashing water out of the bath at him as hard as I could. He ran out laughing, leaving a lake of water slopped all over the floor, my clothes and the towels.

'Stupid tosser,' I giggled and wandered out naked to find my cigarettes. Eden was sitting at the computer, typing frantically, as though he'd never left it. I wrapped a sheet around myself and lit a cigarette, my hair in heavy wet springs dripping on to the bed.

'What are you doing?' I asked.

'Checking my emails,' he said, putting his cigarette out and reaching for another.

'You smoke too much,' I said. He stopped typing and looked round to stare at me.

'OK, OK,' I admitted.

There was a knock at the door and I padded over to open it with the glow and the smile of someone who has just had lots of great sex. There was a short bald man in a black suit standing there. He was pale as death (i.e., just got off a plane from London) and as grim.

'Miss Zanetti. Commander Whitehorn. Scotland Yard,' he said, flashing a card. A wave of light and heat swept into the room and Eden stood up from the computer. Ah ha. Here he was.

'Sorry. If it's inconvenient—' Whitehorn offered, peering in to look at Eden.

'No. No. Of course not. If you wouldn't mind, I'll see you in the lobby in ten seconds,' I said. He strode away.

'You see,' said Eden. 'You look like a normal person, but really you're the Angel of Death.'

I pulled my wet jeans on and tried to dry my hair with a towel.

'Bugger off. He may want to present some prestigious award to me, for all you know,' I said, well aware that in fact Whitehorn had come to see me in my capacity as Angel of Death. He was one of those types who travels the world investigating atrocities, usually committed against Brits. He'd worked on the death of that ambassador in Athens. Not only worked on, but got a conviction, if I remembered rightly. Scotland Yard still has a reputation good enough that local police forces around the world are always clamouring for their help. Not that they don't do their own thing too. It can be worse for the families that way. One autopsy here, one back in Britain. Poor Shiv. They shave your hair off, you know. So that they can see if there are head injuries. The body people bury is not the body they first identify. I grabbed a handful of my own hair at the thought. Once, when she was pissed, my mum said she'd cut my hair in the night. I still feel that its continued existence is somehow precarious.

I sat down with Whitehorn on one of the stupidly grandiose lobby armchairs where I'd sat with Yo, and I ordered us both a beer. His face glimmered briefly with the inner conflict of whether to drink on the job or not, but he decided to go ahead and drink it, as I'd known he would.

'Miss Zanetti,' he began.

'Faith,' I said.

'Faith,' he began again. 'We have reason to believe that Siobhan Boucherat was murdered on 26 August in her room at this hotel.'

'Oh Jesus,' I said quietly as two glistening glasses of beer were expertly lowered on to our table.

'It would be immensely helpful to our inquiries if you could provide us with any information that might be relevant. That is, even if it does not seem relevant to you. Stories she may have been working on? New acquaintances she may have made?'

I barely heard him. Estuary English. A whine that usually comes out of the mouths of London disc jockeys. People who call university 'Uni', not that they've been, and put question marks of intonation at the end of their sentences. They say things like, 'How cool/bad/good/late/ early/cute/weird is that?' In policemen, though, and in Commander Whitehorn, it had been flattened into an endless, though minor, complaint.

'They hanged her?' I asked, meeting his eyes with horror.

He looked away, ashamed. I thought it must be awful having to provide people with the ghastly details of death as though somehow, through the translation, it becomes your fault.

'It would seem that she may have been manually asphyxiated and was then suspended from the door hinge by the belt which was subsequently removed from the body by police pathologists,' he told his beer. 'The belt belonged to the victim.'

'She was strangled?' I breathed. Whitehorn nodded.

'So, was she dead when they put her up there?' I put my hand to my mouth and shut my eyes for a moment.

'It would seem not. Unfortunately,' Whitehorn told me. 'The body is still being examined.'

'Oh God,' I said.

Eden came and sat down with us. He put a hand on my shoulder.

'Shiv was murdered,' I said and he stroked my hair. He was right. It is a horrible world, and there is nothing we can do but mourn. Right all along.

So I sat in the lobby and I told Commander Whitehorn about Misha and the trafficking stuff.

'Shiv was having a thing with him,' I began, leaning my elbows on my knees. 'She had a lot of things . . .'

I told him that Misha had been investigating the story on Svyeta's behalf and I gave him Svyeta's phone number at her friend's house.

'I just feel . . . no. I know that if we could find Sasha we'll have cracked it. What happened to Shiv must fall into place,' I pleaded. And I do hate to plead.

I was ashamed at my lack of progress. Would I have put more into it if it were my own child? Of course I bloody would. I wouldn't keep filing the daily stuff, taking orders from Martin Glover. But then, I persuaded myself, if I had dropped my job, I wouldn't have been able to stay. Scant consolation to anyone. I told Whitehorn I was sure Shiv and Misha's deaths were linked. I told him about the list and the ransacked flats. I told him about my break-in and that I'd moved rooms. He took a few notes and looked sympathetic. There was something beaten about him. He travelled, he investigated the deaths of dead Britons. Every day he faced grief and gore and every day he found out a tiny bit more about the various kinds, or perhaps the one kind, of sickness that makes people do these things to each other. Perhaps he was a bit like us, really.

CHAPTER NINE

The Gaza trip was undertaken with an air of sheerly professional duty. Except by McCaughrean, whose zeal was irrepressible. He was impatient, waiting for us. He leant out of the window to shout us on as Eden, Grant and I came together out of the hotel.

'Women, eh?' he jeered. The suggestion was presumably that my toilette had been responsible for the delay. Hassan was waiting nervously outside the hotel entrance. Father Bryan had been happy to get him out doing something constructive and he'd been willing. He knew Gaza well, he said. I thought he might do. He bowed his head when he saw me.

'Forgive me,' he said, stepping backwards as though I might punch him or something.

'Of course,' I said. 'I wouldn't have phoned if I didn't.'

I introduced him to the boys and they shook his hand like an adult, an equal. You could see he was flattered.

I opened the door and we climbed in, Hassan gangly and teenaged, shy.

I leant forward to whisper the bad, though not completely unexpected, news to Don: 'Shiv was murdered,' I told him.

McCaughrean started to wheeze. He dragged his camera bag on to his lap and rummaged around for his blue inhaler. Putting it between wet lips he sucked hard at it, sweat beading on his forehead. The driver flashed him a quick glance as we skidded off the decent road and on to the potholed stretch to Gaza. Were these people gravely ill as well as wanting to go to the last place on earth?

There was a spectacular sunset over the Mount of Olives, that we didn't comment on. The beauty of Jerusalem always seems in slightly bad taste, considering. Like babies at funerals.

Eden looked up to take it in and seemed to wince in pain.

'Think he'll come today?' he wondered.

'Who?' I asked, blowing my smoke out, slumped and exhausted.

'The Messiah,' Eden said, not so much as a twitch of irony.

'Shouldn't have thought so, why?' Grant said.

'Well, when then? Look at them all, waiting up there,' he smiled, inclining his head towards the thousands of tombs on the slopes of the hill, positioned so that when He does come they'll be the first to know. Or something.

Other times it could have been funny. Now though it was just sad. I flicked my cigarette butt out of the window into the heat and the driver turned his radio up. Some kind of Egyptian pop. Hassan mouthed the words to himself, unconsciously. I hate it here, but in London, when I occasionally hear it on the Edgware Road or somewhere, it gives me a thrill of butterflies in my stomach by association. Association with chaos and heat and fear.

Recovered now, McCaughrean lit a cigarette and drew a big mouthful of smoke in, coughing.

'Shit,' he breathed.

'Sorry, Don,' I said. 'I know she was a good friend.' Actually, I knew she hadn't been particularly.

146

McCaughrean was emotional, sure, but there had been a moment just then when I actually thought he might die of shock.

'Hardly knew her, really,' he choked, tears streaming down his face.

Eden looked at me in despair, unfairly holding me responsible for McCaughrean's presence and personality. I shrugged. The rest of us held ourselves together in our grief, but there seemed no reason why McCaughrean should if he didn't want to.

When we passed the final checkpoint, the driver pulled over and refused to go any nearer. He warned Hassan off in darkly whispering Arabic. Already people were firing into the air and the tension was thick. It wasn't quite dark and the streets were seething with men. Everyone seemed to be shouting and going in different directions – a teenager in a green Hamas headband waving a gun, an old man with a rippling banner, a blank-faced, black-robed woman carrying a portrait of one of the dead, his ammunition strapped to his body. It was a cheap-looking copy, printed out on glossy paper, the colours lurid and blurred into each other.

The first road we came to, picking our way through the crowds and across piles of bricks and stones, had a few buildings on it that were just heaps of rubble and tangles of wire. The green and red neon of some shop signs still flickered into the darkening night and the scream of Quranic chanting blared out of every radio and television in the area.

The rage of revolution was in the air. Intifada. As we walked towards the main road where the funeral procession was supposed to be happening, a group of young men, high on anger and impotence, ran up to us screaming, 'Fucking Americans! Fucking Americans!' Their eyes were wild with loathing and they shook their fists as though they were about to pummel us to death. Hassan shouted back at them in a vain attempt at mollification.

Two old men were sitting in a doorway just near us, playing chess and drinking mint tea, the hems of their robes stained yellow by the sand. One of them looked up and spat something at the young men who immediately backed away, jostling and muttering.

'You must excuse our youth. They have all turned into extremists while we weren't looking,' the man playing black said to us in perfect English. 'Tea?'

We thanked him, but didn't stop. McCaughrean had already waddled on ahead, his camera bouncing on his chest. He had flicked into work mode and was invincible.

'Don McCaughrean – laughs in the face of fear,' Eden said.

'The Duck,' I smiled.

We both blinked hard with each volley of shots we heard, trying not to look up. Hassan's face froze. He was scared, I thought. Only young. Stray bullets from these parades kill a couple of hundred people a year. Nobody seems to appreciate that they come back down again. A band of about a hundred men in black stocking balaclavas came pounding past us shouting 'Allah' hu Akbar!' over and over again, their Kalashnikovs clattering against their chests, reams of bullets wrapped around them. They wore white headbands splashed with black allegiances and they punched the air with a grunt every few bounds. They swept McCaughrean up with them while Eden, Hassan and I pressed our backs against the wall. Then we followed them at a run.

'Keep up, Zanetti,' Eden shouted, excited.

'Yeah, yeah,' I grinned. Shiv, Misha, little Sasha – put aside until we were safe again. And that's the attraction on the job, isn't it? Always a new excuse to put other things aside. A new crisis every day, wiping out the old ones, at least for a while.

We turned a corner and were engulfed in the procession. The coffin bearing God-knows-what bit, if any, of the man we saw blowing up the army base at Gesher Haziv was held high above the heads of his male relatives and his Al Aqusa colleagues, if colleagues is the word, some of them too in balaclavas. The coffin was tipped and tossed in the crowds, swathed with green cloth, and bearing a photo of the man inside (not that he can possibly have been in there since he must have been wiped off the walls of the cafeteria by forensics).

I shoved my way forwards to where the mother was walking, grim-faced but dry-eyed. Martyrs are not to be mourned. Even martyrs whose fat little hands you used to hold and whose pudgy tummies you once tickled. I thought about the woman I'd interviewed years ago, hoping her little boy would be a doctor and not a martyr like Daddy. She looked as though she might faint with contained sorrow.

'We are proud of him!' his sister told me as we were pushed into each other, washed forwards with the crowd. 'I want to die for Palestine!' she smiled, pleased to be showing off her English, to be accompanying her brother's coffin, to have decided to martyr herself to her cause. She looked about thirteen.

It was dark and I felt bruised when I wrestled my way out of the mass and got to the place where the Fatah meeting was being held. It must have been a cinema once, I thought. When it still had a roof and a screen.

Hustling on to the floor in front of four or five old men on a rostrum, I thought how much Shiv would like to have been here. She would have filed one of those pieces Barbara-Ann quite often made her write, very Sunday-ish, that always begin with 'It'. And then they wouldn't have run it. Or they'd have run the first and last paragraphs on page 714 and Shiv would have railed about it all night in the bar. You know the kind of thing. The Sunday papers are full of them – starting with a dropped intro: 'It was the party of the decade. Everyone wanted a ticket.' New par.

'In downtown Los Angeles last night fourteen of the . . .' Blah blah blah.

Basically, to achieve this effect, you put all the who-what-why-where-when, that would normally come first, in the second paragraph, and a silly incomprehensible piece of rubbish in the first one.

'It could not have come at a worse time for the peace process.' Drop. 'Last night in Gaza the body of suicide-bomber Yasin Al-Kassab was laid to rest, and the old guard of the Fatah movement told demonstrators to fight on to the death for a free Palestine.' Hey. You've read it a million times and, let's face it, you didn't get past that paragraph the first time.

Pieces like that are always full of words that nobody ever uses in life – 'downtown' (in the centre of town), 'penned' (written), 'jetted off' (set off in a plane), 'tucked into' (ate), 'the bard' (Shakespeare), 'the pontiff' (the Pope). It's the same pieces that end: 'Only time will tell' or '. . . remains to be seen'. One of the American news networks banned their correspondents from saying 'only time will tell' at the end of their pieces to camera because everybody was signing off with it. Unable to think of a proper alternative, they all switched to 'remains to be seen'. Brilliant.

I went into alert when someone trod on my toe. The men smelt of sweat and fear, the night was dense with heat and the stars hung low.

'Our mothers can't have loved us much,' Eden said, appearing in front of me accompanied by Hassan, who now looked almost panicked. Unlike us, he didn't have any emotional distance from this. This was his crisis. He whispered translations of the various chants into Eden's ear, eyes flitting about wildly.

'What?' I asked, hassled, irritated. I mean, I knew he was detached from the present, but this was insane. We were in a dangerous, or at least volatile, situation and he was going on about his mother.

I nearly fell as a new wave of men crushed in and we were pressed closer to the stage. The shouting was loud and frightening in its zealous lunacy.

'That we need to be here doing this. We should be at home in Putney with our families, reading each other amusing bits of the Sunday papers,' he shouted. We had been separated now.

'What amusing bits?' I yelled back.

'Fair point,' I heard him say as he disappeared from view. My face was squashed into the sweating back of a teenager screaming for Israeli blood.

Fucking typical of Eden to start going on about Freud when we were about to be trampled to death.

I stamped the heel of my boot into the floor and tried to stay still, not to be pushed forward any further. I caught sight of Grant Bradford's shock of hair over to the right and tried to wave to him, but he disappeared in the swell. One of the old men, some side-kick of Arafat from the early eighties, got up and started speaking. He wore the tea-towel headdress and a cheap grey suit with a checked shirt under it. He had thin plastic sandals on his feet, like the kind of thing people wear on the edge of swimming pools. He didn't have the statesmanly gravitas he needed. Stained stumps of teeth, chain smoker's skin and exhausted eyes. I didn't understand what he was saying, but I understood what the audience thought of it. Not much.

A couple of blokes started firing upwards and people ran out in panic, unsure that an actual gun battle hadn't started between crazed factions. The speakers bothered to try and calm everyone down for about twenty seconds and then ran, or hobbled away themselves, leaving the rest of us to it. To my horror, the guy in front of me started chanting something about America. Something not good. Seeming to feel my fear, he span round to face me. No point telling these people that we're not American. They don't distinguish. We have to take responsibility for the economic colonization of the world and the unpleasantness that has accompanied it. After all, we know the risks when we vote to emulate them.

I was looking for a gap in the crowd to run into when the madman grabbed a handful of my hair and pulled my head into his chest. He fired to draw attention to himself and his hostage. A space cleared around us and I could breathe at last. I looked wildly for Eden and Hassan but I couldn't see them. Where the fuck had McCaughrean gone? Grant? My new friend put his gun to my neck and dug it in.

A Makarov 8mm, I thought. Standard police issue in Moscow, though I couldn't be sure. This guy was shouting his victory and a lot of others were cheering, egging him on. To kill me? I don't know. Some were rushing forward to drag us apart, begging him, perhaps, not to make more trouble than there already was. Oddly, as I inhaled the stale and spicy breath of this boy whose sweat was soaking my shirt, I began to agree with Eden. What the hell were we doing here?

He was pulling my hair hard now and had forced me to bend at the knee so that I was uncomfortable and getting scared. Then, to my complete astonishment, I saw Yo. I was sure it was Yo.

'Yo!' I shouted. He was wearing a green Hamas bandana and his chest was bare. This Israeli special forces soldier was shouting in Arabic with the rest of them. Even in this situation, my mind was racing with the story. If I could get Don to take a picture of him they would run the piece. I could write it tonight. If I was still alive.

'Yo!' I shouted again. He met my eye for a flicker of a second and then shoved his way out of sight. Why was nobody helping me? Come on, somebody. Do something.

So somebody did. Leaping out from behind the stage, Hassan came flying through the air to crash down on us, screaming something about Allah and holding a Kalashnikov up in one hand. He landed hard, smashing us to the floor, and someone fired, perhaps by accident. Was he saving me in apology for attacking me out at Father Bryan's? His nerves had made him invincible. He sat on the other guy and poked his gun in his eye. He seemed to know him.

I thought I perhaps wouldn't hang around. I scrambled up and ran as fast as I could out into the pounding street. I wondered if I was at last going mad. It's not uncommon. Look at Edmonds. I lit a cigarette and leaned against a wall, ruffling my hair and rubbing the patches that had been wrenched. I felt as though I'd been beaten up in that crowd. Bruised and kicked and humiliated. I inhaled hard and let my breathing calm. Maybe my desperation to see someone I knew had produced Yo for me. Could it be a symptom of fear?

The more general madness though seemed to have abated and there was a bloke with no teeth selling tea from a huge copper samovar. Over the road, someone had lit a fire for his kebab stall and ordinary Egyptian pop was playing from a radio in one of the bombed-out buildings. The enraged youths who had been baying for blood fifteen minutes ago seemed to have come down a gear or two into jostling, laughing bands of teenagers with nothing to do on a Thursday night. I'm sure I spotted one of the Fatah grandfathers buying himself a cone of sunflower seeds.

I let myself smile and was pleased to see Hassan coming towards me now from out of the hall where he had presumably fought his friend off. He saw me and held up his hand in recognition, making his way over to me. I threw my cigarette down and trod it into the dust before I realized that Hassan was staggering, lurching, falling towards me. And I had taken a step to catch him before I saw that he had been shot in the stomach or chest. He fell heavily into my arms, choking on the blood that bubbled up from his lungs. People started shouting and crowding.

I held Hassan to me and shut my eyes. Hugging him as tightly as I could, we collapsed to the ground together and I knelt there supporting him, desperately trying to absorb some of the agony.

'Oh, Hassan,' I whispered, kissing his head.

I stroked his hair and felt the shudders of death rack his body. He seemed so tiny and childlike now, not the warrior who had just come to my rescue.

'Fuck,' he gurgled through the blood.

'Ssshhh. It's going to be all right. You're going to be all right,' I said, tears forcing their way out through my closed eyelids. Tears that acknowledged the miserable flimsiness of my lie.

'Fuck the Russians. Fuck Meier,' he spat before going into Arabic mumblings.

'Yes,' I said. 'Fuck them.' The death rattle sounded in his chest and I relaxed my hold, crouching over him.

'Hassan, I'm so sorry,' I cried as we huddled together, the living and the dead in a heap in the dark on the Gaza roadside.

It could have been ten minutes or an hour later that Eden was helping me up, wiping a smear of blood off my face with his thumb. Some people in vaguely medical costumes were hauling Hassan away. McCaughrean coughed awkwardly and shuffled his feet. When I looked up at him, he raised his camera to his eye and shot a few frames.

'Are you mad?' I asked him.

'Sorry,' he apologized, as though he'd accidentally spilled his drink in my lap.

Someone pinched my arse when I was on the way to the loo in a restaurant in London once and when I turned round to look at him, baffled, he said, 'Oh, sorry, love.' I could just imagine Don doing that.

I noticed to my shame that I was still snivelling.

'Did you know him well or something?' Eden asked, leading us all towards a car and driver he'd found.

'Yeah. He tried to kill me at that orphanage on the West Bank,' I explained, fishing for my cigarettes.

'I see,' said Eden, who didn't, but gave me a light. He looked shattered in the brief flicker of flame that lit up his stubble, the shadows under his eyes and the crinkles of his forehead.

We were quiet all the way back. Even the driver didn't switch his radio on. It was only when we were rolling through the lights and noise of Jerusalem again that the air of violent unreality seemed to slip away.

'God, I hate this job,' I said.

McCaughrean snorted. Or maybe he was just clearing his throat.

'You love it,' Eden told me.

I blew my smoke out with a sigh of admission.

'You know, I saw Yo there. Shouting in Arabic. Wearing a Hamas bandana.'

Eden swivelled round to stare at me, stunned.

'No?!'

'Yes,' I nodded. 'I thought I'd imagined it at first, but I didn't. It was him.'

Eden lit a cigarette frantically and started rapping his fingers on his knee.

'So it is him, then? The traitor we're all after? Yo's been blowing his comrades to smithereens?'

'I didn't know we were all after him,' I snorted, almost annoyed that this was a general story and not my own private investigation. 'But I suppose with him trying to stitch Meier up and stuff . . . Well, it makes sense. And the ringside seats to everything . . .'

Eden's whole face was ablaze with excitement.

'But if it's true about Meier and him having all that contact with the orphanage—' he muttered to himself.

'I think Father Bryan must know something. Even if he doesn't know he does. It's worth another go,' I said. 'Tomorrow.'

The bar seemed empty without Shiv. We got revoltingly drunk. Eden started telling plane crash stories and McCaughrean got photos of his children out of his wallet. Salim brought me a new vodka seconds after my old one was finished and I was chasing with one of those Mexican beers in a bottle. Grant kept starting a story about eating a worm out of the bottom of a bottle of mescal, but nobody was interested.

I hadn't had a bath and was all scratched and bloody and dusty. I pulled my hair back into a ponytail to make myself feel more alert. It didn't work.

Eden was talking about a plane he'd failed to get back on in Rwanda because he'd gone for a pee behind a tree on this airstrip in the middle of nowhere. The thing had a petrol gauge that didn't work and a cracked windscreen, but the propellers had seemed reasonably serviceable. Anyway, by the time he'd run out to chase it, raging, down the runway, the tail fin was already on fire and it lurched up off the ground and ploughed into a mountain with Eden's suitcase and translator on it.

'Fuck,' said McCaughrean tearfully.

When I started considering sex with Eden, I knew it was time for bed.

'Night,' I said, stumbling off my stool. I mimed typing with a flicker of my fingers before disappearing. It was true. I did have to knock something off about Gaza, not that much had happened in any news kind of sense. I got Hassan in anyway – another tragic casualty of the Middle East's ongoing blah blah blah. They probably wouldn't use The Duck's depressing pictures though.

I went to my day room and had a shower, vaguely hoping to osmose some of the moisture into myself and avoid a hangover. The water that ran between my toes was brown with Hassan's blood. I wrapped myself in a towel and smoked a cigarette on the edge of the bed. I obeyed the phone's flashing message light and listened to a frail Svyeta asking me if I had any news for her. That someone in my state was being relied upon for anything made me want to weep. I needed to ask Whitehorn what he'd got. It was pathetic, really, to have passed the buck to him when I'd got nowhere. Just some empty flats and some corpses. I took a couple of diazepam with a glass of water – the alcohol hadn't wiped out the day's nightmare.

The phone ringing woke me up.

'Shit,' I muttered to myself. It was stupid to have fallen asleep in this room. I meant to get dressed again and go upstairs.

I rolled across the bed to answer it. It crackled and I didn't say anything.

'Faith, lovey?' she said.

I hadn't heard her voice for more than ten years. Before any other feeling could leap out, I got angry.

'What?' I asked.

'Faith, sweetie . . .' She went on, audibly bursting into tears.

'Mum. Go away,' I said and put the phone down.

It rang again immediately and I stared at it for a couple of seconds before I picked it up.

I didn't have a chance to speak before Evie exploded into my ear.

'Honey, I am so sorry. I am so so sorry, honey. Listen, she called me and said it was real important and did I have the number and I said I didn't know where you were and she was so desperate, hon. As soon as I gave it to her, I knew I shouldn't have. Honey? Faith?' I reached my cigarette packet from the floor, put one in my mouth and lit a match, my lips trembling. Fucking pathetic.

''S OK,' I said, blowing the match out.

'You OK?' Evie asked, guilt pouring out of her mouth.

'Sure,' I said, coughing to cover anything else that might have wanted to express itself. I sat up.

'Actually,' I said, pulling myself together and shaking my hair which was still wet, 'things are a bit rough here. Something weird going on and we can't work it out.'

'We?' she asked, immediately hitting on the one word in the sentence that was significant to her.

'Me and Eden,' I said, crawling under the covers.

'Ah ha! It's about time you settled down, darling,' she said, satisfied.

'Hello?' I asked, laughing now.

'Well, didn't you guys once have a thing?' she demanded.

'Not really,' I said. 'Listen, it's late.' I looked at my watch. Three-thirty.

'OK, pumpkin. Forgive me?' she asked. I groaned.

'How come she's got your number?' I wanted to know. Sort of.

'We talk,' Evie said quietly.

'You do what?' I nearly choked on my smoke. I had been lying happily on my back, but now I sat up, spilling ash on to the sheet.

'Listen, baby. What can I do? I'm a mom too. I know how it feels,' she said. 'She just wants to hear how you're doing, hon.'

'You haven't got a fucking clue how it feels to her. Plus which, you see Mo and Tita practically every day, which is hardly the same thing as trying ... Anyway. Sorry. It's fine. I didn't speak to her anyway,' I said.

'Oh pumpkin—' Evie implored.

'Oh, Evie,' I said straight. ''Night.'

''Night, baby,' she kissed.

I put my cigarette out and dragged a clean pair of jeans on. I zipped my jacket up without T-shirt or anything and crept barefoot out of my door, across the courtyard and along the corridor to Eden's room. I knocked and turned the handle.

'Hi,' I whispered. 'It's me. My mum phoned.'

I padded across the rug towards the bed in the pitch night, crickets screaming outside.

'I thought your mum was dead,' he said, half-asleep.

'Not yet,' I told him.

He sat up, tanned and lived in. He ruffled his head.

'Faith,' he said, in a pre-emptive apology. I flicked out of clambering-into-the-warmth-of-his-bed-and-losing-myself-in-him mode and switched on to disaster impending.

She threw a sheet off and poked her head out, long brown hair, messed up from sex, falling into her face. About twenty.

'Motek?' she asked woozily, throwing a sleeping arm round her lover. I was out of the door before any new expressions could fly on to our faces.

'Faith!' I heard Eden shout after me, but he didn't come out of the door. He'd never have caught me anyhow.

I dreamt I was half-animal and crawled around the floor biting chunks out of people's calves.

CHAPTER TEN

I woke up with that hyper-efficient hangover thing. I feel so rough and so incapable of action of any kind that I end up doing far more than I'd ever have done if I'd felt normal. Proving to myself that I'm not as much of a wreck as I feel.

I phoned Commander Whitehorn on his mobile and got him in the middle of a meeting with the Jerusalem chief of police.

'I'll call you back—' He started to say.

'No you won't. Talk to me. Did you find the Russians?'

He coughed and lowered his voice.

'Not exactly,' he admitted.

'Yes or no? Listen, Whitehorn, you need our cooperation if you're going to get anywhere with Shiv. Help me here.' Well, it seemed worth a try.

'Miss Zanetti, I will not be harangued . . .' I heard him excuse himself and slip into a corridor. 'The Russians whose flats you visited were Israeli policemen working undercover on the child-trafficking

159

ring. You are right about that. It looks as though their cover was broken by our friend Misha. Now I really must . . .' He was desperate to get rid of me.

'What about Sasha? Svyeta?' I hounded him.

'Mrs Karamazova will be kept up to date on the whereabouts of her son should any information be forthcoming. I believe we have an appointment for seven a.m tomorrow,' he said, and hung up.

We did? Apparently we did.

In my efficiency glare I moved straight on without pause. When I tried to get in touch with Father Bryan, I ended up with Adam on his mobile.

'I'm so sorry about Hassan,' I said. 'I feel it was my fault. I never meant him to—'

But Adam interrupted me.

'Faith. Listen. There are some Russian children at the orphanage. I don't know where they came from. Meier brought them,' he said, urgently, in that way people have when they don't want anyone near them to hear.

'Thanks. I'll be right there,' I said and hung up. Sasha! I wanted Eden to come with me, but I wasn't about to go and wake him up. I lurked about pretending to have breakfast and put Svyeta on automatic redial on my mobile.

It's not as though we have any claim over each other. By the time I'd drunk my second espresso, I was already wondering why I had been stupid enough to go running to him in the middle of the night anyway.

'Listen, I'm so sorry to have disturbed you last night,' I smiled up at him when he came out into the morning sunlight, shirtsleeves rolled up, clothes creased as though he'd slept in them. I knew, of course, that he hadn't.

'Faith—' he started, patting his shirt pocket for his cigarettes.

I held up my hand to stop him.

✻   ✻   ✻

When I finally got Svyeta, she could barely speak with the effort to restrain herself, to keep her hope well in check.

'Svyeta,' I said. 'I don't want to promise anything, but a group of Russian children has turned up at the orphanage in Bethlehem. I'd like you to come with me, if you can face it.'

After all, he might not be there.

'Oh. Vera! Vera! Thank you!' she cried. She got in the first taxi she could find and appeared before I'd lit my third cigarette.

She staggered into the courtyard, escorted by Zahir, as though she had at last been let out of a darkened cellar into the light of day. She seemed to have lost about three stone. Her clothes hung off her bones like an anorexic's. Her eyes were sunk in her head and her skin was grey. She was keeping it together, though. She had put on some very pale pink lipstick and had put some sticky stuff in her hair. If she lived in the West, she would be the kind of woman who watched adverts about lipsticks that don't rub off. Eden once told me that there are women who don't drink fizzy water because they think it gives them cellulite. Who are these people? Why don't they have anything else to worry about? Jesus. If I looked after myself so well that the type of water I drank was a worry . . .

She didn't know whether to kiss my cheek or shake my hand and, as she lurched towards me at the iron table, her movement turned into a faint, her legs buckling at the knee, her eyes rolling back in her head. Eden just about managed to catch her and we walked her inside and sat her in the armchair under the enormous brass ceiling fan. Zahir brought her a globe of brandy on a silver tray and a slice of pistachio halva.

'*Prostitye*,' she whispered to me in apology, coming round quickly. We sat there while she ate and drank.

Eden leant his elbows on his knees and smoked. His face had frozen solid in grief for this woman who couldn't find her little boy. It made me want to hold his hand for all the good that would do. When his brother was killed, he'd told me, his mum had refused to let the body be buried.

'He is scared of the dark,' she screamed, when the undertakers came. He was twenty. She held on to his body for three days, refusing to leave her bedroom. In the end, a doctor sedated her with an injection and they buried her son without her. Afterwards she didn't speak at all for two years. She would open and close her mouth like a fish, Eden said, but nothing came out. Svyeta had dark sweat marks in the underarms of her blouse.

Eden helped her out of her seat and into the front seat of the hotel's Volvo. I'd requisitioned it for the day. We didn't talk. There was nothing to say until we'd seen the children.

I looked down at the sleeve of my jacket, my dad's jacket that he had leant out of hundreds of car windows in the heat, just like I was leaning it out now. I flicked my cigarette into the road and watched it in the rear-view mirror bounce and spark under the wheels of the car behind. I glanced back at Eden. He shut his eyes.

I noticed people were picking the olives already. Spindly arms reaching up to spindly branches. Summer nearly over.

I smoked and fidgeted my feet around in my boots. I fiddled with the radio and found a station that played us Bollywood hits all the way through the checkpoints and grey olive groves, rubbly hills and biblical sites. Must be a lot of Indian Jews here, (from Calcutta?), I thought. I wondered why so many religions had begun here. Perhaps there was just madness in the air. There are whole psychiatric wards here spilling over with people who come to Jerusalem and start to believe that they are the Messiah. Men, women, people from all over the place. They call it Jerusalem Fever. Maybe they've always had this kind of trouble here. Millennium after millennium of lunatics claiming to be the son of God. Or maybe they all actually are the son of God. Hey, who am I to judge other people's sanity?

Bryan came out to meet us, but the place was deserted. There was nobody about at all. Nobody tending the vegetables, no children playing, no cooking smells. It was eerily quiet, except for the occasional tok of an Apache overhead. The retribution for all the bombs had begun. Of course. You scratch my back, I'll scratch yours. Or is it an eye for an eye? Whatever. The thing that nagged at me was that if Yo really did have something to do with all the things that had been happening, how did he get through the psychiatric checks for his elite unit? It didn't hold together. And yet he'd been there in Gaza.

'Thanks for coming,' Bryan said, stony-faced. He said he had hoped our working with Hassan might have been a new start for the boy. Apparently, since punching Meier in the face, he had started saying he was going to do something for Palestine. 'Do something for Palestine' inevitably means die. Why it can't mean start fundraising for a new hospital or get the roads into some sort of manageable state, I don't know. How dying is going to help, remains unclear to me.

I once met a bloke in Chechnya painting white lines down the side of the road outside his house. His house was surrounded by rubble. The road had been completely destroyed by mines, the city (Grozny) no longer existed. It had been obliterated by war. 'I need some sense of order,' he said. I could get to grips with that. More useful than dying, by a long shot.

'I'm so sorry,' I said. I hugged the priest, feeling the hot weave of his black jacket, smelling the stale sweat of his old body, the brush of his bristles against my cheek.

'Peace be with you,' he said and led the way, Eden helping Svyeta to walk, as though he were dragging a skeleton across the sand. I explained to him as succinctly as I could.

'Svyeta is looking for her son,' I told him. His nod was so grave and so full of understanding and hope that I began to truly believe that little Sasha might be only a few feet away from his mother. Traipsing through the shimmering heat mirage that seemed to sweep up off the ground, we stood, all four of us, outside Father Bryan's hut. He gestured us in.

Bryan sat down on the edge of a wooden stool. In front of him, the Russian children sat meekly cross-legged on the floor. There were six of them, shabby and fidgeting, like puppies at Battersea Dogs' home waiting to be chosen, trying not to seem too eager, trying not to hope too much. Svyeta was breathless, squinting to adjust her eyes and look closely at each pathetic child. Eventually she gasped and pushed a sob back into her mouth with her hand. With the slump of her shoulders and the blankness of the children's faces, we saw that none of them was her boy.

But they could have been. They were all Russian, they were all her Sasha's age. They all looked at her with an orphan's mixture of hope and despair. They know it isn't their mother really, but they can't quite kill the desperate millisecond's thought that it might be. Bryan was clearly exhausted, a few day's stubble on his face, the horror of what was becoming increasingly obvious as the truth lurking behind the mask of his expressions.

I would have liked a drink. I put my shades on top of my head and squinted around in the darkness for a proper look. They weren't like normal children. That sallow Slavic look – high-cheekbones, wide eyes and skin so incredibly pale it might be made of snow. They were so quiet and still. There were things very seriously wrong with them. Now I thought about it, I realized that they had the dead eyes of the street-children Svyeta had mentioned. That was who they were.

I crouched down near Svyeta next to a little boy with dirt-coloured hair. We both watched a big brown beetle walk slowly across the floor. 'Where did you live before?' I asked him. He glowered at me without the slightest trace of trust. I was just one of the scumbags in the world who wanted something from him.

'With a guy,' he said, staring at his toes. Filthy toes. Bare feet. He twitched them.

'What happened to the guy?' I asked.

'How the fuck do I know. They took him,' he told the floor. Svyeta winced audibly as he swore. He was about five.

Svyeta knew we were close now. You could see her arms dying to clasp her son to her, wherever he was.

'But before that. In Russia?' I asked.

'Nowhere,' he said. 'In the cellars.'

So it was true. Svyeta's husband had been bringing street-children over. The old buildings in Moscow all have huge, mostly disused, cellars. All kinds of tramps, street-people, rats and dogs live in them. Soon, I suppose, they will all be converted into windowless basement flats and sold for a fortune.

Eden knelt down and held hands with a blonde girl in plaits who immediately started to cry. Bryan too was crying silently, huge tears pouring down his raddled face. He had realized what he was a part of and his heart was not going to be able to cope. He put two pills into his mouth and swallowed, wiping his face with the back of his sleeve. He seemed to be muttering a prayer. Adam helped him back on to his stool.

Svyeta hugged as many of the children as she could. She kissed them and cried. I tried to speak coherently and not to lie down on the floor and scream and rage at life. If God exists, I thought, He's a bastard. There's a poem by Mayakovsky on this theme. Mayakovsky who, unsurprisingly, killed himself.

I listened to Svyeta ask them over and over again if they had seen Sasha. She showed them his picture but they didn't seem to dare say anything about anything much. They couldn't even say where they had been held because they didn't know. They wouldn't say what had been happening to them. By the look of them, they didn't much care any more.

But then one boy with short-cropped sandy hair and a black eye grunted loudly. 'I knew him.'

We held our breaths.

The boy nodded and bit hard at one of his nails, dragging a piece of it off into his mouth.

'Sasha. He was with me at the last place. Went with the Arab boy.' Well, it was better than nothing. He was alive, he'd been paired up with another kid and taken on by a 'big guy' according to our tiny source.

Bryan deserved an explanation. In the dark, there, over a cup of tea, I told him about stuff. About Shiv and Misha and the Russians' empty flats. I told him what Hassan had said and what Adam had told me about him. His face tightened as I spoke into the heat. His clothes hung more loosely on his body and his watch began to look too big for his wrist. 'Yes. Adam is more perceptive than I am. It is him you must talk to now.'

His lips pursed and his face drained of its last remaining trickle of colour. 'Poor Hassan,' he said. I wonder whether dying trying to say something is worse than dying with nothing to say, babbling madly in a hospital ward. I had a friend whose mum died of cancer after saying, 'There is someone in the garden.' There wasn't, and somehow it was that absence of anyone in the garden that made the words so meaningless and so sad.

I peered into Father Bryan's face, but he turned away from me and pushed open the door.

As I walked out towards the car, shading my eyes from the sun with my arm, I saw Bushra, the little girl who had fallen over at my feet when I first came here, sitting on a wooden bench under the sparse shade of an apricot tree. Its branches were bending with the weight of its fruit. A whole tree full of apricots. She looked up at me and I waved, trying to look cheerful, a normal adult on a normal day.

I would take the priest's advice and talk to Adam. He hadn't clarified his thoughts in his own mind, but, if anyone, he knew what was going on. Eden stayed behind with Svyeta, trying to talk to the children. Meier himself, Bryan confirmed, had brought them in.

I like seeing Eden with children, even in circumstances like this. His height and his presence always make him seem like an adult amongst children even when he is actually amongst adults.

I was in a shop in Paris once and they were having a sale of children's stuff. There were elegant black-bobbed mothers, slim again already, the baby in a sling round their chests. Fathers in new loafers and beige slacks pushing pushchairs, brothers and sisters in white socks and patent leather shoes, neat hair clips, kicking the crap out of each other. Anyway, in the middle of the room there was this enormous table. It had bowls and spoons on it and was built to look like a giant's table in a fairy tale, towering above the heads of the adults. Or, I thought, like an ordinary table must look to a child. I reached up my hand and stood on my tiptoes to touch the enormous cutlery and I found that there were tears in my eyes. No man could be big enough or brave enough or kind or funny enough to replace my father. There isn't anyone that big, because to a child her father is simply all-encompassing.

Nobody except, maybe, Eden Jones.

The Volvo rattled and shook its way towards Adam who, I assumed, would be getting ready to croon at the King David. I was pushing the accelerator so hard it might have gone through the floor. I lit one cigarette off another as I rammed the car into the road, my sweating palms clamped to the steering wheel, my heart pounding. I tried to file the information in my brain. The children and the General. Misha and Shiv. Yo. It was one story that made a kind of sense, but that turned my mind to porridge when I tried to piece it together logically.

It's like people explaining to you that the universe is curved. You listen to them and it sounds reasonable enough. Then, seconds later, you try to describe it back to yourself and it doesn't make sense. Your brain isn't having it. Or trying to think rationally about God. The ontological proof about perfection and how there must therefore be a god or something. It sound OK, but it won't work if you're actually trying to convince yourself. A stone shot up from the road and cracked the windscreen. Then a bird slammed itself into the bonnet and left a stain of blood.

The King David didn't seem to be affected by its relative emptiness.

167

Only 20 per cent full, they said. The lobby was still swarming with people and the staff nodded as deferentially as ever. Adam was waiting to start his act, sitting, conspicuous in his solitude, up on a high stool at the bar.

'Adam!' I shouted, the revolving door still spinning behind me. He was chatting to the barman. The air-conditioning was extremely extravagant and I shivered as I ran towards him across the ice-white marble. There were little glass bowls of nuts on the bar.

'I met the Russian kids. They wouldn't talk to me. What are they doing there?' I said, breathing hard.

He took a second to recognize me before processing what I'd said.

'This is Yehudi,' he told me, introducing me to the barman. It was an odd response. I nodded to Yehudi.

'Vodka, please,' I said, for want of anything more friendly.

'Yehudi loves me. I'm the only person who ever orders alcohol. I drink the most complicated cocktails I can to keep him happy.' He pointed at his drink. It was blue and had a plastic elephant in it.

I smiled weakly.

This is a very frum hotel. The lifts stop on every floor on the Sabbath.

'Please, Adam. It's important. I'm looking for a friend's child. A Russian. Alexander – Sasha,' I said. So she wasn't a friend, but somehow the mission to find Sasha had become so connected with Shiv and what had happened to her, that I felt as close to it as though we had been looking for Shiv herself.

Adam went quiet for a bit and poked his elephant around with a novelty palm tree stirrer. He had some coloured bits of string round his wrist and badly bitten nails. He sighed and I could see his brain working, clunking round like something in a museum about the Industrial Revolution.

I continued to stare at him. Yehudi poured some orange juice for a group of Hasidic wives in cheap wigs and floral skirts.

I climbed up on to a stool. It had a fat leather seat. I thought he was about to run away, or kiss me or something, but when he stood up, he just looked at me.

'Excuse me,' Adam said.

He walked over to the piano and picked up a microphone that was lying on top of it. To a largely oblivious lobby, Adam sang 'Fly Me to the Moon'. He had a nice voice. When he had finished, I clapped along with the Hasidic ladies. He inclined his head, put the mike down and came back over.

'Sorry,' he said, as though he'd just been to the loo or something.

'The boss is standing over there.'

'Sure,' I nodded.

In between doing 'Love Me Tender', 'My Way', 'Luck Be a Lady Tonight' and 'Unchained Melody', Adam told me he'd left Father Bryan's because Bryan refused to refuse the General's money or the children Meier kept turning up with.

'I told him. I said: "Bryan, that bloke is bad news." But he trusts everyone.'

'You don't think Bryan is doing anything . . . underhand?' I asked, by now ready to believe almost anything.

'No. Of course not. But Meier just brought these Russian kids in. I mean, where the fuck did they get orphaned?' he wondered, twiddling his elephant. 'Not in this country, I don't think.'

'Exactly,' I said. I told him about the information Yo had been giving me, though not, of course, the source.

'Fucking hell,' Adam said, biting a nail. 'But if we can't find where the kids are coming from, he just looks like a friendly philanthropist.'

I nodded. 'That's why I need Sasha. We know where he came from and how he got to Jerusalem. The others are street-kids. They won't say who brought them here, but we do know who brought Sasha, and that he brought others. And then Meier seems to take them either to people's houses or to the orphanage.'

'He's a low-life specimen,' Adam said, shaking his head. 'Sometimes, when he finds homes for the kids, we never hear from them again. I reckon he's feeding them to settlers' families or something. Like those people in Chile. Or Brazil.'

'No you don't,' I told him, offering him a cigarette.

'No. But maybe he's placing them with settlers, or army families. Somewhere their parents would rather have died than send them. You know?'

I did. It was astute of Adam, I thought. Exactly the kind of perverse thing I could imagine the General doing. But I was pretty sure it was something worse.

'And Bryan doesn't check?' I wondered, leaning my elbows on the bar, finishing my drink.

'He's too trusting. He thinks everyone can be redeemed. He'd rather hope for the best and lead by example. If there's evil in the world, he thinks that by laying good alongside it, it might be transformed.'

'Not any more, he doesn't,' I said. And it was true. I had seen Bryan's admission to himself that things were not what they had seemed in the tears that ran down his face. He had let himself believe what part of him must always have suspected – that the General is someone who wanders around with the blood of innocent souls dripping from his fingers. Stumps.

The Hasidic husbands had come to join their wives, locks of devotion swinging at the sides of their behatted heads. I mean, you'd have to really believe in God to go around like that, I thought. But then again they were probably looking at me thinking, 'You'd have to be a real atheist to allow yourself to go around like that.' Not that I am a real atheist. At least, I wouldn't like to try and stand it up in an argument. When people who've been raped and macheted by marauding drug-crazed armies passing through the village smile up at you and say, 'God exists and He loves me', it's difficult, not to say patronizing, to tell them He doesn't: 'Actually, I've had a perfectly nice life and I know the truth – He doesn't.' It doesn't work, and, hey, they should know.

We sat in silence for a while.

'You don't think he's prostituting them, do you?' he asked, begging me to laugh it off as impossible. But he'd said it. And he believed it. It was out there.

'Yes,' I said. 'I do.'

Eden was in his room when I got back to the hotel. He'd beaten me home. He was hunched over his computer in boxer shorts and a shirt. Bare feet on the tiles.

'Hey,' I said, pushing the door open and peering in. He smiled.

'Another cutting-edge piece, pushing back the boundaries of modern journalism?' I wondered.

'Yes, actually,' Eden nodded, standing up.

I perched on the edge of the bed.

'The Palestinian authority's given BP permission to drill for gas. The Israelis need gas. It looks like peace,' he said.

'Wow,' I said, and meant it. 'When?'

'Dunno. Just spoke to the BP man,' he said, pacing down the room for his coffee cup and back to the computer to save what he'd written. 'You?' he asked.

'I don't know. Adam thinks Meier is a player in the child-trafficking. Basically, if anyone knows where Sasha is, it's him.' I said.

'And if anyone's not going to tell us, it's him.'

'Yeah,' I agreed. 'That's right.'

'Think it's worth doing a hospitals search?' he suggested.

''Spose,' I conceded. I didn't really, though.

I kicked something with my foot and leant down to pull it out from under the bed. It was a high-heeled shoe. It had the name of a designer written inside it with an italic flourish. I felt myself click into coping mode, a little bit of defensive electricity firing off in my brain.

'Girlfriend coming over later, motek?' I shouted to him. I wished I hadn't straight away. Can't I just leave him to his own devices? Do I want him to apologize and say it's just because I won't have him?

171

Yes. I do. A lizard ran across the room and I threw the shoe at it. I missed, of course, but it was a pathetic thing to do.

'Haven't got a girlfriend,' he said, walking back into the main room, a towel to his face.

'Faith, if you want me to apologize for getting laid and tell you it's just because you won't have me, I will. But I don't see what good it will do. If you want me to lie here every night hoping you might come in and try to fuck me just because your mum has called you out of the blue, I will. Frankly though, Zanetti, I'd rather have a bit more notice. You are a self-centred bitch.'

I laughed and put my right boot up on my left knee.

'Nice little shoes she's got. What did she do? Go home barefoot?' I asked.

'She had a pair of trainers in her handbag,' Eden said. He pulled the curtains open and let a blaze of sunshine into the room.

I blinked.

'No?'

'She did,' Eden said, but he couldn't keep a straight face. Laughing at the poor woman who had been stupid or gullible or miserable enough to follow him home to bed, he came towards me, not taking his eyes off mine. He pushed me back by the shoulders and kissed me. He smelt of beaches.

'I can't,' I said, rolling him off.

'You can with everyone else,' he sighed, throwing his hands back behind his head.

'Exactly,' I said. 'And so can you.'

I closed the door quietly and then leant against it. I could hear Eden on the phone to London, arguing about what they'd done to his piece the day before. I needed a drink.

Yo picked up his mobile phone at last.

'Faith Zanetti,' his voice smiled. Salim put a shot by my free hand and I winked to thank him.

'How's it going? Have you recovered from the kibbutz?'

God, but he was going to seriously try and pretend he hadn't seen me in Gaza last night.

'You're not seriously going to pretend that you didn't see me at the meeting in Gaza last night, are you?' I asked.

'Not pretend, no. I really didn't see you at the meeting in Gaza. You mean the Fatah thing where the boy got shot? I read about it this morning,' he said. He put his hand over the receiver for a second to issue some kind of order to a third party.

He was so certain, so relaxed, that I doubted myself rather than him. Briefly.

'Did you know that three quarters of the world's cranes are in Shanghai?' he asked when he came back to the phone. His trademark had lost its charm. I could see now that he used it as a way to get out of talking about things he didn't want to talk about. He had been there last night and now he was really scared.

'No. I didn't know,' I said. 'Yo—'

'Have you made any progress?' he asked, breathless now. I looked out at the pool. Someone in shorts and a straw hat was fishing flies off the surface with a big net.

'Not yet. I got your message, but couldn't find anything concrete. I'm having dinner with our friend tonight.'

'Meier?'

'Yup.'

He paused for too long.

'Faith. Faith, I don't want you to do that. He's dangerous.'

'Already set up. I'll see you afterwards,' I said, waving over at Salim for another.

But Yo hung up. When I called back I got the answering service in Hebrew and English.

I was nervous now. Yo had sounded scared. Scared for me? For himself? I couldn't tell. And I couldn't cancel dinner. God knows, I needed all the information I could get. All I could do was to sit in the golden evening light of the courtyard, watch lizards and smoke.

With a deferential bow of the head, Zahir told me that the General had arrived. I was reading a British tabloid left behind by a tourist. A columnist was stamping her feet about asylum seekers and how nobody spoke English at her son's school. It made me wish refugee status on her. I'd like to see her learning Arabic in a fortnight and having to clean people's toilets to feed her son who was being bullied at school for not speaking the language.

It's not that I don't get homesick for all that. The luxury of worrying about cholesterol levels and things. Or, to be honest, homesick for HP sauce (I love HP sauce, I have been known to carry bottles of it around in my suitcase with me, but one broke once, so I stopped), but complaint columns make me want to weep. No offence. Still, not as bad as those ones whose headline ends with the name of the politician to whom they are directed, as though the politician gives the slightest toss what some space-filler has to say to them. You know the kind of thing: 'Na na na na naa, Mr Brown', 'Na na na na naa, Mr Blair.' People who hang out at the Groucho Club and hope someone notices.

I looked up and saw his repulsive figure striding towards me. I had dressed up as a woman and he was as delighted as ever. When he kissed my hand, I could have sworn I felt a trail of tongue. I shuddered.

'Getting cooler already,' I said, though it must have been a zillion degrees out here.

He took this as an invitation to put his arm around me as he led me out of the hotel. I almost wanted to tell Zahir that this was a purely professional relationship.

This time there was half an army standing round his car. The other half was in a blacked-out car behind. Some kind of support vehicle.

'Jesus Christ,' I said.

'It's nothing, Miss Zanetti,' the General oozed. 'We have to take threats seriously. Traitors in our midst.' He laughed at what seemed to have been a joke of some kind. Certainly, if I were him, I'd be taking any threats extremely seriously indeed. As he edged towards me across the back seat in the icy chill, I considered making some myself.

We went to a French place this time, where the sommelier wore one of those silver tasting cups round his neck and a man dressed in a sort of P.G. Wodehouse butler's uniform was making crêpes Suzette at someone's table. They were elated to have the custom after all the recent suicide attacks, so they were being extra specially nice to us. This was quite something, considering how nice people usually are to the General and his guests. I could barely get my cigarettes out of the packet before someone hurled themselves forward with an obsequious scrape to light it for me.

The General put his hand on my knee under the table.

Now I know I should have flirted like mad, and tried to pretend to like him and stuff, but what I knew now had tipped me over the edge. There was nothing I could think of to do but confront him.

'Why did you take those Russian children to Father Bryan?' I asked him. It worked. At least as an effort to shake him off physically. His hand reappeared beside his fork.

He laughed with blank eyes.

'Miss Zanetti. You are always at work. Let's relax this evening,' he said, taking a slurp of his champagne.

'I am relaxed,' I said, tapping my foot a hundred times a minute under the table, picking at the skin around one of my fingers above it and smoking with a barely concealed urgency. 'Who are they?'

He was a bit put out. He didn't know I'd been back there until now and clearly had no desire to talk about the place. As far as he was concerned, he had set up the meeting for me and given me on- and off-the-record quotes consistently for years. Quite apart from the flowers, champagne and dinners. His patience, apparently, was wearing thin.

'They are children of some friends of mine who sadly passed away,' he said, looking down at the menu. He was the sort of man who would have rillette followed by chateaubriand.

I coughed, incredulous.

'What? All of them?'

He stared me down.

'Do you doubt my word, Faith?' he asked, all arrogance and false hurt. Shit, yeah! I wanted to say.

'Hassan died last night,' I challenged him, leaning back as the waiter poured me more champagne.

'Most regrettable,' Cyclops said, waving his mutilated hand around as he ordered his rillette and chateaubriand. There was a lady playing the harp in the corner and heavy green velvet curtains hung over all the windows.

'And I saw Yoram Jakobs shouting in Arabic and wearing a Hamas bandana.'

Meier raised his eyebrows and smiled.

'Did you indeed?'

'You knew about this! Are you setting him up on purpose?' I was pretty stunned and Meier was enjoying it.

'My dear,' he said, relishing the tone he was allowing himself to use. 'Armies are complicated machines. You cannot expect to understand them fully from the outside.'

'Try me,' I offered, but he only smirked and leant over to stroke the back of my hand. I could tell when further questioning wasn't going to get anywhere. Still, it was fascinating that Meier was obviously in on whatever Yo was up to.

I stabbed a snail with the special snail sword they'd given me and I realized what the General's seduction technique was missing. What men usually do is they give you two pieces of information. They'll say something like: 'I used to be in the army' or 'I go running in Hyde Park.' This is designed to tell you that the man is in perfect shape, looking good under these here clothes, and that he is super-virile.

He can keep going for hours. Then he will give you another piece of information. For example, 'I did a philosophy degree' or 'I do the occasional yoga class.' This tells you that although he is very hard in all departments he is also sensitive, i.e., he will let you have an orgasm first. The General never gives the second piece of information. If a woman is going to get drunk enough to go back home with a man and take her clothes off, she needs both pieces of information. The first alone would be no good (thug). The second alone would be worse (wimp). The General tries to suggest sensitivity with his oily attempts at chivalry but he never provides the facts to back his suggestion up. So as a woman you are left with the impression that sex would be quick, aggressive and completely without any satisfaction. I swigged at my wine, forgetting to sip it like ladies do.

The General had seen someone. He smiled at the door and I turned round. It was Moshe, Yo's captain, and a woman who was obviously his wife. She had a big hairdo and red lipstick. It seemed as though the army was leading by example and getting on with life as usual – suicide attacks or no suicide attacks.

Moshe approached our table.

'Shalom, General Meier,' he said to Cyclops, shaking his hand.

'Miss Faith Zanetti,' Cyclops told him, indicating my head.

'How are you, Miss Zanetti? I am sorry you had to witness our tragedy at Gesher Haziv,' he said, taking my hand kindly, as though he really felt responsible. 'This is Esther,' he said, and I shook hands with his wife. She had big emerald earrings on and eyes like Sophia Loren.

Cyclops looked annoyed that Moshe and I already knew each other. He didn't have a chance to say so, though, because it was at that second that the sommelier pulled a machine gun out from under a table and started firing at us. You'd have thought I might have been expecting this sort of thing by now, but, as always, it had come at a moment when I really wasn't thinking about it.

I lay flat on the floor and shut my eyes. I have no idea how I got there. It was like on the *Bad News Bible* course. I was going out for dinner and didn't want my T-shirt covered in mud. We were doing field training with explosions and gunfire and things and I'd decided I'd stand and watch. As soon as the first shot went off I found I was lying face-down with a mouthful of dirt. It's an instinct.

I tried to feel my whole body bit by bit to see if I'd been shot. I wriggled my toes. One of my shoes had come off. The General's bodyguards fired back straight away, an explosion of retaliation, and I had seen the sommelier thrown backwards, his torso plugged with bullets, even before I hit the ground. The screaming switched to moaning and shouting and some soldiers were helping us to our feet. I trod on a snail that must have fallen to the floor with the table. The feeling of it on my bare foot made me shudder. It could have been an eyeball. Esther was dead.

CHAPTER ELEVEN

The General only said one thing on the way back to the hotel. He said, 'Mother fuckers.'

I asked him who, but he didn't even hear me.

His mobile phone rang over and over again in his pocket, but he ignored it. This must have been about as far away as the man had ever sat from me. A relief in some ways, though it made me feel self-conscious about my short skirt now that it had been made redundant. Especially since I had a huge graze on the front of my left knee. That's the trouble with skirts. They don't protect you much.

The driver was shaken and went too fast, honking the horn and swerving round dawdlers. Our escort vehicle was close enough to brush bumpers.

Before I got out of the car at the hotel, Meier leant over and kissed me on the cheek. He put his left hand on one of my breasts and squeezed it hard. I didn't push him off. I knew this was a cursory gesture designed to show me that things were as normal. I waited for him to remove himself and then I stepped out. He inclined his head to me slightly before screeching off into the night. The muezzin was calling to prayer over the crackling loudspeaker and a few old men hobbled towards the mosque.

Eden was in the seething bar with Don. They were talking about Commander Whitehorn.

'If that twat had any idea the things I've seen . . .' Don was saying. A few bevs already sunk, apparently. Once he gets on to the things he's seen, there's no stopping him till morning. No surprise there. What was vaguely surprising about the bar scene, though, was that the woman from Eden's bed was sitting there with them in the smoky fug. This was quite a major breach of protocol. We normally keep our liaisons to ourselves, Eden and I. I sat down with them and Eden raised his eyebrows at me. McCaughrean smiled drunkenly. The woman was finishing a story, pouting her opinions out of painted lips.

'Anyway,' she said, heavily accented, 'I think it's terrible what the Tibetans are doing to the Chinese.'

Eden coughed slightly and Don blushed on her behalf. Or maybe he was just getting redder anyway after another day in the sun and another ten beers.

'Oh, I do!' I agreed. Eden kicked me under the table. 'I mean, all that passive-aggressive stuff. Enough to drive anyone insane.'

Don spat a mouthful of beer out, laughing. It made wet blobs on his trousers. Eden smiled.

'Yes,' he said. 'Very provocative use of purple and orange. And those silly trumpets.'

The woman looked confused. Her name was Ronit. She was twenty-three and a post-grad student at the university. Not in international relations, apparently.

'So how do you know Eden?' I smiled encouragingly.

'I waitress at the Pizza Piazza on Monday evenings,' she explained. Yes. I knew she looked familiar. She had served me and Svyeta that time. Not as mundane a job here as it might have been somewhere else. I mean, you have to really want the money to risk the bombs. And considering she could have done phone sex like normal students.

'Uh huh,' I nodded, beaming falsely at Eden. 'I see.'

I did, but she didn't. This was Eden's five million and forty-second waitress. He'd lived with one in Reykjavik for a few months once. She was a roller waitress in an American diner. Her name was Anika. He brought her over to London to meet his friends and they split up because she hadn't heard of Humphrey Bogart. Well how would she have heard of him? She was eighteen.

I felt guilty as soon as I'd started teasing Ronit. I didn't care if she thought Tibet was in Canada. Certainly, knowing their capital cities doesn't seem to do many people much good. I was just pissed off with Eden for being so depressingly predictable. I got up and bought her a drink – a cranberry juice with soda – and then I told them about my evening.

'You wouldn't know it,' Eden explained to Ronit, 'but Faith here actually is the Grim Reaper. I'd keep away from her, if I were you.'

'Listen. It's got fuck all to do with me,' I said. 'I'm not usually around when people try to assassinate Cyclops. Have dinner with him more than once, and the odds are against you.'

McCaughrean was cleaning behind his fingernails with a match.

'It's like sitting next to Pip Deakin on a plane,' he said, to nobody in particular.

'Why?' I asked him. I lit a cigarette and sipped my vodka. I was sure I'd sat next to Pip before, not that he'd have me nowadays. He'd probably move.

'He always chunders,' said Don, pleased with himself.

Eden nodded.

'It's true. I've never known him not use the sick bag,' he agreed.

'God. That's so seventies,' I said, stunned.

'Yeah. When flying was a bit new and everyone thought you had to make use of all the amenities,' Don chortled.

I didn't even know they still had them. Hey, don't throw up in there it's a collector's item. It's probably true that someone's got an actual collection of them – Laker 1979, PanAm 1982, TWA 1990, Swiss Air 2002. It's odd that it's now called Swiss. I always think people are having some kind of brain seizure and haven't been able to finish their sentence when they say, 'I flew Swiss.'

'That's repulsive,' I concluded. Ronit looked a bit shocked. If she ever had actually been sick, she was definitely going to keep it to herself.

I went back to my room to file a piece about the restaurant. I called Yo, but got his answering service. In the end, I just had to do a straight assassination story, with only the faintest suggestion, in the form of a made-up quote from 'a source close to the Israeli military', suggesting that it was a Mossad inside job. The thing about the mole story, and the desk in London was still hassling me about, the Lord knows, is that it just came too easy. Too many tip-offs from Meier, too much evidence, too much carnage just thrown in my face.

I suppose everything was affecting me more than I thought, because I fell asleep at the computer and I've never done that before. I find it hard to sleep at all, in fact. Since the thing with my mum. Not the phone call. The other thing. The reason I won't talk to her.

This thing. Basically, she tried to kill me when I was little. Not many words. You can say it quite quickly. It's about as much as I can say about it, though. As long as you don't think while you talk, it's OK.

I never told Dad or Evie. I couldn't. In fact, I didn't speak at all for a bit and they all thought it was the trauma of Mum drinking and of leaving her to go and live somewhere else. I wanted to tell Eden, but the words didn't come out. People say you forget things like that in an attempt at self-preservation, but I haven't. I dream about it a lot. Or, at least, I dream about not being able to breathe, about having something in my mouth suffocating me. I prefer to sleep without bedclothes if I sleep at all. And I haven't tried going to bed sober since I was about thirteen.

Anyway, there you are. Or here I am. So I fell asleep with my cheek pressed into the keys. And I dreamt about the little blonde Russian girl whose hand Eden held at Father Bryan's. Snub nose and a scar above her eyebrow. I saw her with a picture frame around her face. She was trying to pull it off, but it was part of her skin and it bled when she scratched at it.

I woke up breathing hard, an imprint of my computer all over me. I glanced around befuddled.

The first flat we'd gone to. Petr Kolbasov. He had a picture of the same little girl on his wall.

'Ugh,' I said to myself, standing up. 'Fuck.'

I lit a cigarette and paced around the room, knocking the heel of my shoe against the tiles. I went upstairs and stood outside the door of what had been Shiv's room. The police tape had gone from the door and the barriers that had been put up in the corridors had been taken away. I leant my back against the wall and looked out at the stars. I used to find it comforting when I was little. Depressed people are supposed to have a centre of the universe complex – they feel the plane will crash because they are on it, or that everyone is looking at them, thinking about them, obsessed with them. I think that the sanest people are the ones who are acutely aware of their own absolute insignificance. Looking up at the stars and knowing that their light is already millions of years old makes me feel insignificant and comforted. It doesn't matter – a tiny little life, nearly over in the enormity of time and space. It feels awful and unbearable, but it doesn't matter.

I stood there until an Italian television correspondent, who I've always thought was very handsome, came out and closed the door behind him. He looked at me, surprised, and I tried to smile.

'Hi,' I said. I think he thinks I'm stalking him now.

So they've cleaned up her room. Is there anyone staying here for non-journalistic purposes, I wondered. I doubt it, actually.

I woke up before dawn, feeling that someone had been leaning down over me, their breath in my face. I lay still for a minute or two, listening to the silence, and then sat up and switched the light on. Tangled up in my hair was a pink rose. I had to wrench it out of the curls. One of the thorns scratched my temple.

CHAPTER TWELVE

By half past five, I was sitting on a sun lounger by the pool, smoking cigarettes and watching the ripples on the water. Even in my jacket and jeans, I was freezing cold. The white sky was beginning to seep away and the blue was creeping in.

One of the kitchen staff, a fat lady I'd never seen before, came out of a back door for some fresh air. She paced up and down a bit before she saw me under my palm tree. Straight into work mode, she came up and offered me some coffee.

'Thanks,' I said, smiling. My fingers were cold.

I was on my fourth cup when I was accused of murder.

Whitehorn came out and found me around quarter to seven, as arranged. I'd moved to one of the tables and a few boys in starched aprons were putting towels out and checking the chlorine levels. An American man was doing lengths. It's another world, this getting up early thing. I was genuinely surprised when he appeared, abs gleaming. He leapt in with a 'Morning, ma'am.' When did I become ma'am?

Surely I ought to be miss still. He didn't seem to have a hangover or anything. He wasn't shaking with the need for a strong coffee. He didn't have the hunched shoulders of someone who has seen the evil of the world and will probably be seeing it again by the end of the afternoon. Perhaps he was a businessman (what business? Arms?) or an airline pilot.

'Miss Zanetti,' Whitehorn said, sitting down with me on a plastic chair. He was more confident now. He'd got a bit of a tan and his suit wasn't quite so suffocating at this time of day. Also, he was accusing rather than apologizing. Well, he didn't exactly accuse, but he didn't have to. It's all in the tone.

'Listen, sweetheart,' I said when he'd got to the point. I often call people sweetheart when I am particularly angry with them. Like married couples who use each other's names as an insult.

'I did not kill Shiv. You know that. For a start, I couldn't have lifted her on to the hinge. Anyway, I adored Shiv. She went off her head after something happened with or because of the Russian. Misha. If she was murdered, it was by someone connected with him. You know it. I know it. So get rid of that tone of voice.' He didn't answer. Was this part of a bad cop routine?

The American got out of the pool, dripping and breathing heavily. He was the colour of honey. 'Ma'am,' he said again and walked back into the hotel leaving wet slops of footprints on the tiles, a fluffy white cloud of a towel round his waist.

'We need to eliminate you from our inquiries is all,' Whitehorn said, sounding like an English policeman again. 'Israelis are insisting on it. Only a formality.' It didn't sound like one.

'Great. Eliminate away,' I said, rapping my fingers on the table. Everything is so clean and pale and clearly defined at that time in the morning. 'What did Glover say? He must have been pretty pissed off.' I was angry enough myself to be having this conversation when there was so much he ought to be finding out, and I thought Martin would be even less impressed. His girlfriend was dead, after all.

Whitehorn smiled lightly.

'I have yet to interview Mr Glover. We have an appointment for this afternoon.' He opened his diary and a tiny picture of Jane Austen fluttered down into the swimming pool. We both pretended not to have noticed.

'You'd be lucky. East London's quite a walk from here,' I said, standing up to go in.

'Indeed. Room seventeen, however, is just along the hall,' he replied. Touché.

That was weird. It was surely about ten seconds ago that Glover had last spoken to me from the office. I would have thought he'd never want to see this place again as long as he lived. On the other hand, maybe he'd already completely recovered from his bereavement and was on holiday with his new girlfriend. After all, as he was always telling us, he'd been brought up in a draughty stately home and that had made him tough enough for anything. Indeed, that was the main premise of his book.

Just like all those explorers who went off on a camel across the desert in the nineteenth century, and those billionaires who try to balloon around the world. There seems to be a consensus of opinion that they are incredibly brave and mould-breaking when really they have got toss all else to do. Their lives are so otherwise perfect that they have to create adversity for themselves. Let's hop across the Sahara with only a hip flask full of Fanta. Why? There are perfectly serviceable planes that get you across far more effectively. And alive with no need for dramatic rescues at the expense of the local tax payer. Mountain climbers too, for that matter. Why do you want to traipse up the Matterhorn? Because it's there. So, look at it. I mean, that coffee spoon is there right in front of me, but it doesn't mean I have to poke myself in the eye with it.

He was doddering about in the lobby when I went to find him.

'Faithy, Faithy, Faithy. How are all you girls?' he asked, hugging me.

'Fine. What are you doing here?' I wondered. Despite everything, I did have the faintest inkling that he might be trying to bigfoot me. He was worked up about the mole story, even though I'd been getting pretty fucking award-winning scoops, if you asked me. Whenever things are really happening, you get people like Glover trying to take the story over from the assigned correspondent. The telly people hate it most because it's the one time they can get their pieces on air regularly and then some idiot who knows nothing about the region but is really famous (if you're American, it's usually Janet Fischer) arrives in a flak jacket and stands there looking intrepid until the trouble blows over. Then she goes back to her nice flat in Little Five Points, Atlanta, and the rest of us have to stay in the cockroach-infested slime-pit we've had to make home.

'Don't worry, Zanetti, you silly tart,' he said fondly, detecting my worry. 'Just come for some – you know, catharsis.'

'Liar,' I said, walking off towards Eden's room and laughing. I could hear Glover laughing behind me, so I knew I was right. Well, he wasn't going to tell me what he was up to, but I'd find out in the end. It was probably the paper's lawyers sending him over to clear up some detail that would wheedle them out of coughing up Shiv's life insurance.

Eden was listening to a Schubert nocturne on his Discman, which he'd attached to mini speakers on top of the television. He lay sunny side up on the bed staring at the ceiling and blowing smoke rings.

'Hi,' I said, creeping in. 'Has Whitehorn tried to accuse you of battering and hanging Siobhan yet?' I sat in an armchair and put my feet up on the coffee table with a clunk.

'Yes,' he sighed, not looking at me or moving.

'And did you?'

'No,' he said.

'What are we going to do about Svyeta?' I wondered, not really expecting an answer.

'I've got someone searching the hospitals for the boy, but—' he didn't need to say it was pointless.

We sat quietly for a bit, listening to the heat. I shut my eyes too and thought about drinking whisky in a stifling Moscow flat one summer. Listening to Patsy Cline. There was a thunderstorm outside and we'd all got soaked. We sat there, me and some bedraggled students, steaming by a mountain of bootleg cigarettes that were piled up in the corner of the kitchen. They would be sold at a kiosk. It was in the days when kiosks were firebombed in the middle of the night. Some kind of protection racket. You'd go out to buy cigarettes in the morning and only the charred remains of your local shop would still be there by the side of the choking road. There had been this feeling then of calm in the centre of a storm. A few surreal seconds of fantasy before life smashed back in. 'Crazy for cryin' and crazy for dyin' and crazy for looooovin' you.'

When I looked over at Eden again, I noticed he was wearing an orange shirt. He saw me see it.

'Bought you a present,' he said, nodding over towards the television. My new shirt was sitting on top of it in its plastic sheath. I shook my head.

'Thanks,' I said. I picked it up and put it under my arm. 'I'm going to go back and see what Glover wants me to do today.'

But right now he was being eliminated from Commander Whitehorn's inquiries. He was sweating and shuffling around in his chair. There was something about his posture that shouted 'not eliminated'. Sod it, though. He was with me when they got her down.

On the other hand, you always get those people making appeals on television when it's obvious they're guilty. There was that man who killed his student girlfriend and hid her under the floorboards in Oxford. You could see he'd done it soon as look at him. It's ridiculous that the police don't have powers to arrest the generally shifty-looking. As a barrister friend of mine says, 'They're always guilty of something.'

And there was the road-rage woman who stabbed her boyfriend. Maybe Glover's horror at Shiv's death was all show and he'd actually hauled her up there himself. No. I raised my eyebrows at him in sympathy as I walked past. Whitehorn was becoming a bit of a pain in the arse. But the look Glover flashed back at me was one of panic.

I made a big effort not to absorb the implications of this and instead took it as licence to have the day off and work on the paedophiles. I went back to Eden.

'What time does Saddam Hussein have his dinner?' he asked me as I pushed the door open. He was shaving now, a towel round his waist, his face covered in foam, a razor in one hand. His left one.

'I don't know,' I admitted. 'What time does Saddam Hussein have his dinner?'

Eden grinned. Delighted.

'The same time as Tariq Aziz,' he said, and ducked back into the bathroom.

If it's possible, I was smoking even more at the moment than usual. Two nights in a row I had had to skulk down to the machine outside the bar in the middle of the night.

I once got thrown in prison in Moscow for buying cigarettes in a curfew. It was while the White House was burning in 1993 and a photographer friend of mine had been killed in the fighting.

It was weird. I was stringing at the time and I couldn't rustle up that much interest in the whole thing. I mean, everyone was running pictures of the burning building and all that. Abroad, it seemed like people thought Russians were always fighting each other. When actually it was the first time there had been any military violence in Moscow since 1917. For locals, it was the same as if there had been fighting on Whitehall in London and the Houses of Parliament were on fire.

Nobody in Moscow believed it, so they all went down to have a look and a lot of them got killed in crossfire. My friend Didi was shot out at

Ostankino, the television centre. Anyway, I crept out at two o'clock in the morning and got arrested within about eight seconds. I spent all night talking to a drunk prostitute with track marks in her arms. She'd been working since she was nine.

CHAPTER THIRTEEN

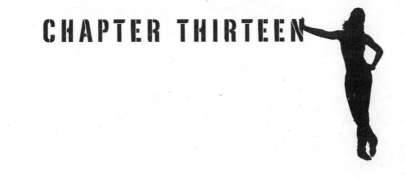

Glover and McCaughrean were wrecked by the time we sloped down to the bar. Grant Bradford, barely on speaking terms with any of us for keeping our stories to ourselves, was more sober, listening with a slight sneer. Martin appeared to have recovered from his interrogation and the three of them were having a who-knows-more-about-Jerusalem competition. McCaughrean was telling his favourite story – about a Jew who lived here in the year 70. The joke is that his name was Ananus.

Martin nearly choked laughing. But when he saw Eden and me, his face lurched into an attempt at a new expression. It went mirth – surprise – composure – fake mirth.

'Afternoon, girlies,' he said, holding his glass up. 'Won any awards for us today, Zanetti?'

I winked conspiratorially. Not out of any genuine good humour or complicity, but because I thought it was the kind of gesture that would shut him up.

'Bin Laden not getting a second's peace with you around, eh?' he went on.

I shrugged my jacket off. 'I am covering Israel, Martin. Honestly, I don't think he's here,' I reassured him.

'Could do with another Bin Laden myself, actually,' McCaughrean chuckled, taking his pint glass off towards the bar.

Don has quite a good story about some session at the UN where he ended up talking to a delegate who turned out to be one of the Bin Laden brothers, a Harvard-educated smooth-talking man in a suit. Anyway, just as Don was leaving for the airport, this Bin Laden asked him what airline he was flying. Terrified him out of his mind.

McCaughrean slurped the foam off the top of his beer, the glass resting on the camera bag he hugged to his chest.

'You want to try one of those new digital things, Don,' Grant suggested with a malevolent grin.

'Yeah. Right,' Don nodded, squeezing his bag closer to him.

Then Glover, his lips wet and his eyes glazed with alcohol, began to sing. He wiggled on his stool so that he shook like a blancmange and red patches appeared in the flesh of his face with the effort of breathing deeply.

'I've got a Niiiiiiiiikon camera, I'd love to take a pho-o-o-tograph, so Mama don't take my kodochrome awaaaay.' Don does indeed use a Nikon F100. Although 'use' probably isn't the right word. Work with. Love. Respect in the morning.

Eden and I sat as still as possible so as to avoid looking at each other. It wasn't the end.

'If I took all the girls I knew when I was single, brought them all together for one night – You know they'd never match my sweet imagination, everything looks better in black and white . . .' Martin went on.

It was supposed to be funny, but when he finally stopped, Don was crying.

'I love that song,' he burbled, rubbing a sweaty palm along an enormous thigh.

'Oh, Jesus,' Eden said, and stood up to go to the bar, smiling.

I lit a cigarette and sat back. The correspondent with different-coloured eyes glanced wearily over at me, begging me ocularly (is that a word? I once tried to read a book by Henry James, but had to throw it across the room when I got to a bit about a woman who 'raised her ocular surfaces', I mean eyes. Eyes, for Christ's sake) to save him from an academic from the university who was banging his fist on the table, the stirrer wobbling in his gin and tonic.

'Trying to find a Palestinian partner for peace is like a blind man in a dark room looking for a black cat that isn't there,' he said.

Good line, I thought. I shrugged at the French bloke. Can't help you, mate. He leant back towards his date and nodded sagely as though he'd been listening.

I didn't feel like playing humour one-upmanship with the boys. I drank my vodka like a Russian and wiped my mouth.

''Night,' I said, and went upstairs.

I lay there in my tiny room, boots on the bed, and stared at the television. There were lots of news pieces on all the flashing urgent channels by people who were down in the bar right now. The way the CNN woman stood there on a pile of rubble with sirens screaming behind her, her flak jacket strapped on, uniformed men with machine guns and reflector shades twitching nervously at the edge of the shot against the white Jerusalem stone, you'd think she stood out there the whole time, constantly digging out the story, talking to contacts, diving behind cars as explosions ripped through buildings (they always rip, explosions – in the news media, anyway). In fact, she's drunk and trying (usually succeeding) to get laid at least half the time.

Eden knocked on the door just as I was throwing one of the hotel pens at the television. I put my cigarette out and went over to let him in. I knew it was him from his footfall on the flagging.

'Come up for a quick one?' I asked.

'No,' he said, 'but if you're desperate.'

Necessary badinage done away with.

'Svyeta phoned me. She wants to tell you something. Said you weren't in your room,' he said, sitting on the bed and flicking through some Israeli military report I'd pretended to myself I might read.

He handed me a scrap of paper with her number on it, efficient of him, though of course I had it already, and I leant over to call her. Eden put two cigarettes in his mouth and lit them. One for me. One for you. I winked to thank him.

'Vera?' she said the second she picked the phone up. She was breathless, smoking, crying.

'Wait there. We'll come straight round,' I told her. I mimed to Eden to pick the pen up and chuck it to me and I scribbled her address down.

''S go,' I said to Eden, picking up my jacket and cigarettes.

'Let's get that story,' he smirked.

'It's not a story. It's a child. Or it was one,' I said from the other end of the corridor. Self-righteous bitch. Normally, that's what he would have said. He should have said it now. I almost wished he would. That he didn't meant he knew what I was thinking about. Maybe he'd been thinking about it too. So I was pushing on a bit. So perhaps I wouldn't have time to do it now. Only another decade of child-bearing, give or take a year or two, and disgusting procedures I wouldn't want to endure. Don't want to be one of those crones you see on the Upper East side in New York. Women with expensive little snub noses and every last wrinkle strapped behind their ears, pushing strollers full of IVF triplets down Park Avenue.

I probably shouldn't have done it. But the doctor said its brain might be damaged by the alcohol. First few weeks are pretty key, apparently. Well, of course I would have stopped drinking if I'd known. Anyway. I didn't tell Eden until afterwards. He punched the cigarette machine in the Mille Colines in Kigali so hard his knuckles were bleeding.

He didn't say anything. What's to say? Neither of us has referred to it since.

I think the worst thing about it was lying there waiting for my turn. There were ten of us in there lying in a little row like a children's rhyme. It was somewhere in Ladbroke Grove. We could see each other and did a bit of cursory smiling. You know, all in the same boat. Sympathetic but determined. Then one woman – one girl (she was about sixteen) – said, 'Fuck this. I'm having the baby.' She leapt out of bed, put her clothes on and walked out. It was that more than the operation itself, more than the preposterous counselling they put you through (woman asks you if you're sure ten times and then you sign a form), that made the rest of us aware of what we were doing. Three of them burst into tears. The one I liked best though was a girl who looked at herself in a compact mirror and said to me, 'I just want to get rid of these spots.' This was her third.

'Self-righteous bitch,' Eden said under his breath as we walked down the stairs. I wanted to turn back and kiss him.

'Fuck yourself,' I said, instead, but I was smiling.

It was a great night. The sky was bright and black and it was almost cool. The crickets were singing.

'Nice evening for it,' I said and Eden snorted. There is something wonderful about this city. You can sort of see why the Messiah might choose it.

'Maybe I am the Messiah,' I told him. 'How would you know? I mean, what are the signs?'

'Giving a toss about other people. Having a beard,' he explained.

'Oh,' I acknowledged.

There was a policeman standing outside the hotel door, very obviously guarding us.

'Have there been threats?' Eden asked him, surprised. We are an unlikely target. An entirely Arab staff.

'Murder suspect. Not allowed to leave,' the boy told us.

'Oh shit,' we said in unison, walking on as if unconcerned.

I put both hands through my hair and Eden pushed his shirtsleeves up although they were already up.

'So. Not us, then,' I said. We both knew who the suspect was. There was nothing to say.

There seemed to be even more road blocks than usual and hardly anyone out on the streets in the west. The Russian ghetto was livelier. Threatening in an indirect way. I prefer places where the men carry guns and the boundaries are clear. You know where you are if the dangers are obvious. Look, there's some fighting over there. Here is a big tank. This area just had an atmosphere of menace. Small groups of Russian men. Young, dehumanized by life, unpredictable. The worst.

Svyeta's friend opened the door of her ghastly flat. A nondescript slime pit in a nondescript block. Satellite dishes, white stone, a Soviet smell of cabbage in the hallway, shouting and children crying behind the walls. Walls that themselves gave off a stinking heat. The friend – Masha, her name was – was tired and fat. Her face was doughy and puffed up with alcoholism. Her apron was dirty and her husband was unconscious on the sofa.

Svyeta sat meekly on a greasy armchair.

Eden drew his breath in and I said, 'Oh God.'

She had been badly beaten up. Her face was purple and swollen, her lip split, her eyebrow bleeding. She had a bandage round one hand and she was bent in the middle as though she'd been kicked in the stomach.

I knelt at her feet and took the unbandaged hand.

'Svyeta,' I said, but nothing else would come out.

She didn't bother to cry this time. She just spoke as though she was talking about something else.

'They took me from the hallway here. Three of them. They said they knew where Sasha is. We went in a car. To a nightclub. Not far. At first they sat and drank and then when I asked about Sasha they beat me. Nobody helped. People pretended not to notice.' She winced in pain and her forehead crumpled. 'They said to stop making trouble for them. Said a British policeman had been to see them. Then one of them took me from the floor to the toilet and raped me. The others too. They say Sasha is dead. One of them – Tolik – said he killed him himself.' It was now that she started to cry. Messy, wet, snotty, red-faced wailing. Real crying. She could hardly speak any more. 'I don't know why they didn't kill me. I asked them to. Maybe that's why. Or they want me to tell you to stop. To tell the policeman to stop. So I'm telling you.'

We stood frozen in silence as she spoke. When she had finished her friend said, 'Get her out of here.' Not a close friend, apparently. Or just a very frightened woman. A child shouted 'Mama' from a door to my right. So fair enough.

Masha let me use the phone and, panicked, I called Whitehorn. I knew he had been following the child-trafficking thing because it was the link to Shiv. He'd looked into the missing Russians, the undercover people who had still not turned up. I couldn't imagine a child-trafficking Russian being very sympathetic to an undercover policeman. And it was Misha who had led them to them.

Now it was clear that neither Eden nor I was remotely suspected of killing Siobhan, perhaps Whitehorn would be more communicative. He was terse, but aware of the gravity of the situation. He was probably perfectly nice when he was off duty. He gave me the name of a woman at a police station in the centre and said I should take Svyeta there to make a report. He stressed, and I mean really stressed, that I was in no position to prove a link between Shiv and the missing Russians, let alone start writing about one.

And then quietly, so quietly I might have missed it, he tipped me off.

'You might try the Ulysses nightclub in East Jerusalem,' he said. 'It's just a thought.'

And that was it. All he would say. It sounded a likely enough venue for the attack on Svyeta. By name, at least.

There used to be a club in Moscow called that. It was owned by a very frightening Serb with a metal hand.

'You could be more helpful, you know,' I told him, annoyed. I needed help with these fucking Russians and he knew as well as anyone that the Israeli police had enough on their plates.

'You are entitled to your opinions, Miss Zanetti. I am doing my side of the job and the Israeli police force is doing theirs,' he told me.

'Thanks,' I said and hung up.

Svyeta bent forwards and had her head in her hands. The husband rolled over, snoring. He stank of whisky. Thick and sweet. They were showing *Baywatch* on television, dubbed into Hebrew with Arabic subtitles.

'He's not dead,' I told her. 'He's not dead.'

I believed it was true. She looked at me with the last bit of hope in her soul, but it died as soon as it had risen.

'Help us,' I asked, pulling her up out of her chair. Eden came to lift her from the other side.

'Some Russians kidnapped and raped her. They've got her son,' I explained to him. He got the abridged version.

Svyeta weighed nothing. The street lights, ads and shop signs a blur of despair on the way. She wandered into the police interview room across town stupefied by misery. She was followed by a young woman carrying a steel tray with forceps, scissors, swabs and cotton buds on it. Svyeta sank into a metal chair, not caring any more what happened to her. The Russian translator was bleary-eyed, drinking a paper cup of espresso. We left them to it.

*   *   *

There was a fight going on outside Ulysses. Two men beating the crap out of another one who was lying on the floor. A couple of stray dogs watched them from across the road. The bouncer on the door, a fat man with a shaven head and gold chains, wasn't even looking at them, let alone thinking about intervening.

He was looking at us, though. We were dramatically out of place. Or maybe it was just me. The kind of women that came here, such as they were, didn't wear jeans and boots. Eden paid a heroin addict behind a bullet-proof window and we had our hands stamped. With a swastika. I looked at the bloke with almost admiring awe. I mean, this was truly psychotic.

'Joke,' he said, without so much as a twitch of a smile.

'Ah,' I nodded.

Inside, it was so dark and smoky it was hard to make out the people from the walls. A little boy leant out from behind a curtain and stared at us. We weren't the usual type of customer. The bar was over in one corner, lit by a red neon strip around the edge of it, that flashed on and off with the music. Russian pop. When my eyes had adjusted, I could see a couple of tables with unconscious heads slumped on to them. Big fat ham heads, close-shaven to show off the scars. Next to them, enormous hands clutched mobile phones. One man lay face down on the sticky lino. There were a few couples writhing about on the dance floor. The women were fairly obviously prostitutes – too young and too good-looking by far. They would not have been dancing with these men for the good of their health.

There was almost no security here. Obviously, nobody imagined that this was somewhere worth bombing. They were right.

'Over there,' Eden said. Over there was where three enormous men sat at a table reigning over the club. They were trying to frighten people. Trying to make their position clear. That being the aim, it was going pretty well. One looked Palestinian, the other two were fine examples of the Tambov-mafia look. Necks thicker than heads, sloping shoulders like Tupulov cargo planes, army and prison tattoos, shredded knuckles, guns openly strapped to their waists, deeply scarred faces, a few too few fingers (they chop them off each other when they're drunk), and little leather handbags on straps. I've never known why they choose to demonstrate their feminine side in this way. Standing, or rather undulating, near them was a girl taking her clothes off to the music. They weren't paying much attention, but it seemed they had probably paid her to stand there and do that all night. Some sort of kudos-enhancing activity. We stood still watching until she had finished. She picked her clothes up off the floor and stepped back slightly to put them back on. None of the ceremonial wriggling around this time.

I went to the bar and got us a couple of beers while Eden introduced himself. By the time I turned towards him, a bottle in each hand and a cigarette between my lips, he had been lifted up by the Arab and one of the Russians and was being dragged out towards the door. I followed them and watched him be tossed into the middle of the road. A motorbike swerved to avoid him.

I leant against the outside wall of Ulysses while he picked himself up and came over. I handed him his beer.

'Thanks,' he said.

'What did you say, for God's sake?' I asked, a police car screeching up at our feet.

'I said: "We have reason to believe that you are selling children for sex. Do you deny it?"'

I spat my mouthful of beer out. Four policemen ran into the club.

'You said what?'

'I said: "We have reason to believe . . ."'

I interrupted him.

'Yes, I know. Why? Now they'll just get rid of the kids, go back to Moscow or Tambov or somewhere and we'll never find Sasha or Shiv's people or anyone.'

'Sorry,' he said, testing his fingers for brokenness.

Our three friends were brought out into the night, their wrists cuffed behind their backs, guns to the nape of their necks.

'See,' I said.

'What are you talking about? Svyeta's given a statement,' Eden complained. He was probably right, actually. She would have given the police enough information to know where to come for her rapists by now. Eden wandered off to find a taxi and I stood around smoking. This area was a shit-hole by any standards, I thought. Looked like some sort of suburb of Bradford, except for the heat, and the depth of the night. Part of me wanted to give up and go home. I'd like to have checked into a nice clean hotel in London, eaten a curry, gone to the cinema, done something normal. It was not to be, though. Of course.

I thought at first it might be a cat. A cardboard box a few feet away from me, next to a heap of rubbish bags by a lamp-post, moved. I flinched away, expecting one of those moth-eaten one-eyed things to leap out at me, yowling. But the more I looked, the more I could see that it was something bigger and less agile. Maybe a bear or a badger. Or . . . When it finally scrabbled its way out of the cardboard, I could see that it was a little boy. The same one I'd seen in the club. He looked at me for a while, mistrustful, terrified actually. He looked around as though for an assassin at his shoulder. He was probably six, wearing a Brazil football shirt and some tracksuit bottoms. Bare feet, dirty hands, but not a street-child. Then, when he had satisfied himself that there was no one else around, that I looked, I suppose, as I had sounded inside, he ran at me as though he was going to rob me or something. It was hard to believe that he could have made the decision to trust me in that instant. That he was not so appallingly traumatized that he would never knowingly go near another human being again. All I can say is that he did.

The force reminded me of the gypsy children in Moscow. They used to stand at one end of the metro underpasses and run at people, their arms linked together as though they were playing British Bulldog. They'd knock you over, crawl all over you like Lilliputians, and take everything you owned. It was pretty non-violent and almost funny. If it wasn't so sad.

Anyway, this boy grabbed my legs, shut his eyes and wouldn't let go. He pointed inside, shouted in Arabic, wailed and cried. I picked him up and he flung his arms round my neck and his legs round my waist. I put my hand up to his head and hugged him towards me as he shook with crying. I was about to start myself when a car appeared and Eden leaned out of the window.

'I think he likes you,' Eden said. 'Get in.'

The boy must have seen us in the club and taken us for potential rescuers. The thought occurred to me that he had chosen me for my femininity. I think it must have been that. Men were not to be trusted, but I, even in my jeans and boots, even with the least maternal attitude in the world, I was a woman and a potential nurturer. Not a woman enslaved by his own captors, but someone from outside. He'd spotted his chance to escape and he'd gone for it. Gone for me. I was ashamed to feel my eyes watering. I wondered if there were others in there. Sasha? We'd have to come back.

I kept him on my lap in the taxi, stunned by his trust and tenderness, and, as we rushed through the night, he fell asleep on my shoulder. I had to bite my lip hard now in order not to cry. I must be tired.

'Eden, what am I going to do? I can't take him back to the hotel. Everyone knows we're there.' I fiddled around for my cigarettes.

'You can't smoke in his face,' Eden said.

'Oh. No. That's true.' It was. I raised my hand to bite my nails instead, but there was a smear of blood on it.

'God, I wish I'd looked for a flat,' I sighed, looking out at the neon swirls of Arabic on the shop fronts.

'What about Edmonds's place? Isn't it still empty?' Eden suggested.

'You're right!' The accounts woman on the foreign desk had been pressuring me to move in because they were paying rent on it for another couple of months or something. I argued that it wasn't my problem, but now I could score points for frugality with the paper and be slightly more convincingly in hiding. I bit the inside of my cheek and decided I wouldn't be telling Martin Glover where I was going for the time being. It was in the pit of my stomach, but I wasn't about to let it rise any higher into my consciousness than that. His guilt, that is.

I wondered, as we travelled, the little boy sobbing softly on my chest, what kind of reaction we would get when I finally did make them run the Meier rape acquittal story Yo had leaked me. Trouble is, the papers do hate paedophile stories. And cannibals. A real turn-off. I was doing this appalling cannibal story once in Russia along with a friend of mine who was working for one of the big Americans. Basically, this lunatic and his mother had been eating street-children and when we went round to interview them they were cooking one of them up in some sort of stew. When Kattie tried to file her story, the paper told her it was too tasteless. 'People are reading this over breakfast,' her editor said.

'He didn't even seem to think it was funny. Americans are so weird,' Kattie complained. She's English. On the other hand, it's better than Russians. Russians don't run any kind of paedophile stories because they don't see that it's a story. They just kind of shrug and say, 'But everyone knows that alcoholic fathers and step-fathers are all screwing their children.' It's not that they think it's OK, it's just that they see it like putting every car crash that happens on the front page. I've noticed, actually, that plane crashes only make the small print on page 4, nowadays. Unless they involve Brits or Americans.

Edmonds's next-door neighbour was, it transpired, a drunk woman wearing a lot of make-up and a babydoll nightie who appeared from under her entrance-way palms with a huge cocktail in her hand. She called us motek and fairly openly tried to have sex with Eden, despite the fact that we must have looked like husband, wife and sleepy child. Although I suppose the little one might have seemed a bit swarthy for us, but it was dark. When I asked if she had the keys to the empty house, she was suspicious in an overly aggressive way. Heavily accented she shouted that she couldn't be doing favours for anyone who rolled up at her door. How did she know we weren't about to rob the place?

We both showed her our press accreditation and I explained I had come to take over from Edmonds. This settled her down a bit and after we'd agreed to come and get pissed with her as soon as we'd moved in, she handed the keys over.

Inside, there was no trace of Edmonds. They say he took his mattress into the bathroom so that the aliens wouldn't get him. Evidently, aliens don't go to Rome. Which is odd. Surely it's about the first place on earth you'd go, as a first-time visitor. The whole house had been professionally cleaned so that when we switched the hall lights on, we were faced with acres of gleaming terracotta tiling. The ceilings were low, the walls were bright white, and neat, seventies furniture stood lonely in the vastness. A dark brown sofa with wooden arms, matching armchairs, and a squat coffee table in smoked glass. A few palms lurked in their pots by the staircase. Even from the front door, you could see the city twinkling through the sliding doors to the back terrace. I pointed at myself over and over again and said, 'Faith', until the boy eventually pointed at his own chest and said 'Marwan'. Marwan hid behind my legs. In a gesture that I have obviously inherited from some apes, I reached back to put my hand gently on his head.

We crept upstairs, obeying the house's command of silence. There were three big bedrooms, all of which had bathrooms attached, slatted cupboards under the sink full of airline toiletries. Marwan leapt up on to a bed and put his head on a pillow, immediately smearing it with black dirt. He clamped his eyes shut in a signal for me to go away and leave him to sleep, so I pulled a sheet up over him and kissed him on the filthy cheek, because I thought that was what I was supposed to do. Eden screwed his face up as if to say it didn't suit me.

'Fuck off,' I hissed. Marwan, apparently, was already asleep.

I called the hotel to pick up my messages and Zahir read me out a note from Yo. 'Yoram wants to speak to you urgently.'

'Shit,' I said, fishing in my pockets for my phone.

When I got him, Yo's voice was flat and frozen. But urgent. He didn't sound like someone about to tell me an interesting piece of useless trivia. None of his jokes this time.

'You've got to come and meet me. Somewhere public. Outside,' he hissed.

'There isn't anywhere public at this time of night,' I said. 'Yo, come over here. It's safe.'

'No. Meet me at the Wailing Wall. They'd never dare kill me there,' he said. Cold, but certain.

Eden, for a brief moment, standing there in his white shirt and jeans, beautiful and sad, got competitive.

'Come on! Share!' he said, already knowing he didn't stand a chance.

'Jones, you tosser. The guy phoned me not you,' I said, about to walk out of the door.

'Fair point,' he said and sat down. 'I'll stay, then.'

I slipped back out into the night. Eden was babysitting. Not that he would ever actually say 'babysit', of course.

The Old City was deserted and full of night noises. Creaks and clunks and bumps like ones in books to frighten children. I always thought it was odd that I was supposed to be scared by shadows behind the cupboard. I can't remember a time when I wasn't aware that it is people who are frightening. Alive ones. I flinched stupidly when two fighting cats rolled out in front of me, screaming and scratching, a spiky ball of teeth and claws. I was pathetically pleased to get to the Wailing

Wall piazza, well-lit even now as Yo had suggested and patrolled by flak-jacketed soldiers. Yo was smoking on a bench, acknowledging me with a shift in position rather than any more traditional kind of greeting.

I sat down next to him. He was drenched in sweat. He had come in uniform and even his jacket was sodden.

'Faith. They are going to kill me,' he said, darting not looking at me. He had developed a kind of pallor that was almost green. Frankly, I was surprised they hadn't killed him already. He was still and rigid.

A Hasidic Jew with ringlets was praying by the Wall. What a time for it.

'Who is?' I asked.

Yo looked slowly about him to take in every possible point of assault.

'Mossad,' he said. The first thought that flashed into my head was: conspiracy theory. Loonies always think the secret services are after them. Admittedly, they are usually loonies who don't work for an elite army unit in a country permanently at war. I always liked that film called *Conspiracy Theory* where there's a taxi driver who sees high-level plots all over the place and it turns out they're all true and he is at the centre of them or something.

'Why?' I asked him. Would he confess to blowing up his own colleagues? Might he? 'Off the record,' I added, stupidly.

He spoke steadily and quietly. I could hardly breathe. I was terrified he might just stop and run away.

'Because I found out about General Meier,' he said. He paused to draw breath. I noticed he had a scar across his cheek, as though someone had slashed him with a razor blade. I lit a cigarette, trying to affect some degree of nonchalance. As my match hissed into life, a couple of the soldiers looked over. Like everybody around here, they were expecting the worst. And they could be pretty much assured that it would come. That's what Eden would say.

'Bethlehem. The Intifada. 2002. The Church of the Nativity,' Yo said. He sounded like one of those films where the times and places are flicked violently up on to the screen as though being typed. Films about Vietnam. Saigon 1968. Chkkachhkachka. Some helicopter gunfire. This could be the beginning of a film, I thought. Tough-looking woman, perhaps like the love interest in *Raiders of the Lost Ark*. No make-up, deep tan, hard drinking, butch dressing. But, of course, she'd clean up all right. She's sitting on a bench with a handsome, but nervous, Israeli soldier. It is late at night and a Hasidic Jew is praying by the Wailing Wall as we zoom in to focus on them. The soldier starts to talk and we fade into Bethlehem 2002 as the date and place tickertape up on to the screen and we can see that one of the soldiers toting his gun outside the church is the same man we just saw on the bench in Jerusalem. A voice-over as the action plays.

But it's not a voice-over. It really is Yo and I am sitting next to him.

'I was outside the church and all those people were in there, maybe starving, maybe bleeding to death. There was some kind of demonstration. A distraction, I think, so that they could drag out an injured bloke and we were all nervous. The captain, Moshe, you know, told us to fire. And I fired. And I killed someone.'

I wanted to say, well, Yo, you're a soldier. That's what you do. It's not the end of the world. It's your job.

'I know. I'm a soldier. That's what I do if I have to. I'm not stupid,' he said. Oh good, I thought. A small group of women in headscarves and long skirts were coming to put their prayers between the stones of the wall. They passed us and went in through the cordon. In the film version that plays simultaneously in my head, one of them would be strangely beautiful and she would give Yo a long, slow look of gratitude or pride or something.

'Meier was there. I don't know what he was doing there. I saw him. He was in uniform and this man, this man I had shot, was dying in front of me. I couldn't stand it. I was sick. I went behind this wall, just near the church doors and I threw up. And Meier was there. He was talking to an Arab boy, one of the Palestinians from inside the church.'

Well, that didn't sound like such a big deal.

'I didn't immediately understand the significance of it really. He was giving him details about where Israelis are stationed. I think I trusted him enough to assume it was somehow . . . above board.'

Yo stopped here. It was as though this was the story. Maybe it was, but I didn't get it.

'Yo, I don't get it,' I said. I was terrified he'd leave me there, feeling he'd confessed, me barely any the wiser.

'He doesn't want peace, Faith. He encourages Intifada so that he can keep his political leverage. He is killing us.'

OK. I get it. And I didn't need a Dictaphone. I wasn't likely to forget a single word now. And I knew it was true. When someone's telling you the truth, you always know. When someone's lying, you can be unsure, but the truth is as clear as water.

'I've been an idiot. He had to involve me before I believed it. And it's not just me. He tells us we're infiltrating Hamas, but we're not. We're letting Hamas infiltrate us.'

'Why didn't he have you killed before?' I asked, as quietly as I could. He was in the kind of state I couldn't imagine. Already dead, almost. I couldn't see how he stood a chance. Yo carried on looking straight ahead at the wall and the few faithful. His face expressionless.

'He doesn't know I know. Or at least, he didn't. I got tipped off. He thinks I'm behind the restaurant bomb, but I swear to you, Faith. I would never . . .' He turned to look at me now. 'Don't you think people hate us enough? Don't you think we have a bad enough press, trying to defend our country?' Tears started to pour down his drawn face. 'I had my loyalties, Faith,' he said, his chin quivering. 'Have my loyalties.'

I was looking up at a light flickering in the sky and trying to decide whether it was a plane or a shooting star. The shimmering heat made it hard to tell.

'And now? Why are you telling me now?' I put my cigarette out

210

under my boot and exhaled the last of my smoke. I already wanted another one.

'You've got to understand. In the army, especially in the elite units, you know, like mine, we know each other very well. Meier is ex-special services, Faith. You've got to help me. He's going to kill me,' he whispered.

I reached for his hand and held it, for all the good it might do.

'What can I do?' I begged him. And Christ knows I wanted to do it.

'You've got to run the paedophile story. I've tried to help you. If he's publicly shamed, at least if he has to leave the army. He won't be able to do it.'

I lit another cigarette.

'You're not the mole?' I said, not expecting an answer.

'Nobody is. He sent us undercover as secret agents. He wants war, Faith. He needs war. I was on a job when you saw me in Gaza. He's been planting me in these situations, Faith. I never would have killed my own people. Never.' He sat up now. Grave. 'What could I do?' he asked. 'What could I do?'

I took his hand and we stood up together. Arm in arm, we left the Old City and walked out into the street lamps and traffic of the new.

Slowly, we went back to the Colony. Speaking to no one, I took Yo up to my little minaretted room and told him to sleep. I shook a couple of diazepam out of the brown plastic bottle in my jacket pocket and handed them to him. 'You're safe here,' I said. I hoped it might be true. I suppose I knew though that he was no longer safe anywhere.

I went downstairs to pack my stuff up and take it to Edmonds's. Depressingly little, really, for moving into a house like that. A short-wave radio, two pairs of jeans, my skirt and silly shoes for the old men, some T-shirts, some pants, a wash bag and a few books. Was that really it? The hotel was quiet and the only person around was the man on the door who was holding Martin Glover prisoner. On what evidence? Did Whitehorn have something concrete?

Even the lizards were asleep tonight.

My key in the lock back at Edmonds's sounded too loud and I pushed the door open to find Eden asleep on the sofa, an ashtray under his dangling hand, a bottle of beer on the coffee table. I went off to the kitchen to see if there was another in the fridge. It didn't occur to me until I found a bottle opener and wandered back into the front room that I should probably check on Marwan. That's what people with children do, isn't it? They check on them. Make sure they haven't suddenly died in the night. Admittedly more relevant in this case than it might usually be.

I crept upstairs and heard some shuffling and rustling. He wasn't asleep. This is when I should feel a bit cross: 'Go back to bed!' parents say. Don't they? If I've told you once, I've told you a thousand times. No telly until Christmas . . . I hadn't actually experienced that kind of parenting, but I had friends who had. You'd go for tea at their houses and they had to share the biscuits out and put their plates in the dishwasher.

I opened the bedroom door and saw a trembling lump under the sheet. Was he crying? Oh Jesus. Comforting someone who has endured that degree of trauma was just not going to turn out to be my forte. Gritting my teeth, at least metaphorically, since I'm not sure quite how one literally does it, I pulled back the sheet to find not one, but three quaking boys. One of them was Marwan.

They were huddled there, clinging on to each other with grasping fingers, dirty and chaotic. Their very existence was making a mess in the clinically clean house. They were the mess. All three so impossibly dirty and generally scraggy. They looked as though they had never eaten properly. You know how those little girls in Chinese orphanages are always two or three years smaller than their contemporaries? Never breast-fed, nobody mashing up bananas for them or opening little jars of faintly custardy mush. The result is such a skimpy slip of a child, so spidery and cold, somehow.

'Where the hell did you come from?' I said to the others. But I was smiling. Marwan, infinitely pleased with himself, mimed having gone to get them. He pointed to the bedroom window, propped open on the slant of its big hinge. He must have been pretending to be asleep when I left. He had broken his mates out. Of where?

'Stay there!' I said to them. They clung together, jutting elbows and knees.

'Hey! Eden! Get up! They've multiplied,' I said, dragging him up off the sofa by the arm.

'What have?' he mumbled.

'Marwan has. There are three of them. How long have you been asleep?' I pulled him upstairs to come and see, as though I were showing him some kind of unusual insect in the bath.

'There!' I said, pointing.

'Oh yes,' Eden admitted. 'Hello.'

'Khello,' they chorused, smiling nervously.

'Do you want some cake?' he asked, in Arabic.

They nodded and he took them, one on his back, the others holding a hand each, down to the kitchen where, apparently, there was a ginger cake in a packet in the fridge. I wondered if they knew he wasn't going to abuse them, or if they didn't care any more either way. Or if they completely expected it and so thought they might as well have some cake first.

One of the boys staggered as though he'd been on drugs or was still. I hardly dared think.

'Yo's not the mole. Or, at least, he's being set up by Meier who's apparently trying to scupper the peace process,' I said to Eden, spitting it all out at once. 'He seems to think he'll be dead by morning. Yo, that is. He's in my room at the hotel.'

'Jesus,' Eden said, spitting out his mouthful of beer, more surprised by that than he was by the multiplication of the children.

They sat cross-legged on the floor, stuffing their faces. Marwan was clearly the leader, doling out the cake fairly and nodding to them that they should eat when the other two looked a bit worried.

'Shouldn't you get back there?' Eden asked me.

'Yeah. Shouldn't we put these kids in the bath? They stink,' I suggested. Well, they did. Maybe then we could start asking after Sasha. Clearly none of these was him. They were all as brown as nuts.

I put four bottles of miniature hotel bubbles in and turned the taps on full. The three boys leaned over the edge of the bath and watched as though I were performing some sort of operation. I bent my head over to one side to demonstrate that they should get in and went outside to leave them to it. I didn't want to confront getting them undressed. Obviously.

I put my back against the white paint of the bathroom door and smoked a cigarette. I could hear Eden downstairs, rinsing cups out or something. It was an odd instant domestification. Like that film with the three mustachioed blokes who get left with a baby and are suddenly warming bottles and arguing about who has had the least sleep. Here we were, Eden and I, in a big family house with three children and it was bath time. In a minor act of rebellion, I stubbed my cigarette out on the tiles at my feet and stomped back in. The boys were crouched silently in the bubbles, not moving, their eyes glazed.

'Hey. It's OK,' I said, kneeling down. I got a handful of bubbles and put it on my chin. 'Beard,' I said. They laughed. So I gave them each a beard of their own and waited for the water to turn black before I hauled them all out and wrapped them in a white towel. They seemed bulkier and more normal that way. Should I have washed their hair? Next time, maybe. No! There wouldn't be a next time. They would have to go somewhere else.

At this point, Eden came in with four cups of sweet milky tea on a tray. They sipped it suspiciously.

'Go on. Ask them about Sasha,' I nudged. 'Go on.' After a jerky conversation I didn't understand, Eden said yes, there were Russian children at Ulysses, including a boy.

CHAPTER FOURTEEN

I had never been into McCaughrean's room before. He opened the door on to the cool corridor wearing baggy Y-fronts. Inside, there were a dozen pairs of very smelly socks on the floor, a few scrumpled balls of pants. Ten or more trashy novels strewn about the place – the kind of thing that has flames and a helicopter on the cover. And on top of the television a carton of cigarettes, the end ripped off and half the packets gone. I helped myself to a pack and put it the back pocket of my jeans.

'Don, I've got a job for you. Can you come?' I asked.

'With you, Zanetti, anywhere,' he said, stumbling into his trousers without even asking for details. I thought I'd best give him some anyway though.

'Listen, I want you to hang around outside Ulysses nightclub with me. See who we can see. They've got children in there. Not nice. Can you lurk behind a corner and take some pictures?' I pleaded.

'I'm not a fucking paparazzo, you know,' he told me, smelling the armpits of a T-shirt he'd picked up off the tiles. 'Long lens, then,' he muttered, fiddling about in his equipment.

'Yes. I should think so,' I said. How would I know? Long lens. Short lens. Just take the picture. I get sick of the whole artistry of it.

'Oh, for Christ's sake,' he said, looking at his watch as he put it on.

'Yeah. Sorry,' I admitted. It was about four in the morning. Not getting light yet.

I took the keys to the Volvo from a hook behind Reception. The computer was winking, but there was nobody around. It seemed easier than getting a driver to skulk there with us. We could be there for ever.

Nothing much was going on outside Ulysses. 'No wrecks, nobody drownded, nothing to laff at at all.' A poem my dad used to read me about a boy called Alfred going to the seaside. I think it's the one where he gets eaten by a lion. '. . . And he lay in a somnolent posture, with the side of 'is face on't bars.' You have to say it in a Yorkshire accent.

In fact, the nightclub looked closed. There was a bakery a bit further up the road with its lights on and bready steam pouring out of it, only a bit hotter than the night air, but here – nothing.

'You stay there,' I said to McCaughrean, who was wheezing in the passenger seat.

'What am I supposed to be doing?' he asked.

'I don't know. Take photos of anyone who comes out,' I hissed.

'What is this? Infra red?' he growled, hauling bits and pieces out of his bag. 'Last stake-out I was on, someone punched me in the head,' he told his lens box.

While he was grumbling, a huge black beetle of an assassinate-me car drove up with an escort. It was familiar in some way. In one way.

'Oh, holy fuck,' I said. 'Duck.'

'Yes?' McCaughrean answered.

'No, you idiot. Duck down,' I said, dragging him beneath the window frame by his shirtsleeve.

'Well, I'm not going to get much of a picture from down here,' he whispered, his sweating cheek brushing against my forehead.

'Good point,' I said, and let him sit back up. I crawled into the back so I could lie down flat.

Don poked his camera out of the window and clacked the shutter up and down a few times. Clunk. Clunk. Clunk.

'What can you see? What can you see?' I asked. I felt like a child watching a Jubilee procession.

'Guy with one eye. Israeli General. Your friend. Some Serbs. Jesus. Big Serbs.'

'Russians,' I corrected him. He'd been in Bosnia.

'An Arab. General's got his arm round his shoulders. Bet that's a first,' McCaughrean commentated as his camera whizzed and whirred.

'Oh my God, oh my God, oh my God,' I said to the sunroof. 'We've got him.'

McCaughrean flew backwards into the car and shouted, 'Drive! Zanetti! Drive!'

'What? What? You drive!' I screamed, feeling the urgency, hearing the heavy boots running towards us. The General's bodyguards shouting.

'I can't, Zanetti! I can't drive!' he yelled at me.

'Oh Jesus,' I said, scrambling over into the driver's seat, but knowing I wasn't going to make it in time. They dragged me out of the door, two of them, the nozzle of an M16 in my face. With McCaughrean they were having more trouble. He wouldn't budge.

'Don't touch my fucking camera, you poof!' he shouted as a couple of enormous, reasonably heterosexual-seeming soldiers tried to haul him from his seat. It was then I realized that his attack on the air steward on the way over had had nothing to do with the trolley-dolly's actual sexuality. It was just something he said to anyone who went near his equipment. His camera equipment. I could see from my position in the dirt that he was trying to shove himself over into the driver's seat.

'McCaughrean!' I screamed at him. 'Put it in D. D! D! Press the pedal on the right!'

With a soldier sprawled across his lap, McCaughrean drove the Volvo round the corner at a screech, lurching and jumping it into life. His passenger was thrown out at the first turn.

The General, who stood watching from the doors of Ulysses, waved his arms to his men in a cut-off gesture to signal letting McCaughrean go. He can't have registered the camera, then, I thought. They had let me stand up now, but they surrounded me like some kind of dance troupe doing a military-style number, their guns pointed inwards at me as I pirouetted in the middle or something.

'Miss Zanetti,' the General smiled, walking slowly over to us. He pushed an M16 out of the way to get to me and he took my chin in his mutilated hand. 'Silly girl,' he said. I had two options here, I realized later. I could have smiled and been cute and sexy, told him I was just doing my job and we could come to some agreement. I swear, had it been any other story, that's what I would have done. I am more than happy to compromise myself for safety. Principles come pretty low on my agenda. But this man, as far as I could make out, was having sex with children. Or at least pimping them. So I took option B and spat in his face.

Not unpredictably, it didn't go down very well. I thought he might punch me. I wanted him to. But of course he doesn't hit women. The fucker. 'Ali. Look after her, would you,' he said to the Palestinian, a man with green eyes and badly rotten teeth. He smelt faintly of urine. At least, the small of his back did and this was where my face was. I think it is called a fireman's lift.

He carried me on to and across the Ulysses dance floor in this position. Svyeta had been right about the clientele here. They were keeping themselves to themselves. On the other hand, I wondered if anyone would really come and help you, wherever you were. People quite often describe awful things happening to them on crowded streets in London and people just walking by. Like that poor little boy in Liverpool.

I hit the guy in the back.

'Put me down. I'll walk, OK?' I shouted. I was probably heavy. He put me down and pushed me up a flight of stairs at the back of the club. They were narrow and dark and painted red. Behind a flimsy door three men in black leather jackets were smoking. They were young and Slavic with gold jewellery and dead eyes.

'Don't let her leave,' Ali told them in barely comprehensible Russian and went out, slamming the door. These weren't Svyeta's rapists. They were, by the look of them, more junior slime-balls.

They stared up at me, surprised. I know I should have been terrified, but it just didn't click in. I think if they want to keep you somewhere, then it's because they aren't going to kill you. I didn't believe the General would have me killed. I don't know why, but I just didn't. He liked the game of it all too much.

There were a couple of empty vodka bottles on the floor and some posters of naked women on the walls, torn out of magazines. These men were obviously more used to having to beat the crap out of their captives before they could be persuaded to stay. One of them dragged his gun out of his belt as though it were the last thing in the world he could be bothered to do. A teenager forced to pick his socks up off the bathroom floor. He pointed it at me and said, 'Sit down.'

I walked forwards, towards the sofa, and he rolled his eyes, flicking his wrist to the corner. 'Over there,' he said. 'Fuck.' The kind of 'look at what idiots I have to contend with' type of obscenity.

'She Russian?' the one with a bird tattooed on to his neck asked.

'Hardly,' the gunman sneered.

They seemed to be doing the ex-pat thing of claiming their girls are the most beautiful in the world. I wish they all could be Californian. That kind of thing. I thought about that singer in the Beach Boys who took so much acid that he now has a live-in shrink. I can think of plenty of people who could do with one of those.

I sat down on the floor and leaned back. I lit a cigarette and let them bicker about whether or not I was allowed to smoke. There were no windows in here. Another door, though. Maybe a loo.

They turned the vast television back on. They had been watching some porn video that they'd turned off when they heard the boss coming. Occasionally flashing a glance over at me (I smiled amicably), they watched the grotesque writhing and groaning without interest. Genitalia aren't attractive in themselves at the best of times, and when six times larger than life . . . they were obviously bored out of their minds, watching because they can.

'Hey! Can I have a vodka?' I shouted in Russian.

Somebody pressed the pause button, leaving an enormous dribbling erection frozen on the screen above the grimacing face of a teenaged girl. The men looked at each other and back at me.

'You ours?' the gunman asked, meaning, are you Russian?

'No,' I said. 'But I want a drink.'

He shrugged, hauled himself up and passed me the bottle without a glass. I swigged at it and shut my eyes. What am I supposed to be doing? Make friends with your captors. That's what the *Bad News Bible* advises. Bloody hell. OK.

'I once knew a man in Novyoskol who made the best samogon I've ever had. One shot completely blew me away,' I said, trying to get on their wavelength.

'Yeah,' said the bird one. 'You can't get decent stuff here. We have this flown in.' He picked a bottle up off the table. It was the cheapest, vilest, most scabrous kiosk vodka in the whole of the Former Soviet Union. People will do anything for a taste of home. ''S delicious,' I smiled.

It's the total mundanity of these things that is so strange. When you hear about people being taken hostage on the news, it sounds so incredibly apocalyptic somehow. As though they are having their ears sliced off and are locked in a freezing cellar with no clothes on and only rats' shit to eat. Of course, sometimes they are. But in general they are sitting in a small room being guarded by a moron. Nothing to do, nothing to say. They have never thought before you get there about where or how you are going to go to the loo. They have never decided who's going to feed you or what the guarding rota is. They stand around arguing and hassling and wondering whether or not they ought to be brutalizing you more. That's what everyone says. Especially in Beirut in the eighties. I knew people who got out complaining only that they had never been so bored in their entire lives. It's not everyone who can play mental chess or knows enough Shakespeare to act it out as a one-man show.

'Toilet?' I asked.

All three of them pointed to the door I hadn't come in by. All three of them had been missing the bowl for some months now. However, there was a window in here. Worth knowing. Who was it? Phil Gold who escaped through a window in Beirut.

We must have been doing shots and playing gin rummy for about six hours by the time Ali came back in. We were all very drunk. There was no way of knowing what time of day or night it was. For these low-level thugs it was always three o'clock in the morning. Time for more cigarettes, vodka, porn. Bird, I had noticed (it was a swallow, I think), was a bit younger than the others, with less of a taste for it all. He was slighter, less scarred, fewer fresh wounds. The other two had the knuckles and black eyes to show for their profession. And it was Bird, thank God, who was left to guard me while Ali and the other boys went off to half kill someone.

If one was going to judge the whole of humanity by Eden's baseline thesis, then this was the boy whose mother had loved him the most of the three. I told him my name was Vera. He told me his name was Gleb. He was from a town with a number rather than a name. A closed place fenced off from the world where they produced plutonium. Now that the factory is derelict and the state benefits dried up, the whole place is an enormous allotment where the women grow vegetables and the men drink until they die. Gleb and two friends had shared four bottles of vodka and then circumcised each other as evidence of Jewishness for the Israeli embassy.

'It's not too bad now. Want to see?' he asked.

'No. You're all right,' I said, wincing. 'Did anyone check?'

'Of course not. I had to invent a grandmother in the end. Then I found out I was Jewish all along,' he laughed, pouring himself another drink. This is the sort of thing that Russians actually think is funny.

'Jesus,' I said. I needed to get out quick while I was still sober enough to climb out of the window.

'Why don't you do something about the children?' I asked him, pretending to know more than I do. Largely effective. Unless the subject is nuclear physics or something.

'What about them?' Gleb dribbled. Oh, don't pass out. Please don't pass out.

'Well. Couldn't you stop them doing it?'

'Look, it's no worse than their life in Moscow. Probably better,' he shrugged. 'Film them, don't film them. What's the difference?'

Oh God. They were filming them. I needed not to be sick.

'Filming them?' I said. The pounding music from the club, I noticed suddenly, had stopped a long time ago. Maybe when the others were still here.

'It's a live web cam,' he said, almost impressed by the technology, though trying to pretend he took hi-tech for granted. I don't suppose they have live Internet porn in Town No. 793. Or perhaps these days that's all they have. Russian for web cam is 'ueb kam'.

I looked around for the camera, pretending to think it might be here that they do it.

'Where's the camera, then?' I asked, not too interested. Just idle chat, like the circumcision story. He laughed.

'Not here. The back room. They'll be doing one now. That's where the others have gone. I don't usually get involved. Just the older girls sometimes,' he said. He was talking completely casually. Just doing his job. Sometimes I do the photocopying. Sometimes the faxing. Other times I rape children. I wondered about microphones. Whether people are more turned on if they can hear the screaming child. People. They are not people, strictly speaking.

'Listen. I need to get out of here quickly while I'm still sober enough to climb out of the window,' I told Gleb. He beamed happily and tapped the gun at his waist.

'I'll kill you if you try,' he said – perfectly friendly, though not lying.

This is a thing I learnt in my early teens. Never lie, and people always think you're joking. It's like coming home and telling your dad you've had sex with two boys and drunk fourteen Southern Comfort and lemonades. Everyone just laughs and you go off to bed unmolested. Or shoplifting. If you just pick up the clothes you want and walk out of the shop, nobody tries to stop you. The theory being, I suppose, that if they do, you can just plead mitigating dippiness and say you forgot to pay. You've got your period.

'Just a sec,' I said. 'I'm going to see if I can squeeze my arse out of that window in there.'

Gleb laughed and lit a cigarette butt. We had reached that stage. I think he thought I needed a piss. I creaked the door open and held my breath against the sweet smell. Night to day. It was broad daylight in the loo and I realized only now that the other room was very air-conditioned. In here it was festering and fuming and congealing and steaming. I held my breath and climbed up on to the rim. I held on to the cistern and hauled myself up.

Gleb dragged me down and bashed me across the face with the back of his hand. He pulled me by the hair back into the main room and then fate smiled on me. Well, it was about bloody time she did. She'd been scowling at me for years. He wanted to kick me, I think.

He sort of walked backwards across the room as though he planned to do a kung fu kind of running kick in the head. Do not try this when inebriated. Surely he knew this. He landed on his back so I could almost hear his spine crunch. He hit his head on the corner of the table and I wasn't about to hang around to see if he was going to be OK. Sasha was in this building. I just knew it.

I ran back into the loo, one hand to my swelling cheek and would have just hurled myself out of the window if it had been big enough for hurling. I went out feet first, and nobody followed me. Maybe Gleb was dead.

I let go of the pipe I was holding and dropped much further than I had expected out into the blistering heat and blinking light of the day. I landed hard and I think I fucked one of my ankles. In any case, it hurt as I staggered around in the heat, trying to get as far as possible away from Ulysses. I took my phone out of my pocket, but the battery was gone (what kind of idiot takes a hostage and lets them keep their mobile phone? They could probably have stolen the few shekels I had on me if they'd had the sense as well).

People were staring at me and I thought I might pass out. No self-respecting taxi was going to pick me up in this state. Eventually, or probably fairly immediately, but every step really hurt, I stumbled into a phone box. The only person who picked up was McCaughrean.

I walked frantically away from the club along the road I knew Don would have to take. Every step I heard was some Russian chasing after me with an Uzi.

'My hero,' I said, when the dust cleared around my saviour's car, shimmering in the heat. 'Thanks for rescuing me.' I climbed up to my feet and fished my sunglasses out of my pocket. Feeling better already now I wasn't alone.

'We were trying, you silly cow,' Don complained and pulled me along into a taxi. 'I called the police hours ago. They said they'd deal with it. Wouldn't let me get involved. Had to give a statement and stuff. What perfume is that, Zanetti?' he asked.

'Bugger off,' I apologized, pulling a packet of cigarettes out of his shirt pocket. I made the cab drive back round to the club and I watched for a bit. I really needed to get these arseholes now, it was making me foolhardy. I wanted to see the arrests about to take place. Needed to see them for myself.

There were families walking around near us. I hoped Eden had dealt with the creatures in his charge. Taken them to Bryan, perhaps? Finding out could wait until I'd recovered a bit. After all, he'd seemed like a competent enough father.

I saw a little boy eating a slice of pizza, a mother adjusting her daughter's hair clips. So close, but in a whole nother universe. A police car pulled up with some flak-jacketed hard guys in it and two very senior types in suits. One of them female. One of them Whitehorn. The sky was offensively blue. Like at my father's funeral.

Don and I waited in the car. There was nothing to say. Don blinked very hard when the shots were fired and I let the tears spill out of my eyes. I couldn't remember when I was last asleep.

Minutes later, two of the heavily armed policemen appeared carrying a pair of children each. I was saying 'Sasha' to myself over and over again. I had really lost it now. I craned to see, but the children's faces were a blur of fear and tears. I leapt out of the car.

'Please. Can I talk to them?' I asked the suit lady to whom they had been handed. They were shading their eyes from the sunlight, off their heads on something or other, one of them wrapped in a police blanket that looked as if it had blood on it. 'Please. Please.'

'I'm sorry. We need to process them first. The police station. The hospital,' she said, starting to help them into the car. I wanted to say they'd been processed enough.

'God, you bitch!' I snarled at her, feeling like a lioness trying to get her cubs. A hungry lioness at that. I shoved her out of the way and pulled at one of the children, staring into her face. Her face. No; a girl.

'Sasha! Sashenka! Alexander!' I shouted, as though it was my own son I was trying to save.

And at that, a small voice, a tiny smudged blond voice said; '*Ya. Ya Alexander.*' I looked down into the car where he was huddled in the corner.

'Sasha!' It was him. The boy in his mother's photo. I smiled as though I was having a religious conversion. I'd found him! He was alive and he was going to see his mummy again. By this time, the insulted woman had righted herself and taken charge of the situation by pulling me away from the car door and slamming it hard.

'*Tvoyu mamu skoro uvidyesh!*' I yelled after the screeching vehicle. 'You'll see your mummy again soon.'

We didn't hang around to see who was dragged out or who had been shot. Certainly, I didn't care now we'd got the boy. At all. An ambulance pulled up as Whitehorn started the engine and the crew got out in yellow and green uniforms, as efficient as paramedics at a car crash or a natural disaster. Perhaps they didn't even know who they were dealing with. I suppose they wouldn't have done. They'd just get a phone call saying 'a shooting in Ulysses' and the address. Something like that.

'He's alive,' I said to Don, leaning back in my seat, shattered but happy. Weird to be happy over something like this. But it could have been worse. He could have been dead.

'So, something good's come out of it, then,' he said, trying to be jolly.

I tipped half a litre of shower gel into my bath and ran it without any cold water at all. I felt as though I might never be clean again. Like Macbeth. The multitudinous seas incarnadine.

And then I remembered Yo. For Christ's sake. Yo!

I leapt out and into a robe, running wildly through the hotel slapping wet footprints on to the floor. I dashed up to my minaret and shoved the door open, breathless, wet hair straggling over my face.

Yo lay on the bed which was soaked so deeply in blood it looked as though it must be fake; a work of art. The smell of the room made me retch. He had a bullet hole in the middle of his forehead and his eyes had been closed. It looked as though he had been asleep when it happened. I hoped so. Sitting on a chair by the bed, pale and quaking, was Zahir. He held a rose in his hand. When I stepped towards him, he held the hand out and opened it, palm up. I took the flower and saw the blood from where he had clutched the thorns. How long had he been here?

'Miss Zanetti. Help me. I didn't do it. This how I find him. An Israeli solider. They will torture me,' he said, begging me, holding the sleeve of my robe with his bloody hands.

'Of course they won't, Zahir. Nobody thinks you would have done it,' I told him, pushing my hair back and removing him from my robe. I found I was shivering.

'What the fuck were you doing up here, anyway?' I asked him, though I knew. I can't believe I hadn't guessed before.

'I love you,' he said, bowing his head to his chest and blushing. There was a soldier's corpse lying beside us and he was making his declarations.

'Zahir. Go back to Reception,' I said. 'Call the police.' I kissed him lightly on the cheek as he walked away, shoulders hunched. This hotel's body count was becoming less than acceptable.

CHAPTER FIFTEEN

I was still in my bathrobe watching a programme on BBC Prime where people have to cook things really quickly with fewer ingredients than they would ideally like. I tried to get to sleep, but the more you want it, the more it slips away from you. So I just lay there watching crap, smoking and drinking sweet tea.

Zahir, who bravely had gone straight back to work, recommended it for shock (and he should know) and brought it in quietly on a tray with a bunch of roses. He was drawn. Shattered. The hotel was swarming with policemen, but Zahir, so easily convinced by my platitudes, wasn't worried. Helped, I suppose, by the fact that I had let him tell the police I had found Yo. That I had been alone. I imagine that the army had been quick to declare Yo their double-crossing traitor on the run. I wondered if they believed the lie.

'I am sorry,' Zahir said. 'I never meant to frighten you.' He didn't meet my eye.

'It's OK, Zahir. You could have just spoken to me though,' I said. And he laughed.

The fat man who made a Thai chicken curry won and everyone clapped. Zahir closed the door gently behind him.

When the phone rang, I considered not picking it up, but the noise was annoying me so I took the call just to stop the ringing.

'Yup,' I said, watching the titles to the cooking show. Up next, another cooking show where you learn how to make an asparagus tart. I mean, I know it's a crass point, but people are dying out here. Maybe that's why the world needs its mind taken off the tragedy by this dross.

'It's me,' said Eden.

'Hello, me. Where are you?'

'I'm in the bar. I just wondered if I could pop up,' he said.

'Of course you can. What's the matter with you? You didn't have to phone, for God's sake,' I said, reaching out for my cigarettes.

'Stop shouting at me. I'll be two seconds,' he said. I laughed and put the phone down.

He was outside the door immediately and I opened it to him with my fag alluringly between my lips. I must look like some bedraggled mother of ten on a Glasgow housing estate.

He was holding a big black box tied up with a red bow. And a bottle of champagne with two glasses.

'Hello?' I said, letting him in. He skipped over to the bed and put the stuff down.

'Eden, I'm really tired. I've had a shitty couple of days. Week . . .'

'So? Sit down,' he said. I collapsed into a chair and Eden went into the bathroom.

He came back with my hairbrush.

'Stop it,' I laughed, but he didn't. He tugged every last knot out of it while I sat there, irritable at first, but then smiling with my eyes shut.

'There,' he said, standing back to look at the electric frizz he'd created.

'You're an idiot,' I said.

'Open the box. Open it,' he wheedled, pleased with himself. So boyish and excited that I couldn't not smile.

I put my cigarette out and tugged at the ribbon, lifting the lid off to find another thinner ribbon round a parcel of crisp white layers of tissue paper.

'Eden,' I said, pathetically unable to get lost in the moment. Too much on my mind. 'Where are those boys?'

'I took them to Bryan. They're fine. Don't think about anything,' he instructed. 'Here.'

He shoved me out of the way so hard that I toppled over into my cloud of duvet. He produced a green dress, sort of shiny, the colour of the sea in an English winter.

'Put it on,' he said, grinning like a lunatic. It was quiet outside, somehow. The air seemed thick and dark. It must be night-time, I thought. I had been hiding in here since we got back from the club. For everything else, tomorrow would have to do.

'No,' I said. 'I can't wear something like that. I'll look like a drag queen.'

'Five minutes, Zanetti. Give me five minutes. Put the dress on. Drink a glass of champagne with me. Then I'll go,' he said, sitting down on the bed and flicking the television off with the remote control. A couple walked past the window outside, laughing.

'Promise?'

'Promisk,' he said.

'You're such a lying fucker,' I pointed out.

'True,' he admitted.

I threw my bathrobe over his head and stepped inelegantly into the dress. It was slippery, probably silk. Not that this was really my area. It came down to the floor and had no back to it at all. It just tied round the neck from the front. I felt like a mermaid.

'See. It's not so bad, is it?' he asked.

'Not bad. Idiotic,' I said, and sat down next to him on the bed, slumped and awkward. How do you sit in these things? You can't move your legs properly, you can't slouch around. It's like those Egyptian girls at the big flashy weddings in the Cairo hotels. They are so done up in sequins and netting that they can't actually move. They are just hoisted up on to a dais and people come up to congratulate them.

Eden popped the champagne cork, sitting in the yellow pool of light by the bedside lamp. The only light on in here. This time it was him with a cigarette between his lips. He poured us a glass each. Handing me mine, he got down on one knee at my bare feet.

'No!' I screamed, and leapt up, splashing him in the face with an inadvertent flick of my curls. 'No! No! Don't do this! Stop it!'

'What?' he asked, disingenuously, laughing. 'Sit down, you ridiculous girl.'

I sat down, scowling at him. I sank my drink in one go and burped.

'Faith. Faith Zanetti. Marry me will you?' he asked.

'You absolutely must be fucking joking,' I told him, shaking my head. 'You've completely lost your mind.'

And then he kissed me.

I was too tired not to. Too weak to leave my defences up. Anyway, I love the smell of him and the feel of him. I love that I seem to sink into him as though I belong there. I kissed him back and I put my hands in his hair. When we are like this it almost feels as though we really could drag the pain out of each other and make it all OK again. We tried, at any rate.

Afterwards, I curled into a ball with my head on his chest and he put his arms round me.

'You are an idiot,' I whispered.

'No I'm not,' he said. We could hear the thump of a band out by the pool. There was a wedding party in the hotel. 'If you go in with a high bid you never go away with nothing.'

234

I kicked him as hard as I could be bothered and fell asleep.

I dreamed I was eating ice-cream sundaes at Serendipity with my mum and dad.

It was getting light when I woke up. This was the first time I'd heard a real dawn chorus here. I couldn't tell whether the phone had woken me up or whether it had started ringing just after I'd woken up. It is a long time since I've been as out of it as that. I'm usually just on the edge of sleep – half aware of what's going on. Someone once asked me what time my flight was in the morning. I was fast asleep and didn't remember anything about it, but I told him I needed to be at Terminal Four by six-thirty.

I picked the phone up and coughed a bit.

It was the General.

'Faith?' he asked, knowing it was me.

'Speaking.'

'Expect something from me,' he said, and hung up.

I had been expecting something from Meier for a while. I staggered into the bathroom to splash my face. I made a point of not looking at Eden Jones asleep in my bed. Standing round like a teenager, thinking about how sweet and vulnerable he looks? Nope. I scavenged around for some clean clothes and found them in a carrier bag Eden must have brought back from Edmonds's. Laundered. Pressed. My jeans had a crease down the front. I lit a cigarette and opened the door on to the courtyard.

'Faith?' Eden was calling after me.

I leant back in.

'See you later. Thanks for the dress,' I said, looking at it crumpled on the floor. But in a tiny gesture of thanks, I suppose, I bent down to pick it up and put it back in its box. I didn't fold it or anything, but it seemed too much of a smack in the face to just let it lie there getting spoilt. I'm glad I did. There was a card at the bottom of the box. A scrawl of hurried biro on it. 'R – hope this is the one you were on about. E.'

I smiled to myself and somehow my heart and stomach seemed to relax back into place. I admired him the chutzpah. And now I didn't have to think about him at all. Porcupine. I slipped out of the door, invulnerable.

There were policemen walking around at a near run. One of them passed me, his hand on his gun, his eyes flashing. I put my sunglasses on. The manager ran after a pair of black boots, begging them for a bit more discretion.

McCaughrean was reading the paper and licking some cappuccino foam off his spoon.

'Glover's gone,' he said, satisfied, sucking a sticky finger.

'Where?' I asked, sitting down with a quick glance back at the policeman. It seemed very unlikely to me that the lemon tree in question was hiding Martin Glover. Perhaps he hadn't actually seen any pictures of him.

'Buggered off in the night,' said McCaughrean, folding his paper up and looking up at the sky. There was a cloud in it. The first anyone had seen for ages.

'Cloud,' he pointed. I nodded.

'What? In disguise?' Grant Bradford wondered from the next table, and put my cigarette out in the ashtray. 'The whole place was crawling with guards.'

Don laughed at the idea of Martin in disguise, perhaps dressed as a Saudi woman? He asked me if I was all right.

'Not too bad,' I said. 'Slept well.'

'Where's Jones?' he wanted to know.

I said I didn't know and hoped I wasn't smirking. I also hoped Eden wasn't about to come out of the door of my room. Surely he'd be more discreet than that? He wasn't.

'Morning, Donald,' he said to McCaughrean, pleased with himself.

He was energetic, glowing.

He shouted 'coffee please' to a waiter and smiled broadly, leaning his elbows on the table, eyes glittering.

'Glover's done a runner,' I told him and his face fell.

None of us wanted to believe that Martin had killed Shiv. As the evidence, or at least suspicion, mounted against him, we talked about it less.

'Probably just gone out to do some sightseeing or something,' Don offered and we all mumbled and shuffled and coughed.

''Spect so,' I said, lighting a cigarette. Sightseeing, my arse.

I borrowed Don's phone and tried to find Svyeta. I knew it wasn't my job to reunite her with her son, but I was worried the bureaucracy might be delaying things. I just wanted to put her out of her misery. I'd tried to persuade Eden to find him for me, but he wasn't having any of it.

'What am I? Bill Gates?' McCaughrean kept moaning, tapping his watch to tell me I'd been on the phone long enough, like a parent to a teenager.

'Fuck off,' I mouthed, fishing a few shekels out of my pocket and tossing them on to the table in front of him as payment. I know all the war photographers have been forced to go freelance, but surely they get expenses if they're actually on assignment. He has always been a cheap bastard, McCaughrean. Still, I imagine his alimony is pretty hefty. He is in a particularly good mood at the moment, despite everything that's been happening, or rather because of it. He has got a bad scratch on his face from the retreating belt buckle of the soldier who fell out of the car trying to stop him outside Ulysses the other night.

It turned out, four cigarettes and seven calls later, that Svyeta had been moved to the Kfar Shaul psychiatric hospital where all the messiahs hang out. The policewoman I spoke to told me she thought Mrs Karamazova was a grave danger to herself and had had her sectioned. They don't call it that here, but that's what it is. She was not to receive non-family visitors. I wondered if I could get away with a Russian accent and pretend to be her sister. I flicked the phone shut and bit the aerial until McCaughrean slapped me.

'My phone,' he said.

'Ow,' I moaned, just to keep him happy.

'Not wearing your new dress today, Faith?' Eden asked, trying to embarrass me.

McCaughrean sputtered with laughter, thinking, presumably, that Eden had come in on his hilarious joke about my toilette.

'No. It's true. Eden very kindly bought me a dress, but I won't be wearing it today,' I explained. 'You can borrow it if you like, Don.'

I snatched Don's phone back and tried to ring Bryan. I wanted to check up personally on Marwan. They would have their own lives, of course (I hate the idea of journalist as saviour), but just to check they were safe is all. I'm not about to start adopting every abandoned child I ever lay eyes on. I'm not maternal that way. Really. I just wanted . . . well. To see if they were all right.

I wondered what happens to them now. Do they grow up into normal, well-balanced adults who have put their tragic pasts behind them? Or do they find themselves on a plane to Cambodia when they are thirty-two? Off on a paedophile holiday to a country too poor to care? I mean, are there children who have been raped and tortured who grow up to have a job and a family or is this it for them? Have their lives been finished before they started? I was round at a friend's house in London once, watching her children play. The daughter, who was naked and about two with a dimpled bottom, was showing the paddling pool to her stuffed toys. 'It's all right, little one,' she told a fluffy alligator. It's not a complicated thing. They watch the adults and older children around them and they imitate. So, presumably, abused children play at abusing their toys and then go on to practise on real people. Or not.

'Come and see for yourself, Faith dear,' was what Bryan said.

'Thank you. I will,' I nodded.

I sighed a bit too ostentatiously (the others looked at me with raised eyebrows), threw Don's phone back to him and skulked off to my room to look indecisively at a pile of mail that Zahir must have left and some television news. We despise it and we watch it anyway.

Weirdly, it was showing General Meier himself at a press conference. I thought of him somehow as already arrested, already gone. After all, his accomplices, if that's what they were, would be pretty quick to grass him up for a lighter sentence. I didn't imagine there was a great deal of inter-paedophile loyalty going down. He was shown behind a lectern (was that supposed to make him look more thoughtful?) demanding an end to Palestinian violence or something ground-breaking like that. I didn't listen properly. Abroad, everyone has an educated opinion on what ought to happen in the Middle East. When you're actually here, though, it is much clearer that they are all mad and fanatical and childish. Neither side wants to be gracious because they don't want to be accused of any kind of vote-losing wussiness, so, in order to keep their nutter voters happy, they take the hardest imaginable line and go on fighting. Brilliant. I flicked it off.

The gang story I was doing in El Salvador was a bit like this. Both sides spent the whole time cataloguing the crimes of the other side and explaining the very detailed reasons for which they were going to have to kill them all. Neither had the foresight or generosity of spirit, or whatever it is you need, to realize that some sort of peace deal was the only way that any of them could possibly be left alive.

I remember reading a piece once about Washington DC and the appalling number of murders they had there one summer in the eighties. The journalist did her calculations and concluded that if the murder rate continued at the current rate, then everyone in Washington DC would be dead by 2003. In fact, of course, the killing slowed down a bit and, in any case, hardly anyone white has ever been killed in Washington DC. Hardly anyone white even knows that anyone black lives there. American racial segregation is weird. The land of the free.

Anyway, perhaps this is just what all human relationships are like. Couples who can't be kind to each other because of years of real and perceived slights. 'I would like to have loved him, but he fell asleep straight after sex on our wedding night and we just got off on the wrong foot.' You don't row with someone you don't know very well. Whereas, if you've been bickering over the same bit of stupid land as long as you can remember, there is too much bitterness (and ignorance and patheticness) for anyone to say, 'Oh, no, please, you have it' or 'Don't be silly it's yours too . . . Hey! Let's share it!'

Everything was different out in Bethlehem. The rugged, rustic feel had gone. It seemed like a million years ago that I had first driven out here and seen a few lonely huts, an idealistic priest and some happy ragged children getting a fresh start. Not that I had really thought that for long. Maybe the first hour of my first visit. Still, it's hard not to have a kind of nostalgia for the past, a time when things were more innocent. Or, at least, a time when we didn't know they weren't. Now there were probably four adults per child. A whole line of green crescent vans was lined up under the olive tree where I had first parked. Their back doors were open and a white-coated doctor was rummaging around fetching syringes, bottles of something or other from cold boxes, swabs and bandages. A couple of tents, or more like marquees, had been put up in front of the children's house and Palestinian Authority soldiers were guarding the place along with some Israelis. I was glad McCaughrean was here to catch it.

Bryan hobbled up to us. He was an old man now, all this nightmare seemed to have finished him off, already resigned to the fact that his orphanage was out of his hands. I kissed him on the cheek and handed him the carton of cigarettes I had promised him a week and a lifetime ago.

'Come and join the circus,' he said, smiling. He brushed the

240

biggest grasshopper I have ever seen off the sleeve of his black jacket. A locust, maybe.

McCaughrean, whose excitement I could feel boring into my spine, rushed off straight away at the invitation, his camera glued to his face. Eden shook Bryan's hand.

'Thanks again for helping me with Marwan and his friends,' he said.

'A pleasure,' Bryan told him. 'Marwan is a lovely boy. I think he'll do well, that one.' But Bryan would think that.

I put my sunglasses on my head (they sort of rest there in a wild blonde nest) and looked around. There were little groups of kids everywhere and I scrutinized them all from a distance until I saw him.

'Hey!' I shouted and waved through the blaze of sunlight.

Seeing me, Marwan came running towards me followed by one of the other boys from Edmonds's place. They stopped in front of me and I crouched down longing to hug them but not wanting to breach any kind of protocol. So I smiled instead.

Marwan tugged his chin.

'Beard,' he said and bent over double, giggling with his friend who could hardly contain himself.

'Beard,' the other one repeated, and they ran off.

'Do they recover, then?' I wondered.

'If we didn't believe we could help, Faith, we wouldn't try. Nothing and nobody in this life is without hope,' Bryan explained. I hate the use of 'this life'. The implication being that there's another one. Of course. He believes in God. Which is cheating. On the other hand, it isn't just him, is it? It's Adam and all these doctors and counsellors and volunteers. They aren't doing it for God. They know what they're doing is a drop in the ocean, but they do it anyway. If you can help a little bit it's all worth it. That's the theory, anyway. So hard to practise. That's what Bill Clinton said in the speech I heard him give. He was talking about good advice or something. 'It's easy to give, but it's hard to live,' he croaked. Speech-writer's a genius. Or is it the delivery? Delivery, I should think. He churns out the corniest soundbites as though he is reading the Ten Commandments. Which got delivered just around here somewhere.

Father Bryan introduced me to the child psychologist who had been called out to deal with Marwan and his friends and the Russian children. She'd been working with victims of sexual abuse for fifteen years. She was called Wafa and had big eyes like a deer and gold butterflies in her ears. She said she would show the General's picture to a few of the children for me. I'd brought a head-shot torn out of a paper.

I knew what their answer would be. After all, one of the Russian children had already told me that Meier had brought them out here.

'Trained at Berkeley,' Father Bryan nodded and he went off to talk to Eden in his hut.

It had been cleaned since I'd last been here and now had the atmosphere of a stage set. The bustle and paraphernalia of the twenty-first century made Bryan's monastic existence and the rural antiquity of his orphanage and house look somehow hokey. Mocked up for a performance.

Eden winked at me as I came in. He was trying to preserve last night's intimacy. Keeping a secret.

'Hello,' I said. I wasn't going to tell him I'd read his note to Ronit, but I didn't want him to start introducing me to people as his girlfriend. 'Hi, this is my fiancée, Faith. We slept together yesterday when I seduced her with a dress I'd bought for someone else. Stupid, isn't she?' No thanks.

I gave the first boyfriend I ever had, Tony I think it was, a pine cone and a packet of Space Dust. He left the pine cone round at my house where I'd given it to him and the next day my friend Claudia was eating Space Dust she said she'd got off Tony. 'I don't like it much,' he told me when I confronted him. That was about the last time I ever gave anyone a heartfelt present.

I sat down to drink some tea when we all heard shouting from over at one of the tents. Father Bryan excused himself and Eden and I paced around the hut, looking at each other suspiciously. The heat had become more oppressive since I'd got out of Ulysses. Humid now, rather than dry. The kind of weather that makes me feel tired and gives me a headache. An ambulance drove off with its siren wailing and I could hear the rustle of the white coats, the quick pace of decisive footsteps and the clunk of metal against metal as doors opened and shut and guns were put down and picked up. The sleepy *Children's Stories From the Bible* thing had been obliterated by efficiency.

Bryan came back in with Wafa. He stood deferentially behind her, like Prince Philip behind the Queen. It was dark in here and they were both blinking to adjust their eyes. I could see from her grim expression, though, that I'd got enough confirmation to start writing something.

'Miss Zanetti?' Wafa began, as though delivering an address, but she was finding it hard to go on. 'They all knew him,' she said.

'On the record?' I asked her.

'On the record,' she nodded.

I took her name and job title and stuff down. A few other quotes about traumatized children generally, and her work.

When we left, Eden shook her hand and patted Father Bryan on the back. We rounded McCaughrean up and headed back to Jerusalem.

'Amazing faces, some of those kids had,' he said, lighting a cigarette in the back of the car and leaning forward between us, his face dripping with sweat.

'So would you have,' Eden said.

CHAPTER SIXTEEN

I was standing in the lobby with Commander Whitehorn when McCaughrean came stumbling towards us down the corridor, blood pouring from his mouth and nose, his arm twisted at a hideous angle and hanging loose and dead.

Whitehorn was in a panic at losing his main suspect. He hadn't been allowed to arrest Martin (not enough evidence – I knew it!) and so had held him at the hotel pending permission from London or confirmation from the Israelis that they would accept his own investigation as evidence and arrest Glover themselves. Now he had done a runner and it was Whitehorn's fault. Officially, that is.

He seemed to think that hassling us might make him rematerialize. As though I wasn't as keen as he was to arrest whoever had killed Shiv. Keener, for God's sake.

'I'm telling you, I don't know where he's gone,' I said. I'd already tried suggesting sightseeing, but it hadn't gone down all that well. It's true, I can't think of anyone I know or have ever known who has gone sightseeing. You see them around, tourists. Even in places like this. I suppose the possibility of being blown up makes it more exciting. They have maps and phrase books and ugly American shoes that bounce. Like those sandals with bits of Velcro on them, the wearing of which pretty much ensures you a job on the *Washington Post*. At work, the uniform is suit and tie, and out of work the uniform is baseball cap, khaki shorts, white T-shirt and those sandals. You'd only have to turn up dressed like that on a Sunday and take over someone's desk. Nobody would turf you out. Unless you were black. Or perhaps especially not if you were black.

'It seems less than likely,' Whitehorn said.

He was right. I swivelled on a boot and lit a cigarette.

'He can't do without a drink,' I said. 'He'll be in a bar or near one. It shouldn't be hard.'

So I was taking sides with Whitehorn against my boss. I had admitted that I thought he was guilty. Not directly, but it was enough to make me need a drink myself. I had just turned towards the bar when I saw Don.

He was talking like someone with a mouth full of marbles. He held a hand up to his face, everything about him scrumpled in pain. He looked so pitiful, glancing from one wounded bit of himself to another, trying to decide which to announce as his main injury.

'Toof! Toof!' he said, pointing.

Whoever had attacked him had knocked a tooth out, apparently. Lifting an arm to point though, brought a cry of pain out of his bloodied swollen mouth. More at the sight of his arm than at the feel of it.

'Shit, Zhthanetti, do shomfing,' he sobbed, collapsing on to a chair. Whitehorn was already on his mobile getting an ambulance and wasn't looking when McCaughrean emptied his mouth. Into his good hand he spat what looked like a mugful of blood, half a tooth with a lead filling embedded in it and a Kodak film. I beamed.

'Hey, Don. You're a genius,' I said, and he winked. Or perhaps the purple swelling above his eye just dropped down all by itself. I wiped the film on the edge of my T-shirt and handed it to Whitehorn to pass on. The photos of General Meier, Ali and the Russians outside Ulysses, of course. Commissioned by me and I needed them more than ever. Meier, contrary to what I'd thought at the time, clearly had noticed he'd been snapped. And he'd tried to get the pictures back. Such a hopeless coward most of the time, but McCaughrean knew what was important when it really came down to it. After all, he was living without his kids. It probably takes that to get life's priorities in order. He hobbled outside with Whitehorn to wait for the ambulance and go and get cleaned up. Real injuries at last. And not self-inflicted or anything.

My Russian husband got himself out of military service twice. Once by slitting his wrists to the bone to prove suicidal insanity and once by getting a friend to smash his kneecap. Still limps today.

'I'm going for a shower,' I told Whitehorn, waving as I wandered off towards my room. The maids, I think, had just left. White towels, still warm, hanging fatly on the rail in the bathroom. My water carafe refilled and a bucket of ice glistening by it. The bed was changed – not so much as a whiff of Eden Jones – and turned down, crisp and neat. The television control in its holster, my clothes folded and put away. The folder with the hotel note paper in it lay open on the desk, and the light on my computer winked orange and self-important. So tidy, hotelish and ordinary. No sign of Shiv or of Yo's death, no indication that Hassan had bled into my arms a few miles away, that Esther was already buried, that McCaughrean had been almost killed just across the courtyard by men who had crouched behind his sofa in balaclavas. They had.

I immediately got a call from the desk in London asking where Glover was, and could I write a few hundred words about being held hostage. They had run a piece written domestically about the fact that I'd disappeared in the middle of an investigation into the Russian crime scene. Embarrassing, but I said I'd do it. They loved anything I filed at the moment, plus which I needed to butter them up. Huge, violent scoops with perfect pictures? That's me. I ought to get a raise. I would have hassled Martin about it if he weren't about to go to prison for the rest of his life. Or get shot in the back of the neck. Do they do that here?

'Listen,' I said to someone called Belinda whom I'd never met before. She was covering for Martin – usually did domestic leaders, apparently. 'I've got a really huge story about General Meier—'

'Yidzak Meier?'

'Yes,' I said and lit a cigarette, standing up by the phone, pacing about as far as the lead would let me.

'Jesus Christ,' she said when I'd told her. Then she laughed.

'Oooh! Do you think I can phone the editor and say, "Hold the front page?"'

''S worth a try,' I said and sat down to write. If I call it: Israeli General Heads Child Porn Ring, then the subs would change it just out of bloody mindedness. So I put, General Meier is likely to do life for crimes related to sex crimes against children. That way they could be pleased with themselves when they changed it to, Israeli General Heads Child Porn Ring. It must have been hours later when someone knocked at the door. I'd filed and I'd already had two long conversations with the lawyer who was lawyering it. Honestly, that's what they call it.

I shooed a lizard out from under my feet as I leapt up off the bed to get the door. I was yawning with my hand in front of my face ('Hand to mouth, honey,' Evie used to say) and I squinted into the sun.

Eden smiled softly. He looked as though he might be about to come in and fuck me again but instead he looked down at his right hand. It was attached to somebody else's. A little boy's.

'Sashenka!' I said, without knowing I was going to speak. I squatted down on my bare feet, my T-shirt smeared still with Don McCaughrean's blood, and I kissed him on the cheek.

'*Privyet, malysh,*' I said, taking his hand out of Eden's and squashing it in my own. 'Let's go and find Mummy.'

I led him through the glare of the courtyard and out to the front lobby where we ordered a cab and sat down to wait. Sasha, a freckled little thing with eyes two decades older than his body, sat very still and drank a Coca Cola. He fished the slice of lemon out and put it on the folded napkin.

'Don't like lemon?' I asked him.

He shook his head, solemnly.

'I like ice-cream,' he said, in croaky Russian.

'We'll buy you some,' I told him.

He looked out of the car window with zero interest. None of the things he saw held his gaze. It was almost as though he was blind.

'What happened?' I asked Eden, now that we were on our way. I was sweating in the humidity. Clouds were gathering. My temples were pounding.

'I persuaded one of the shrinks seeing to him that I'd take him to his mum,' he said, staring out at the traffic and the shops.

'Oh gross,' I sighed.

'Didn't touch her!' he smiled, putting a hand through his hair. He wore a white shirt that showed off his tan. Probably not on purpose.

'But how d'you find him?' I wondered, exhausted. I let my hair down. Eden tapped the side of his nose. Irritating. What he meant, though I couldn't be bothered to squeeze the details out of him, was that a police contact had, massively illegally, given him the address before the bureaucratic quagmire could heave out someone to reunite child being processed with grief-crazed mother. Sasha was just sitting watching television in the rec room, apparently.

At the hospital, the boy's weird composure broke a little. He seemed nervous here and hid behind me, clinging to the back of my jacket. His hand was small and dry. I don't like the smell of disinfectant. It has a reek of blood and death about it. I suppose just by association with morgues. Let's face it, the more disinfectant you need to use, the viler the thing going on.

Eden dealt with the official side of things. Sasha and I sat down on blue plastic seats shaped like the imprint of our bums. They stuck out of the whitewashed wall near the drinks machine. A doctor rushed past us, her stethoscope swinging, and her white coat floating out behind her. There was a very old woman in a wheelchair sitting near us, her head lolling over to one side, drool hanging from a corner of her mouth. In her wizened, tattooed and tea-stained left claw she held a Barbie doll.

When Eden had found out where Svyeta was supposed to be, we took the lift up to the seventh floor. I looked at my distorted face in the lift mirror and was surprised at how young and ordinary I looked. I felt a thousand years old. No relation to the darkly tanned woman with blond curls and a bloodstained T-shirt who looked back at me. Sasha stared at his trainers and Eden checked his teeth.

'Got to give up smoking,' he said to himself.

'Ha,' I said.

When we got out, a kind nurse met us and took us down a long corridor, carpeted with blue lino. There were colourful pictures on the walls, scribbled on to sheets of A4.

'The patients,' the nurse said, and he showed us his favourite one. A dog snarling at a soldier, the sky done in purple crayon. He knocked gently on Svyeta's door and turned the handle.

She sat in an armchair facing the window and I could see the straggles of her over-dyed hair waving above the top of the green fake leather. The nurse stepped back into the corridor to give us some privacy and I pushed Sasha forwards a little bit.

'Svyeta,' I said. 'There's someone here to see you.'

She didn't move, so I gave Sasha another little shove and Eden and I stood aside, smiling, waiting for the shriek of joy, the tears.

Sasha had now seen his mum's hand resting on the arm of the chair and finally believed us.

'*Mama! Mamochka!*' he cried, and ran forward, slipping a bit, righting himself and throwing himself into her lap with a sob.

She didn't speak or move. Something, I thought, wasn't right. I suppose Eden and I walked round to face her at the same time. Sasha was buried in her lap and the nurse faced us from his position out in the corridor. Our expressions told him to rush in to his patient. After all, she was on suicide watch.

Running, with a look of grey panic on his face, he stopped in front of Svyeta and stood very, very still, not wanting to disturb anything.

'Oh, holy fuck,' I whispered and walked as slowly as I could round to where he was staring at the boy and his mother. 'Please, no.'

I wanted to delay what I thought I would see for as long as possible, to put it off for another life when I could cope with tragedy upon tragedy and never give up hope.

But Svyeta wasn't dead. Her eyes were huge with tears and she smiled in a beatific way like the Madonna in an ancient icon. God was benign and she knew it. She rested a wasted hand on Sasha's head, a drip strapped into its vein, and breathed in.

'*Privyet, malysh,*' she said, closing her eyes. '*Privyet.*'

Eden was leaning his forehead against the wall, his arms raised above his head as though a policeman were about to frisk him. A tear was trickling down his face. There is some pain that is too much to bear and Svyeta had suffered it, but been reprieved. It almost didn't seem true.

After my dad was killed, I would watch news items about hostages who came home unharmed; missing journalists who turn up, ship-wrecked souls who are washed ashore and make their way home, lost schoolchildren who were just staying the night with a friend. To me, it is those stories that seem unreal. When you are waiting to hear, when your life is being ripped apart by horror, you hope beyond hope that the worst isn't true, that the loved one might pop back up like a flattened character in a cartoon. In my experience, though, they don't. So when I hear or see that they do, it does seem like some mystical and holy reprieve that I was never granted.

I left the room, white and perhaps in shock of some kind. I sat down where I was, on the top steps, and leaned into my knees. I cried so much that when a fat lady in a white cotton trouser suit of a uniform tried to help me up I had almost forgotten where I was. There were sirens out in the street and a commotion as professionals went about their harrowing business. When I met the nurse's eyes – Sylvia, it said on her name tag – I started sobbing again; hysterical, desperate crying. I clung to her arm and she walked me into a side room where Eden was smoking out of the window. He turned to look at me when I came in and his face was gaunt and grey, despite the sun. He smiled in acknowledgement of our victory and I started again, collapsing on to him, clinging to his shirt, wiping my tears and snot on to it. Sylvia handed me a paper cone of water and two pills. I couldn't think of anything I wanted more.

They took about fifteen minutes to work, for the calm to sweep over me. I went to church once with the school and the vicar put his hand on each of our heads in turn and said, 'The peace of the Lord be always with you.' Just what Father Bryan had said that time. I think the peace of the Lord must feel a bit like this. Opiate-based.

'Who do you think will play me?' Don asked, still talking, as he had been for at least six vodkas, about the film he felt sure was just about to be made. His heroism in not giving in to his attackers was not something we would ever hear the end of.

'That fat gay bloke in *Boogie Nights*? Silly name?' Eden suggested.
'Seymour Hoffman,' I said, dragging the words out.
'That's him.'
Don leaned forward and picked up his drink, groaning in agony.

'Fuck off,' he said, through his swollen lips. 'You can be Hugh Grant, then.'

Eden rolled his eyes but it seemed like quite good casting to me, really. I suppose he'd rather be played by a young Robert Redford or Marlon Brando. I think Hugh Grant might do tired and brave quite well. He might never quite manage the background despair, though. Most people don't even notice it in Eden. His act's so good.

'What about you, Faith?' Eden wondered, teasing me with his tone. Were we pretending to be having a good time, for God's sake? My pills were wearing off. 'Minnie Driver? Alex Kingston?'

'Never heard of 'em,' I said.

Don banged his fist on the table.

'No! Jennifer Aniston doing English. Wipe her make-up off, give her a fag,' he said, delighted. I haven't heard of her either, and I said so.

'Don't you read your own sodding paper?' Don complained.

'Not that bit,' I said.

I used to when I was in London. Maybe there was a time when those sections seemed quite new, when there was something liberating about admitting we like soap operas even though we are educated people who care about Palestine. Now, though, it has become depressing. Nobody seems to give a shit about anything except soap operas and what handbag goes with what. Not that I've ever even had a proper handbag. I expect Eden would like to see me carry one.

I think doing features for so long has made me hate them. You know, the pieces that get recycled every two years. Every two years someone finds an issue from two years ago and recommissions the same piece again. Men, students, who decide to become escorts. The seven most go-getting women in the country under thirty (how can we get photos of sexy young women in the paper today?). Is plastic surgery/milk/air travel/sex bad for your health? Young models who become anorexic/drug addicts/both. Pregnant is the new black. Childless people are actually childfree! The agony and heartache of IVF. Is Britain becoming more violent? What does your car say about you? Four women who lost their husbands to AIDS/air disaster/drugs/their best friend speak out. I want to be a man/woman. Students who strip for money. Oh, we've had that one. Two years must be up.

We had just about managed to salvage our fraying pretence at nonchalance when we were completely silenced by the sight of Martin Glover staggering in from the poolside. I knew he couldn't have gone far. I'd even told Whitehorn he must be near a bar. It was, however, on the surprising side to see that he really had hardly gone anywhere and that he was pretty much at the bar. He was dishevelled and filthy, a big yellow petal, browning at the edges, in his hair, a day or two of stubble on his chin and stains all over his trousers. He was carrying a bottle of wine and an empty glass with some dregs in the bottom. Ignoring us, he walked straight over towards the alcohol.

'I'll have another one of these, sweetheart,' he told Salim, who looked at us sheepishly. As far as I could tell, he had been taking wine out to Martin who had been hiding in the bushes by the swimming pool. Insane. Surely someone ought to just come and arrest him. The thing is, much though the idea of him murdering Siobhan was pretty convincing, he doesn't look much like a psycho-killer. What the fuck, I wondered, had she ever seen in this bastard? He had a pathetic air about him. Once so handsome, but now bumbling, pompous, getting a bit old for his job. His style getting more and more old-fashioned with every page printed. It was so motiveless. Was he really so jealous that he had killed her for fucking Misha? But he knew about all her affairs and took it on the chin. That's probably how he would have thought of it. In any case, she had lost her mind before he got here. That's why I got him to come. It didn't make quite enough sense for my liking.

Eden approached him at the bar.

'Won't you join us?' he asked him and the two men put their heads together, talking in a low murmur. Don and I smoked a cigarette and tried not to stare. When Eden led him up the stairs with his arm around his shoulders, we followed, taking this as a sign that it was time for bed. Typical of Eden to gently, sort of matily, take his hated enemy back into custody. Such as it was.

I had a long bath and stayed in until my skin shrivelled. I washed my hair and, for the first time for months, put a little bottle of hotel conditioner on it and combed it through. Evie used to do it once a week. It hurt and I cried. She always gives me a big bottle of poncy conditioner on my birthday. The kind of thing that comes in a glass bottle with a handwritten label. Always from a shop in Paris or New York. The new thing in hair care.

When I got out, I put my old grey T-shirt on, pressed by hotel laundry, and some clean white pants. I sat cross-legged on the bed and drank the whole carafe of water. I lit a cigarette and picked the phone up.

It rang for ages.

'Hello?' she said meekly. She sounded scared. I don't suppose her phone rings all that often.

'Mum?' I asked. She drew her breath in but didn't speak.

'Mum, I just phoned to see how you are,' I said.

She was silent for a bit and I pulled a scrag of nail off my thumb with my teeth and chewed it.

'Thank you, love,' she said and burst into tears. 'I'm fine.'

That night I dreamed I was falling.

CHAPTER SEVENTEEN

Zahir woke me up. He was carrying a huge sheaf of letters and messages to add to my pile. A waiter was clearing the breakfast stuff away. My first thought was: my piece is on the front page today. We're three hours ahead here, but the papers were already on the news-stands at home. I tried to picture it. Six hundred words on the front and then another two thousand, including a big profile, inside. I'd even done a first-person one, 'When General Meier took me for supper in Jerusalem, I never imagined as I swallowed my oysters . . .' Blah blah blah. I glanced outside. There was nobody about and the air was thick and hot. There were dark clouds in the sky.

I ruffled my hair and staggered towards the door.

'There is no more room in your mailbox,' he told me apologetically, not meeting my eye.

'Thanks,' I said, trying to pull my T-shirt down to decency.

I stumbled around for some cigarettes and lit one. I dumped the letters on top of the television and pulled my jeans on before I started at them.

Lots of stupid messages from London about stories they wanted or didn't want, a nice letter from Father Bryan with a card in it, a hideous painting of Jesus on the cross, suffering more than I'd ever seen. Gai Nikolayevich Gai was the artist, according to the back. Trust it to be by a Russian. Christ writhing in pain, the heat palpable, flies settling on his wounds. Really.

Then the big brown manila envelope. It seemed pretty innocuous until I looked at the handwriting. The thing he had been promising me for days now. Here it was. The thick nib of a fountain pen had swept across the paper, the ink seeping into the texture. Miss Faith Zanetti. I put my cigarette out and tore it open. Why couldn't he fuck off?

If this was something about Yo and how really he had been a traitor and blah blah blah. It turned out, however, to have nothing to do with Yo. By the time I'd finished, though, I wished it had had. Inside, was a grainy black and white photograph. In fact it looked more like something scanned off a computer. It was printed on that kind of paper, not the stiff Kodak stuff. I held it sideways to get rid of the sun's reflection and put my hand over my mouth. I could feel the vomit rising in my throat. When police officers have to deal with this kind of material, they get counselling.

'Oh shit,' I whispered to myself as I dropped the photo and ran to the bathroom. I knelt over the toilet bowl and waited for a few seconds while the beads of sweat gathered on my forehead. I think it was while I was wiping my mouth that I realized who the man in the photograph was. A little girl. Two? Three? Not more than that. Still a toddler. And a man. Yes, the picture was grainy and his face wasn't straight to the camera, or the web cam, probably. It was Martin Glover.

I drank a glass of water and tried to control my breathing. They teach pregnant women to do yogic breathing, don't they. Deeply in, but longer out. Something like that. I couldn't stop gasping. I seemed to be crying, though I didn't feel sad. Perhaps this is actually what shock feels like. I thought it was over, but when I walked slowly back into the main room, the tips of my fingers trailing against the walls, just the sight of the photograph on the floor, the shape of it, the flutter of it on the tiles, sent me back in to bring up what was left of my insides.

From a safe distance, I threw a towel over it before I went back towards the phone. I dialled Eden's room number but when he picked it up ('Yup?') I found I couldn't speak. I put my jeans on and lit another cigarette. How was it possible that Martin had managed to hide all this from Shiv? From everyone? Was it that doing it here with children who aren't English somehow doesn't count? You know, it probably was. We all feel separate on a story. Away from home. Things, affairs, things which are such a big deal in suburbia, don't seem to matter when people are dying every day, when every second of every life is danger and uncertainty. Maybe he really believed it didn't matter. We'll all be dead soon. That type of thing. Eden was with me a couple of minutes later, his arm round my shoulders. I was shivering uncontrollably and he held me tight.

'What is it? What is it?' he kept asking. I wanted to tell him, but I couldn't. He offered to fetch me a beer and I nodded. Before he left he lit a cigarette and put it between my lips. I touched his arm to thank him. I didn't want to be sick again.

Eden tied my hair back and put my jacket round my shoulders. I drank the beer quickly out of the green, glistening bottle and felt a bit better.

'You're wet,' I said.

He threw his hand towards the window. I got up and pulled the curtain back. It was pouring with rain. Great big fat drops of it smacking against the cobbled floor, pouring off the citrus leaves, soaking the remaining two tablecloths. Zahir ran out to take a pile of newspapers inside.

'Thank God for that,' I said and stepped outside in my bare feet. I shut my eyes and held my face up. Eden watched from the doorway, smoking. I waited until the jeans would need wringing out before I came back in.

'Silly thing,' he said, and threw me the towel that was on the floor. He didn't even notice what was underneath it.

I dried my hair a bit and suggested we go down to the bar. I could do with a coffee now. We walked arm in arm through the pounding rain to the corridor on the other side of the courtyard, drenched again by the time we got there.

Downstairs, there were two boys dragging a cover over the pool and Salim looked grim as he dried some glasses with a white dishcloth. He had the radio on. Some bleak love songs. When he saw me, he smiled and reached for the vodka.

'Too early. Coffee, please,' I said, and slumped down at the bar. I should tell him. I needed to tell him. It was weird that it was Eden I ached to tell. I didn't like what it said about me. About us. If only Shiv was still here I could have told her and I wouldn't have had to think about what I do or don't feel for Eden fucking Jones. And I would have told him too, if Martin Glover hadn't waddled over to join us.

'Hey,' Eden said to him, slapping him on the back too hard to be genuinely friendly.

'Morning, girls,' he answered, better presented this morning, but still tense and definitely not sober. 'File anything about the hostage thing, Zanetti?' he asked, trying to convince himself he still had a job instead of an impending prison sentence.

'Couple of days ago. While you were in the bushes,' I said to my coffee cup. Eden kicked me in the shin. I couldn't look at Martin. All I could think about were ways to kill him. I wondered what I could do with my coffee spoon. All those big bottles behind the bar. Smash two of them and he wouldn't stand a chance. Perhaps I was strong enough to strangle him. Fat neck, though. Probably not.

''Sup, Zanetti? Seem a bit down today? Letting the story get personal?' he slurred, his cheeks wobbling, even his tongue black with wine. He had aged a decade since last week and he hadn't looked good then.

'Sorry, Martin. The sight of you makes me want to vomit,' I said, standing up. I punched him in the head as hard as I could. Which is reasonably hard. He fell off his chair at any rate and there was blood on the tiles.

'Jesus, fuck, Faith. Innocent until proven guilty,' Eden said, trying to help Glover up.

'Fuck you, Jones,' I spat.

I threw my cup at the mirror behind the bar and Salim swore in Arabic as it cracked. From side to side. The curse has come upon me. I ran.

At the top of the stairs I had to sit down. I should have eaten something. I was feeling weird and rough. Dizzy, shell-shocked. I put my head in my hands.

I was shaking and swimming when Martin took hold of my wrists.

'Faithy, Faithy, Faithy,' he drooled. 'You don't believe all that, do you? I loved Siobhan. She was my girl.'

He was staring at me madly. His blue eyes were swollen and watering. He was begging me to believe him. His use of the word girl made me retch again and I stood up, trying to get away.

'Martin. Get off me. I know. I got a picture from the General.' I was pulling towards my room and he let go so that I fell over into the wet courtyard with the force of my own attempt to escape.

Apparently he hadn't read my piece over the Internet this morning. The hard copy wouldn't be here until tonight. He stood over me and we both froze.

Then he threw his head back and roared. He actually roared. He bared his chest up to the rain, swallowing the water that poured down on us. And he roared like a wounded lion.

I scrambled to get up, but he fell on top of me, lunging at me as though he was playing rugby or something. I could smell the foulness of his breath and feel the sweat from his face dripping into mine. He had his groin pressed into me and his stomach pinned me to the ground. He put his hands round my neck and pressed. His thumbs were already embedded in me before I even tried to scream and he'd winded me when he fell. I could feel myself slipping out of consciousness within seconds, my tongue pushed forward by the pressure. I felt a big raindrop splash on to it as my mind blackened.

I was still wet when I came round so it can't have been long. I was lying on my bed and Dr Ahmed was setting up a saline drip on a stand next to me. I opened my mouth to ask what he was doing and was immediately aware of raw pain in my throat. I put my hands up to my neck and he nodded.

'I've put some arnica on it. But it will remain sore,' he said. Great, thanks. So, I've salved my own professional conscience but done nothing to alleviate your suffering. Is that what you mean?

'What's the drip for?' I coughed, really in pain now.

'You are seriously malnourished, Miss Zanetti,' he said. 'When did you last eat?'

Now he mentioned it, I couldn't remember. With Cyclops at the French place, maybe. God. Was it? I'd had that beer this morning. Did that count?

At the thought and taste of the beer, I remembered what I was doing here and felt sick again. I looked around the room and saw McCaughrean smoking like a schoolboy by the door.

He flicked his butt out into the courtyard. I could hear the rain flooding down still.

'She's up,' he said to me, coming over.

'You're lucky I was around, Zanetti,' Don said. 'Cunt would have killed you.'

I smiled weakly.

'Thanks Don,' I said. 'You're my hero.'

McCaughrean blushed.

'Where's Eden?'

'Ah. Well. Glover tried to run after we'd . . . after I'd pulled him off, and Eden . . . Eden's gone after him.'

'What are you talking about?' I choked.

Apparently they'd left him blacked-out in the courtyard while they dragged me in here and when they went back out to deal with him he was already in a taxi outside, heading for Bethlehem.

'So Shiv saw the picture and went off her head?' McCaughrean said, trying to ease me away from panic about Eden. Or perhaps ease isn't the word, given his choice of diverting subject. He dumped his camera bag on the floor and helped himself to some water. Dr Ahmed taped the tube into the back of my hand and slid the needle out. He can't have had time to attend to any other sides of his practice lately. He'd been here practically every day for ages. I wondered how many years he'd been the hotel doctor, but it wasn't the time to chat.

He smelled of Ralph Lauren Polo today. Nice, really. Half a bottle less and it would have been all right.

'Thanks,' I told him. I was trying to be calm.

'I should think so,' I said. 'Misha must have got hold of it somehow. It must have been what he wanted to tell me.'

'Poor sod,' Don sighed.

'Where is the . . . where is the picture?' I asked.

'Police,' he said, and I nodded.

'And then when Glover came she went for him and he killed her?' he wondered, pacing about.

'Something like that. Must be,' I said, reaching for a cigarette. I forgot the drip stand and it nearly fell over. Dr Ahmed was packing up his bag.

'Naughty, naughty, lady,' he said, taking the open cigarette packet out of Don's hand to stop him offering it to me. 'You need to look after yourself a little bit, Miss Zanetti.'

Why? I thought it, but didn't say it. But really. Why? I remember telling an eighty-year-old Russian woman, a neighbour in Ryazan, that she shouldn't smoke. She had lived through the camps and was hacking and spluttering herself to death.

'Why not?' she asked, and I couldn't think of a reply. The next day I bought her a pack.

I mean, it's not as though I've got children who need me. A tear of self-pity snuck into my eye and I let myself think that Eden's arms look lovely when he leans on the back of a chair.

'I know,' I said. 'I will.'

I leant back on the pillows in a pretence at relaxation.

'Wonder where he's gone,' I said aloud to myself. 'If only there was an El Vino's in Jerusalem, he'd be easier to locate.'

I was beginning to understand, and I had often thought about it, how it was possible to hate someone enough to want to torture them. Had Martin Glover been sexually abused as a child? I suppose probably he had. Was he seriously mentally disturbed? Almost certainly. Did he choose to be a paedophile in a cold rational way? Of course not. Does this make me not want to kill him slowly? No. That's what a criminal justice system is for. To stop people like me getting there first. Obviously, I would never advocate lynching or anything close to it. Everyone deserves a fair trial and no punishment should be cruel or the death penalty. But God, they need to get these people quickly so that I don't do what I want to do. And it's different when you haven't seen it. When you haven't met the kids. Seen the photograph.

Ahmed left. One down.

'Don, luvvie. You couldn't pop down to the bar and get me a beer, could you?' I pleaded, smiling.

McCaughrean hesitated, the buttons on his shirt straining. It must have shrunk in the rain.

'Please?'

He shook his head and laughed. As soon as the door closed I leapt out of bed. The line was harder to get out than I'd thought. I pulled at it and a spurt of blood flew up into my face. I was left with a bleeding gash in the back of my hand. There might still have been a bit of plastic in there. I put my boots on and ran outside, across to the lobby and into the first taxi that skidded over in the mud.

'Bethlehem,' I said. 'Please.'

Agitated, I sat up straight, smoking, licking my wound to stop it bleeding, staring out at the rain all the way. The driver killed a dog on the road. At least, I hope it was dead. There was a big thud.

I overpaid him when we got there, to the square in front of the Church of the Nativity. The stalls had packed away in the rain and people huddled in shop doorways. There were no tourists. Nobody at all on the square, apart from a soaking wet Eden Jones. And me.

'Eden!' I shouted, running towards him, torrents of water pouring down my face.

'Jesus, Zanetti. You should be in bed. You look like shit. What happened to Dr Ahmed?'

'He said I was OK to get up,' I told him and showed him the back of my hand. He kissed it.

'I want to get this fucker myself,' I said.

'Me too,' Eden whispered. 'Me too.'

'What now?' I wondered. I looked around at the rain. A group of old men were drinking tea in a little café, playing chess, eating. People were drawing down the shutters on their souvenir shops. I heart Bethlehem. My sister went to Bethlehem and all I got was this lousy T-shirt. Plastic Jesus in a crib.

We looked into every alcove we passed, making our way round the empty, sodden tourist streets.

'I was right behind him. My cab was right on his bumper. He ran,' Eden said. 'I shouldn't have faffed around paying the driver.'

'Martin Glover ran and you couldn't catch him?' I said, almost smiling. Not quite, but nearly.

'Leave it, Zanetti,' Eden said, and patted the top of my head.

'Look,' I hissed, and flattened myself against a wall. I'd seen him. There was no way he could have waddled far. He was here. Martin was sitting at a low table drinking a beer, talking to a young man. Through the steamed-up windows it was hard to tell if he was dripping water or sweat or both.

'Did he see you?' Eden asked. I shook my head.

'No.'

I leant round again, peering now through multi-coloured plastic ribbons that curtained the door. It smelt of cigarette smoke and greasy cooking. There were a few men playing pool at a knackered-looking table.

'He's giving him money,' I said. Eden smiled in an imitation of politeness as a woman walked past under a big black umbrella, dragging two children behind her like a duck with her ducklings.

'Jesus,' he said. It occurred to us both that even now, even after everything, he might be buying a child for sex. Or at least it occurred to me.

'Shit. Shit. He's coming,' I coughed. My throat was agony. I must have a purple bruise all around my neck.

We dashed through the pelting rain to a crumbling doorway opposite.

Glover didn't notice us. He was white and shaking, walking through the weather as though he didn't even notice it. Creeping behind him at a distance, we followed him back to the church.

'Where's he going?' Eden wondered.

'Fuck do I know?' I said, though neither of us was seriously addressing the other. We hid in a shop now, stared at by a crowd of crones who moved aside for us. Well. Hid. We were on the conspicuous side. The soaked tourists with the frightening injuries. That's me at any rate.

From there, from under the drumming of a red plastic awning, we watched Glover walk into the middle of the square, usually packed full of tourists, and he just stood there, waiting.

'Let's go,' I said. 'Let's get him.' I wrenched away from Eden, but he grabbed my hand and pulled me back.

'Wait,' he said. 'Wait.'

Glover looked as though he thought a bolt of lightning might strike him. As though he wanted it to. He looked up at the sky and then he suddenly sank to his knees, his hands clasped in front of him in prayer. He actually crossed himself.

'Fuck me,' Eden breathed.

And I couldn't wait. I ran out towards him, screaming. Water was pouring off him, he was appalled, terrified to see me.

'How could you?!' I yelled, drenched, running and mad. And then I was overtaken. By Commander Whitehorn and three Scotland Yard men in black boots that splashed through the puddles.

'Martin!' Whitehorn shouted. 'Martin!'

And the shot rang out from up in the belfry. I fell flat on my face, my hands covering two wet cobblestones, my knees stinging from the fall. A crack that might really have been lightning. I looked up, not sure if it was me who'd been shot or Glover. High up on a rooftop, I saw the face of the boy from the café. He pulled his weapon away from his eye to make sure he'd hit the target and he sat there for a minute. Taking a tissue out of his trouser pocket and wiping the rain from his face.

Whitehorn and his men were already seeing to what was or was just about to become a body.

I didn't rush forwards with all the locals to see whether Glover was dead or not. I knew he would be. He'd paid his money. I wandered back to Eden, still standing there under the dripping awning by the tourist shop.

I fell asleep in the taxi back. The rain was somehow comforting. Reminded me of home. Eden must have carried me into bed.

'Switch the telly on, could you?' I asked him later, sipping my sugary tea and stuffing another baclava in my mouth. Dr Ahmed had been none too happy about fixing the drip into the other hand.

'Never, never, in seven years of medicine, has a patient taken a drip out of her own arm. Irresponsible. Insane. What were you thinking?'

On and on like that, he went. Eden winked at me.

He fiddled with the controls until the haranguing tone of a news channel crackled into the room. It was BBC News 24 and they were running an emergency correspondentless piece from here. Pool shots from WTN and a domestic voice-over.

'British journalist Martin Glover was shot dead in the Israeli occupied city of Bethlehem just over an hour ago as he reported on the upsurge in violence in the area. Glover was the *Chronicle*'s Senior Foreign Affairs Editor and had arrived in Israel on Friday to report on the ongoing Intifada. He is the seventh journalist to be killed in the area this year.' No mention of his house arrest for the murder of his girlfriend. Not a peep.

So that's what he was, I thought. Senior Foreign Affairs Editor. Whatever that's supposed to mean. Killed in crossfire, they claimed. My arse.

His death had pushed my Meier scoop down to second item on the news. On the British channels, anyway. Still, the bit of the story that had been mine, the exposure of Meier for what he is, was already secondary now to the General's dramatic arrest. We'd watched it in silence.

Cyclops on grainy film being led from his mansion to some kind of army vehicle. He was handcuffed and entirely bald. He blinked as though he'd been asleep when they came for him and the Arabic voice-over was explaining something about internal betrayal that I didn't understand.

Bald. Astonishing. So, despite having one eye, a face full of shrapnel and only half a hand, he was still vain. Was he trying to make himself more attractive to the drugged and naked child he was just about to rape and torture? Or was this look aimed more at me – foreign journalists with whom he wanted to cut a dash? I pulled my hair back the better to concentrate. I even tried the other channels. Janet Fischer (so she was here then) for CNN said his collection of child pornography was the biggest the Israeli police ever uncovered and it has in itself launched an enormous international investigation. A point scored for globalization. Or is it? We can come together to track down paedophiles, but didn't we create international paedophilia? They showed lots of archive stuff of Meier's famous massacres for which he would never now be tried, despite the decades of work some Lebanese lawyer had put in.

McCaughrean was gripped by the Glover coverage. I think he was glad that they couldn't be described as being of a type any more. He'd worried that they were just a couple of fat old drunks together.

'Jammy fucker,' McCaughrean said. 'Now he's a hero.'

McCaughrean seems to think that the fact that I'm bedridden means he can hang out here stuffing his face.

'Not jammy,' Eden corrected him. 'Suicidal . . . Look, he's dead already.' Eden was pointing at a shot of Martin on a Red Crescent stretcher being dashed from the scene of his shooting. His eyes were open, but fearless and gone, as he was whisked through the WTN shot. The crew had been doing a story about the decline of the tourism industry when they heard the gunfire.

My dad was on television when he died. They showed him being rushed through the grey drizzle of Belfast and into an ambulance. His shirt was sodden and stained with blood. His eyes were terrified, very much alive. Evie tried to stop me seeing it.

It's weird, the suicide thing with paedophiles, I thought, smoking now that Ahmed had gone. The sugar and salt pouring into my pathetically starved bloodstream. Why do they always do it? Is it because they'll have such an awful time in prison, or is it because it's the last taboo and their families will suffer so horribly? At this thought I remembered that he had a wife and children somewhere. Ex-wife and estranged children. Didn't they all?

McCaughrean announced that he was off on suicide-bomber watch. He was just being polite, I think. Nobody in England was going to run pictures of anything today but Glover, and Don didn't have any. Was he giving us some privacy? Ugh.

Eden sat down on the bed with his arm around me and we watched the story develop as the teams of people scrabbled their information together. Within an hour, they'd found Glover's mum and got her crying and saying what a lovely son he was. An hour and a half and they had his ex-wife refusing to comment. A sweet hippyish looking type standing outside a house somewhere like Islington, her key in the lock, distraught and confused, a ten-year-old boy hiding behind her purple and orange skirts. Then the WTN cameraman did a quote about how he'd just been filming a souvenir stall in the rain when he heard the shots 'ring out'. And you know what I thought? I thought, I must get one of those olive wood nativity scenes for my mum. She'd love that.

'I'll get one of those for my mum,' I told Eden, poking my cigarette at the screen. 'Should have done it when we were there. Got a bit sidetracked.'

'Thought you hated her? Thought you were waiting for her to die?' he said, moving one of my curls to look me in the eye.

'We made up,' I said, and stubbed my cigarette out in the ashtray.

CHAPTER EIGHTEEN

It was raining. It's always raining here. When I'm away from England, I picture it as a country of sweet country churches, sunny spring days and green grass. When I am in England, it is always grey and raining. Weirdly toytownish, though. Shiny black taxis, gleaming red buses, nurses looking *Carry On*-esque in their uniforms, scudding clouds and children with teddy bears and sweets. Something so unreal – as though you're just about to see a paper boy shouting out a headline, a cockney doffing his cap, a flower girl with a bunch of lavender, or a man striding across a village green in cricket whites.

The rain streamed down my taxi window like tears.

In the damp church, although it was only about three o'clock, it was so dark that we were all peering at each other for recognition. Hundreds of already drunk newspapermen in their old black suits and ties, shuffling into their pews and veering wildly between making inappropriate jokes and being weirdly reverent to the Church of England. Their suits only ever came out for these events. Memorial services for colleagues. Mostly murdered in the field, but sometimes a cocaine overdose with a call girl. Whatever. They were heroes. Our heroes.

Because in some way this is what we all aimed for, I suppose. This kind of recognition from our peers. But you can only get it by dying. I bumped into Pip Deakin outside on the steps. He had an umbrella and was pulling it down and shaking it when he spotted me, standing in the drenched grey cold. I had managed black jeans and a grey shirt. My boots are black anyway, and my jacket dark brown.

'Hello, Faith,' he said and kissed me on both cheeks. I would rather he'd ignored me. There was something so irritatingly pious about burying our differences for a friend's memorial service. Eden, Don and I had decided to let Glover be buried a hero. What was the point, after all, of torturing his family?

I was nearly late. I got a taxi all the way from Finsbury Park. The driver smoked so that the steamed-up windows went all wispy and blue. It was a good lesson for my third day as a non-smoker. He was wizened and yellow and coughed up sputum from his lungs with every word. And there were a lot of words. But I didn't hear them.

My mum loved the nativity scene. She held all the little animals and figures in her fingers as though they were flowers. Putting them down gently on her sideboard. Jesus in his crib. The three kings and the shepherds standing to one side. The ox and the ass on the other. Mary and Joseph proudly standing at their son's head.

'It's lovely, darling. Thank you,' she said.

She opened the door in a clean pair of jeans and a white T-shirt. Her feet were bare but her toenails gleamed as though they had been lacquered. She had washed her hair and wore a bit of make-up. She had cropped her hair quite close to her head like a man and it was grey as stone. I remembered it so long and curly and dark blond. I remembered the smell of it. She leant forward to kiss me, but I couldn't do it. Instead, I handed her the paper bag with her present in it and she took me upstairs to her flat. We had a mug of tea each (cats in playful poses with balls of wool) when she opened the bag and took the pieces of carved wood out.

'I got you something too,' she said and handed me a present wrapped in flowery paper, the Sellotape clumsy, and tied with a silvery ribbon.

I opened it, careful not to tear the paper. It was a big bottle of conditioner from the Body Shop. She was apologetic.

'I remember how I used to struggle with that hair,' she said. She reached her hand out to touch it, but quickly withdrew it, aware that she might be breaching a new protocol.

Her flat was tiny, but not vile. She slept on a futon on the sitting-room floor and the bathroom and kitchen led off the main room, the kitchen through a beaded curtain and the bathroom through a door that she or someone else had painted purple.

'I always read your stuff,' she said, and pointed to a huge pile of papers on the floor. Years of them. 'I used to stick them in albums, but there were so many . . .' she broke off. 'Evie told me you won an award,' she said.

There were three pictures of me on her mantelpiece. All childhood ones from before they took me away. Took her away. I managed not to cry for twenty minutes.

When I did, she held my hand and started telling me about meetings I could go to for adult children of alcoholics. 'It's OK,' I said.

When I left, she told me she'd hoped she might be a grandmother by now. I laughed and hugged her.

'I've still got a year or two left,' I said.

I stood on the Stroud Green Road for ages, waiting for a taxi to go past. There was an old lady buying sugar cane from a greengrocer's and a teenager with twin babies pausing with her pushchair to light a cigarette, shielding herself from the rain with her hands.

'I didn't have the pleasure of knowing Martin Glover,' the vicar began.

Somebody coughed loudly. You could almost hear the cynicism. Everyone thinking, Well, I did, and I wouldn't have called it a pleasure. The candles made shadows in the vaulted ceiling and the stained-glass windows behind the altar looked dull and shabby with no sunlight to blaze through them. Someone rattled the matches in their pocket.

We sang 'The Lord's My Shepherd' and the organist was very slow, the mourners very reticent, though there must have been a thousand people there. Even up in the balcony. Martin's son read a passage from the Bible: There is a time to live and a time to die. Eccelesiastes, apparently. According to my programme. Eden took my hand and I didn't shake him off. Janet Fischer was crying. Really sobbing. Someone handed her a handkerchief. The fact that she was here meant there'd be a news crew filming us as we left. If nothing big happened, we'd all be on television at nine and ten. Some El Vino's crony got up and told some laddish anecdotes, fond reminiscences, and everyone laughed, glad to break the silence of grief. Even I smiled when he said something about the tongue sandwiches that Glover never touched.

A tramp wandered in and lay down to sleep in the aisle, snoring loudly. The bloke, who now I come to think about it, might well work at the *Chronicle* – listings? Oped? – said Martin would have liked that at his memorial service. All this bizarre pretence that somehow the deceased is with us, sharing in the irony of his death. His suicide, more like. Bastard.

'Not a great loss to the world,' Whitehorn said to me in our final interview. I had to tell him about the attack and stuff before he closed his case. He sat on the edge of my bed, watching the bag of liquid food empty into my arm. He couldn't look at my hands. Either of them. Seemed not to like needles. It's funny how fearless people have such mundane phobias. Like Shiv and her buttons.

The men in front of me, two drunks from home news, talked all the way through. At one stage, the one with the dark brown suit said, 'Hear the rumours?'

His friend hissed back, 'Don't know what all the fuss is about. It was a matter of course for the Ancient Greeks.'

Afterwards, we all went to the Reform Club and stood under gloomy columns drinking gin and tonics from circular silver platters, held out by tightly uniformed waiters. Pip Deakin pinched my arse. That explained a lot. I was fishing the lemon out of my third when Eden came up and put his arm round me.

'You look tired. Shall I take you home?' he asked. I've never been so grateful for anything in my life. Not that I was going home, or anywhere of the kind. I was staying at Browns off Piccadilly. Even staying is a bit of a euphemism. So far I had put my bag down on the bed and washed my hands with a tiny bar of flower-scented soap that I unwrapped from a slip of gauzy paper.

I leant my head on his shoulder.

'Why'd you give me a dress you bought for Ronit?' I asked, looking up at him.

He kissed the top of my head, absently.

'I didn't,' he said.

'I found the note in the box,' I told him quietly.

I put my glass down on the ancient brown leather of somebody's ancestral writing desk.

'Oh,' he said. 'She can't have taken it out. I bought her an answer machine. Same box.'

'Oh,' I said.

We were about to walk out of the dark green room when McCaughrean bumbled up to us, his camera bag bouncing against his hip. His left eye was still badly swollen and he had three little lines on his face where stitches had been.

'Hear about the massacre?' he said. 'See you at the airport.'

I took my mobile out of my pocket and called the desk. Of course there was only a student work-experience boy there because everyone else was here, at the Reform Club. He sounded worried.

'I saw it on Reuters. I've paged Bea but she hasn't got back to me,' he squealed.

Bea put a hand on my shoulder. 'Sorry, Zanetti. Are you up to going back?' she asked.

'Sure.' I smiled. 'I just need to get my bag.' I grinned up at Eden.

'Good,' Bea said. She was new. Brought in from a tabloid. But I liked her. 'Tickets and money at Heathrow. Or they will be.'

Eden, Don and I walked slowly down the carpeted stairs. Outside, London was slipping past in the rain. Black taxis shining like toys, red double-decker buses, a girl actually posting her letters in a pillar box, and cars splashing grime up on to the pavement. Greying couples in expensive clothes were already huddling under their umbrellas and walking towards the theatres.

'Wet as a whore's . . .' Don began, looking up at the sky and holding a hand out to catch some drops.

'Yes, yes,' we stopped him, clamping our hands to our ears.

McCaughrean had managed to persuade Trevor ('Give me them, you nance, or I'll start shouting') to give him six miniatures before take-off and he sank them all while we were taxiing down the runway.

'Tell us a joke, Zanetti,' he said, lifting my headphones out of my ears and prodding me in the ribs. Eden winked from across the aisle.

'Thought you'd given up,' he mouthed, pointing at my shirt pocket. Or rather, the packet of cigarettes in it.

'Just in case,' I smiled.

We had cleared the clouds and Trevor was coming back with the trolley.

'There's this old Palestinian man dying,' I said.

'Hmmm,' McCaughrean pondered. 'Must be a fair few of them.'

'This is the joke, Don,' I stared at him.

'Oh. Right.'

'So, there's this old Palestinian man dying. He gathers his sons around him and says, "Boys. My only regret is that I didn't live to see you married. I have one piece of advice for you – marry Jewish girls." The boys are horrified. "But Dad," says one of the sons, "you always told us to marry good Muslim girls."

"I did," says the father, gasping his last. "But they will grow old and ugly, ill and die."

The sons are upset and confused.

"Surely Jewish girls will do that too?" the youngest boy asks.

"Yes," says the father, "but that doesn't matter so much."

McCaughrean smiled to himself, satisfied, and shuffled further into his seat.

I winked over at Eden and put my headphones back on. Trevor put a couple of vodkas down in front of me.

'Thanks,' I said. I poured myself a drink and took a sip before reaching out to touch Eden's hand.

'OK?' he asked, squeezing my fingers.

'OK,' I said, and I looked out of the window to watch the clouds glance past.